PINECONES AND ORCHIDS

"Ted, I just came over to say I'm sorry. I would never stand you up on purpose; I know we had a date." Robbin had always been totally honest with Ted. "I just . . . when Kent called and asked me out this morning, I was so surprised and thrilled that I forgot all about our plans."

"Thank you for sharing that with me, Robbin," Ted replied harshly. "I'm deeply comforted by that explanation."

"Teddy, I love going out for a pizza with you, but I do that all the time. Having a date with Kent was like – a trip to Disneyland."

Her words seemed to trigger something deep within Ted. "The last time I checked, Robbin, the Pizza Palace wasn't accepting reservations for days in advance."

"I thought . . . when you mentioned reservations . . . I thought you were kidding."

"Well, I *was* kidding, Robbin," he snapped. "I was kidding myself. Now that we all know that the joke was on me, would you *please* go home."

Suzanne Ellison was born in Iowa and now lives with her husband and family in California.

PINECONES AND ORCHIDS

BY

SUZANNE ELLISON

WORLDWIDE BOOKS

LONDON • SYDNEY • TORONTO

All the characters in this book have no existence outside the imagination of the Author, and have no relation whatsoever to anyone bearing the same name or names. They are not even distantly inspired by any individual known or unknown to the Author, and all the incidents are pure invention.

First published in Great Britain in 1988
by Worldwide Books, Eton House,
18–24 Paradise Road, Richmond, Surrey TW9 1SR

ISBN 0 373 50904 9

11–8810

Made and printed in Great Britain

For Tara,
my little rainbow

CHAPTER ONE

SWEAT TRICKLED DOWN Robbin Walker's neck as she jogged the last block of her route. Except for the vague scent of ammonia in the air, which made Robbin slightly curious, it was a glorious summer day, bright and clear and already warm enough to justify a dip in the pool next door. But Robbin didn't have time for a swim today, let alone the cup of coffee that her widowed neighbor would automatically fix if he heard her slip through his back gate. If it weren't for that bed-shaking sonic boom an hour ago, she wouldn't even have had time to run this morning. Robbin knew she should have been grateful for the unexpected wake-up call, but for some reason the vibration had left her feeling as though she'd been rousted from her sleep by a nightmare.

She took a deep breath as she reached her front lawn, and did a few knee bends . . . then froze when she noticed the car in the driveway. It was a Mercedes—golden, gleaming, and obviously brand new. So was the man who emerged from it; a veritable Robert Redford in the flesh. Or close enough, anyway, in the eyes of a thirty-four-year-old divorcée who'd realized just last month that she'd been alone long enough and was finally ready to do something about it.

He looked like a man who did everything according to his own brand of time. Tall, supple, and catlike, his motions were smooth and liquid; she suspected that there were hard and lean muscles underneath his suit jacket. He was no more than forty, and his deep tan hinted that he spent his spare time outdoors...and not just sunbathing on the beach. A flawlessly cut black suit hugged every caressable line.

Robbin wished he'd come an hour later, when she'd be dressed for the real estate office in that gorgeous turquoise sundress she'd bought just last week. She would hardly have chosen to present herself to this tawny-maned creature with her hair in a half-brushed ponytail! But subconsciously she remembered that her pink and purple fleece suit, baggy though it might be, was a stunning foil for her dark hair and ivory skin. Maybe he wouldn't notice the red cheeks or the sweat.

But he didn't seem to notice Robbin at all, even though she stood only a few feet away. His eyes were drawn to the picket fence between her house and Ted's, where Captain, the Ballards's Siamese cat, was imperiously demanding the stranger's attention.

"Mrrroooow?" Captain insisted, waiting for the man to approach him.

Dressed in black, nine men out of ten would have ignored the light-haired cat or told him to get lost, but the movie-star-like vision before Robbin strolled easily toward the gate and reached up for Captain without hesitation. "Meow to you, too," he greeted the Siamese affectionately, his deep voice vibrating in the stillness of dawn. He cradled Captain in the crook of his arm, and rubbed the cat's throat and ears, making the feline purr thunderously and stretch his claws in delight.

In that instant, Robbin would have happily traded places with the cat, but she didn't have long to mull over her fantasy. The stranger turned toward her leisurely, and his eyes focused on the young woman before him.

"Good morning," he said cheerfully, expecting her to reply in kind.

But simple words of greeting failed Robbin. She was mesmerized by his bright, blue eyes and the nonchalant gaze that took in every line of her casual demeanor. She sensed his tacit approval.

Robbin was unaccustomed to having men look her over quite this way. She'd dated very little since Doug had left; the highlight of her typical week was dinner at the Pizza Palace with Ted, his two youngsters, and her own three kids. Of course, lately she hadn't had the pleasure of Ted's company much. During the school year, the whole Ballard clan bopped in and out of her house several times a day, but since her children had gone to their dad's in June, she'd seen precious little of Ted or his kids. Of course, Tina and Larry had been spending a lot of time with their grandmother, but it suddenly occurred to her that that was no excuse for Ted's summer hibernation. She forced her attention back to Captain and Robert Redford.

"His . . . name . . . is . . . Captain," Robbin managed to tell the intriguing stranger, pointing to the cat. "He loves attention, but he can be a bit . . . aggressive at times. He likes to nibble on fingers and toes."

"I remember," the man confessed indulgently, tugging gently on one feline ear. "Captain and I have met once before. We wrestled a bit and, as I recall, he got the better of me." He punctuated his words with a smile that dashed sunlight over his smooth, square features. Deep dimples framed his sensual mouth, giving him an endearing little boy look. "My daughter's cat bites, too," he informed Robbin. "He's a lot like Captain. If he's in the mood for company he expects you to scrap all your plans, but if you're the one who's lonely you might as well be living on a South Sea island." His glorious smile faded as he tacked on softly, "Come to think of it, my daughter's a lot like her cat."

Robbin wasn't sure how to answer that. If Ted had said those somber words, she would have brightened his mood with a joke. But Robbin wasn't confident enough to risk offending this delectable stranger.

"Are you . . . looking for somebody?" she asked courteously. *Please let it be me!*

He looked surprised by her question. "I'm here to pick up Ted, but I'm so early that I thought I'd take a moment to chat with Captain." Suddenly his sunny smile embraced Robbin in a very personal way. "And anybody else who happens to be on the welcoming committee."

This time she had no trouble smiling back, certain she'd misread his earlier moment of introspection. She was about to introduce herself when an old Chevy scrambled into Ted's driveway. Sarah, the college girl he often hired as a baby-sitter, pulled her long legs out of the car and trotted up the walk.

"I'm so sorry, Mr. Ballard!" she bubbled as the front door swung open, revealing just a glimpse of a tall, trim man with a thick shock of brown hair. "I know you told me to be here by six but—" Her excuse was lost as she disappeared into the house.

Robbin didn't need to watch her go to visualize the scene inside. She knew Ted's house as well as she knew her own, right down to the colorful hearts Tina had scrawled on the wall next to the couch seven years ago and the ratty brown towel that had been plugging up the hole in the ceiling since the rainstorm last Christmas. There would be wall-to-wall dirty dishes in the kitchen and clothes strewn all over the bathroom floor. Eight-year-old Larry would still be in his pajamas, rubbing his eyes and complaining about the color of this week's toothpaste.

Small wonder it always took Ted so long to get out of the house in the morning! Instinctively covering for her friend, Robbin turned back to the visitor who was cuddling the purring Siamese. "I'm sure he'll be with you in just a moment, Mr.—"

"Hawthorne. Kent Hawthorne." He glanced at the three wrought-iron numbers nailed over her front door, then back at Ted's porch. "It's been a while since I've been here," he admitted, realizing he'd parked in the wrong driveway. "I'd forgotten how similar these two houses look."

Under other circumstances Robbin might have laughed. Ted's yard was the joke of the neighborhood; he always told people to search for the only house on the block that looked as though nobody lived there. Of course, that new sod lawn he'd just put in had changed the face of 347 Mulberry Lane, as had the bed of roses and hanging fuchsia baskets under the eaves. Robbin had been meaning to compliment Ted on his hard work. After all, who else would?

Their two families had always been close. Her ex-husband, Doug, had once been Ted's best friend, and Ted's wife, Ellen, had been like a little sister to Robbin. After Ellen's death, Ted had had his hands full, struggling with two grief-stricken children and a mountain of medical bills. The Walkers had continued to include the Ballards in all their family gatherings and Robbin, a full-time homemaker in those days, had taken Ted's youngsters under her wing and had raised them right along with her own. She had ferried the two younger girls to dance lessons and the boys to scouts and had represented Ted at the dentist's office, the doctor's office, and parent-teacher meetings at school. Ruth, her eldest, had helped out with baby-sitting on the weekends.

Last year, when Doug had moved out and then taken a vibrant interest in a young woman at work, Ted had quietly mopped up Robbin's tears, day after day, night after night, until the pain began to ease. He wasn't the sentimental sort—his idea of comfort was usually a barrage of silly jokes and a bag of popcorn during a late-night movie on TV—but he was always there when she needed him, demanding nothing and giving her more than she'd ever thought one friend had the right to ask of another.

The golden vision was speaking again. "I hope I haven't inconvenienced you, Mrs.—"

"Walker. Robbin Walker," she introduced herself eagerly. "I'm Ted's next-door neighbor."

"You're Robbin?" As the sunburst smile took over his face again, Robbin decided it was his crowning glory. "I'm really glad to hear that."

Robbin was thrilled but mystified. "Why is that?"

The vibration of his deep voice was even more dramatic when he laughed. "Because Ted's been trying to get me to meet you for months. I was afraid you wouldn't be at all my type but—" his eyes swept over her again with that appreciative glance "—I can see I underestimated Ted."

Robbin grinned, suddenly glowing. If this man weren't single and just as delightful as he looked, Ted never would have tried to wrangle her a date with him! "People do that a lot," she replied, trying to sound calm. "On the surface he's just good old Ted, but underneath, he's—"

"—right behind you, so watch what you say," Ted announced as he crossed his lawn to the edge of the road where Robbin was still standing. His voice was stiff, unnatural. She didn't know why; it just lacked that cozy burr that always warmed her. Her joy dropped a notch or two.

Prepared to throw Ted one of her "Yes, dear" looks when he asked her to check on the baby-sitter, Robbin was surprised as she turned to face him. She'd already noticed that he didn't sound like good old Ted; now she realized that he didn't look like Ted, either.

At least, not the Ted Ballard whom she'd trained to wear black shoes with gray suits, ordered to throw out socks with rat-sized holes, and taught to wash his white shirts separately from the jeans he used to work on the car. She'd spent hours patiently explaining the concept of "ring around the collar." *That* Ted Ballard had slowly added fifteen pounds in the last year, hadn't cut his hair until Robbin tactfully reminded him, and had only mowed the crabgrass once a month.

This Ted Ballard wore a camel tweed suit that set off his perceptive brown eyes. Robbin hadn't helped him pick it out, but every one of the pieces matched, anyway. He'd grown a mustache since she'd seen him last, and lost every trace of that incipient paunch. Either he'd doubled his running time, or he'd profited from her lack of baking while her kids were gone for the summer.

Robbin had only seen Ted a few times since June, usually at a distance, and she *had* noticed gradual changes in his appearance, but it struck her now that she'd never seen him looking so fine.

"Robbs?" he asked softly, studying her face. His chestnut hair showed the mark of professional styling, and the thick new mustache, peppered with red, gave a sense of strength to the firm contours of his mouth. "Are you okay?"

Robbin shrugged, feeling foolish. She knew she should have been pleased with Ted's new elegant demeanor, but for some reason his appearance made her uneasy...as though she were looking at a stranger. "You just...look so different these days, Ted. You look great this morning, and I didn't even help."

It was, she realized belatedly, a left-handed compliment at best, and clearly not the response Ted had been looking for. He tried to grin nonchalantly, but his embarrassed smile was the one that slipped out when he forgot her birthday, or tried to lie about what he'd bought one of the kids for Christmas. She hadn't intended to embarrass him, and if they'd been alone she could have given him a quick hug and forgotten the whole thing. With Kent there, somehow everything was different.

"We've got to go, Robbie," Ted said gently, forgiving her faux pas. "I'll see you tomorrow."

"Tomorrow?" Robbin asked, then winced as she read the momentary hurt in his eyes. Vaguely she remembered talking to him on the phone earlier in the week about dinner on Friday. He'd made some joke about reservations...at least, she'd assumed it was a joke since they never ate anywhere but the Pizza Palace. There weren't many other choices in Coltersville—a truck stop, a couple of fast-food joints, and a teenage hangout—and Ted hated to drive back to Morgantown for dinner when he'd just spent the day there. "Sure, Ted," she answered, hoping her answer would satisfy him without giving Kent the wrong impression about their relationship.

There was something...well, intriguing about the man whom Ted had picked out for her; something that went beyond his striking good looks. It was the smile, Robbin decided. Or maybe the way he was cuddling Captain. Any man who liked cats and kids couldn't be all bad!

"I was just about to tell your neighbor what we're doing out here today," Kent offered as an opening conversational gambit. "There's been an explosion at the—"

"We don't have time for that, Kent," Ted cut him off. "We've got to get over there ASAP." His tone was almost harsh, underlined with some nameless emotion that Robbin had never heard in his voice before. It gave her goose bumps. He pushed past her without a glance and slipped into Kent's regal coach.

Kent gave an amiable shrug and displayed his dimples again. "Duty calls. Sorry we don't have time to chat, Robbin." He could have dropped Captain on the ground, but instead he crossed the driveway to place the cat gently in her hands. It was a gift, somehow, an offering that she found hard to take lightly. For an instant his searching eyes met hers, and once again Robbin thought she saw a shadow of pain in their sea-blue depths. But no more words were forthcoming from Kent.

Robbin struggled for a way to keep him there. "Surely you're not going to drop a teaser like that and just drive off without telling me what dragged you two out of bed at this hour." Her words were soft, meant only for Kent's ears. She'd practically forgotten that Ted was nearby.

But it was Ted who called out of the open car window. "That's exactly what we're going to do, Robbs. I'll tell you all about it tomorrow night."

Fine time for him to start worrying about punctuality, Robbin fumed. She'd held dinner for him dozens of times. Not recently, come to think of it, but . . .

She glanced at Ted in irritation, but held her tongue when she saw that his eyes were full of some tense warning for Kent. Robbin didn't know what problem the two men were off to solve, but she knew instinctively that something more than just the alleged lateness of the hour was bothering Ted. Kent had mentioned an explosion; that must be the key. She knew that Ted had some kind of civil service job that dealt with environmental protection, and she had to assume that Kent worked with him, or he wouldn't be picking him up at dawn.

Her eyes flashed back to Kent's, and to her surprise she saw the same masked concern in them that she'd seen in Ted's. No, it was more than concern; it was fear. And she'd thought he'd just been feeling morose about his daughter!

"Nice talking to you, Robbin," Kent assured her with a smile as he cast a glance over at Ted. But the smile didn't work this time; it was forced. "We really do have to get on over to the refinery."

"The refinery?" She blanched, abruptly recalling the predawn "sonic boom" that had awakened her. Suddenly the wafting scent of ammonia Robbin had noticed earlier threatened to overwhelm her. "Do you mean *our* refinery, Kent?"

It was a rhetorical question; Robbin knew full well that Red Rock was the only refinery for sixty miles in any direction. Less than three blocks away from her home, it was adjacent to the kindergarten-through-eighth-grade school that most of the local children attended. There had only been a couple of minor incidents at Red Rock since Robbin had lived in town, but she'd heard of a terrible accident back in the fifties. Before buying the house on Mulberry Lane, Robbin and Doug had discussed at length the potential danger posed by the plant, but Robbin had shelved her initial concern when Doug had convinced her that there was nothing to worry about.

"Teddy?" she asked, her voice dropping as she turned instinctively to her friend for assurance. "School starts in a couple of weeks. Will it be safe for the kids?"

Ted's eyes met hers again; he opened the car door and marched quickly to Robbin's side. In a gesture of wordless comfort, he laid one hand on her face. Robbin closed her eyes, surprised and moved by his unexpected tenderness. She knew he meant to reassure her, but for some reason his gentle touch was frightening. From jovial Ted, such a sober response could only mean that the danger was even greater than she'd imagined. "I'll take care of it, Robbs. You know I'd never let anything happen to the kids." His voice was low but firm. "And I'd never let anything happen to you."

She nodded, trying to take comfort from his determination. Ted was as good as his word; he was nothing if not reliable when it came to promises. It was just that he seemed so... *different* this morning. He looked so good and sounded so bad.... It was an odd combination. Kent, on the other hand, looked good, sounded great, and would probably feel just terrific if she ever got close enough to touch him. Yet, even he seemed a little frightened by whatever had happened at the refinery.

Robbin forced herself to smile at Ted, then lifted her eyes to Kent's as her neighbor slipped back into the car and slammed the door. For a moment Kent didn't move, his expression indicating a mixture of dark thoughts and appreciation for the woman before him.

"Maybe we'll... run into each other again," he suggested by way of farewell. It was a nebulous line that could have meant anything... or nothing. Ted was always telling Robbin she'd been alone too long. Was her potent response to Kent Hawthorne due simply to her readiness to come out of her shell, or was there really something . . . well, special . . . vibrating between them?

"I hope so, Kent," she admitted more enthusiastically than she'd intended.

But Kent smiled back, clearly pleased by her confession. He gave her a nod, then lifted one hand to wave to someone behind her before he turned away.

It was Larry, Ted's eight-year-old, still in his pajamas, waving goodbye to the two men. With his bushy brown hair and ready smile, he was a miniature version of his fun-loving dad. Robbin had practically raised the child; it was only natural to slip her arm around him as he joined her on the driveway. He wasn't quite old enough to object to the maternal gesture.

Larry waited until the Mercedes was out of sight before he turned to Robbin and whined, "Daddy says we can't go out to eat with you guys tomorrow night because Ruthie and Allison and Jarrod are still with Uncle Doug. Is that fair?"

Robbin smiled and hugged him closer. "You know what your dad always says, honey. 'Life isn't fair; but it's fun.'" *Like today, for instance. One minute I'm glowing because of this new man on my doorstep, and the next I'm shaking in my boots because Ted's afraid we're in danger.* Determined to conceal her uneasiness from the boy, she said, "Mr. Hawthorne acted as though he knew you, Larry. Is he a friend of your dad's or do they just work together?"

"They don't really work together," he answered. "They just sort of do the same thing."

Robbin raised her eyebrows. Obviously there was some reason Kent was on his way out to the Red Rock site, but why was he driving with Ted? "Why didn't they just meet at the refinery, Larry?"

The boy giggled. "Because our car died again."

It came as no surprise to Robbin that Ted's old clunker needed more work, but she was curious as to why he hadn't asked her for a ride as he usually did. They had always bailed each other out in the past, and not just where cars were concerned. Not only did Ted habitually borrow food and tools from his neighbor, but every few months he lost his checkbook and had to borrow some cash from Robbin to tide him over. At least, he used to. Now that she thought about it, Ted hadn't borrowed anything from her since early spring.

Come to think of it, Ted hadn't so much as knocked on her door since April or May. Robbin hadn't realized how much she'd missed him lately until he'd called on Tuesday to make sure she was free on Friday night. It had been an exceptionally lonely summer for Robbin, but since it was the first summer she'd ever spent without Doug or her children, she hadn't looked much further than her divorce to explain her current sense of emptiness. Now that she thought about it, it was unlike Ted to neglect her during such a difficult passage; he must be terribly busy at work right now. She made a mental note to ask him about it. Her kids were due home on Saturday, and they'd be downright hurt if Ted and his youngsters didn't come over to celebrate their return.

"I don't know why Daddy called Mr. Hawthorne," Larry broke into her reverie. "I don't think he likes him much anymore."

"Oh?" Robbin wasn't sure what to make of his comment. Ted hadn't been overly friendly this morning, but she had no idea if that was how he usually treated Kent.

All she was sure of was that Ted hadn't been quite himself today. "Why do you say that?"

"Well, when Daddy first met Mr. Hawthorne they played tennis together a lot." His big brown eyes beguiled Robbin. "You know, since Uncle Doug moved away there hasn't been anybody good enough to beat Daddy."

Robbin nodded. Ted's prowess on the tennis court was his only source of vanity.

"But ever since summer started, Daddy hasn't had time to play. He says that all of a sudden he can beat Mr. Hawthorne all the time, so it isn't any fun anymore."

Robbin studied the child thoughtfully, certain that he'd misunderstood his father. "Maybe Mr. Hawthorne has been busy. He has a daughter; maybe she's staying with him this summer just like my kids are visiting their dad."

Larry shook his head emphatically. "Uh-uh. I heard him tell Daddy that Connie was coming here right after school got out, but the last time they played tennis was on the Fourth of July and Dad said she'd already gone back to Denver."

Stung with a sudden replay of Kent's casual comparison of Captain to his daughter, Robbin was sure she hadn't imagined that moment of pain in his blue eyes. "Do you know why she had to leave so soon?"

Larry lifted his shoulders in childish denial. "I don't know, Aunt Robbin. But after that my dad told me to be careful what I say to Mr. Hawthorne from now on, 'cause people aren't always what they seem."

It seemed a strange admonition for Ted to give his young son, but Robbin assured herself that Larry had simply misinterpreted one of his dad's cryptic comments. Surely Kent Hawthorne was just what he appeared to be: gorgeous, single, and—just possibly—more than a little bit interested in Robbin Jean Walker.

Ted, on the other hand, was just . . . Ted. Good old reliable Ted. No tricks, no surprises. *Until today,* she quickly amended, still troubled by his haunted eyes and gentle touch. Robbin had to admit that she *was* surprised that he'd grown the mustache without asking her advice. And she was even more surprised to realize that, even alongside the undeniably dazzling Kent, Ted had looked—well, to some other woman, perhaps—quite dashing. Quite dashing, indeed.

"Daddy said the new car will be here sometime tomorrow, Aunt Robbin. Will you come and take a drive with us?"

"The *new car*?" Robbin couldn't keep the shock out of her voice. She'd never seen Ted drive anything but that battered old Volkswagen with wire and stuffing hanging out of the seats; she'd never even heard him acknowledge that it needed so much as a bath! Despite his perfectly adequate income, he'd always taken some perverse delight in living like a pauper. "Your dad bought a—"

Before she could finish, the door opened again and Tina, Ted's vivacious ten-year-old, bounded out on the porch. "Hi, Aunt Robbin!" she sang out through a mouthful of braces. "Where's Daddy going so early?" Her innocent joy died quickly as she wrinkled her nose and asked, "Ugh! What's that awful smell?"

Looking at Ted's two beautiful children, it was hard for Robbin to ignore the reason for his dawn trip to the refinery—or his determination to protect them from harm. As a wave of maternal devotion overtook her, the oppressive scent of ammonia suddenly seemed to suffocate Robbin, and the vivid blue sky turned decidedly gray.

CHAPTER TWO

FROM A DISTANCE, Red Rock Refinery was an endless maze of towers and tanks, rails and ladders, pipes and valves. Gray, green and rusty-white blended together in an eerie moonscape of modern technology that had never looked so menacing to Ted Ballard.

He was accustomed to coping with environmental horrors of one kind or another; accustomed to dealing with chronically indifferent officials who became overnight evangelists for the public good when they discovered a publicity disaster in their own backyard. But he wasn't used to seeing naked fear in Robbin's eyes and knowing that *he* might be all that stood between her and danger.

It was an awesome responsibility. Ted had always cared deeply about environmental safety throughout the county—throughout the rest of California, the nation, and the whole world, for that matter—but this...this was different. This time his family was at stake...his children, and—for all intents and purposes—his *woman*.

There was no longer any point in lying to himself; nor was there any point to further pretense with Robbin. He wasn't sure just when it had happened, or whether he would have planned it this way if it had been up to him. He wasn't the sort of man who dwelled on such things. All he knew was that at some point during the past year he'd fallen deeply in love with Robbin Walker. He'd long cared for her as a neighbor, and then he'd cherished her as a friend. Later still, she'd become a surrogate mother for his children. Somewhere down the line, Robbin had become his sunrise and his sunset. It was as simple as that.

Well, *almost* as simple as that. In Robbin's eyes, he was still just good old Ted, the Rock of Gibraltar, her best friend in the world. He'd subtly tested the water many times in recent months, but she'd always remained utterly oblivious to his efforts to kindle a new level of feeling between them. It was time for more drastic action.

It had taken a tremendous amount of self-control to keep his distance from Robbin this summer, but Ted knew that before he asked her to marry him outright, they'd need to break their old habits long enough to make her see him in a new light . . . and give some thought to what life without him would mean to her. It wasn't something he wanted to threaten Robbin with—good God, it would kill him to move away—but he knew they'd reached the end of this road. He just couldn't carry on any longer pretending he was satisfied with their quasi marriage, even though he suspected Robbin still wasn't ready to view him as a lover. The simple truth was that Ted had waited for her just as long as he possibly could. Maybe even longer.

"You never told me Robbin looked like *that*," Kent declared as he pulled the gold Mercedes into the gravel driveway that led up to the refinery gate. "When you said you were looking for a blind date for your neighbor, I figured she was having trouble attracting men on her own."

"Robbin never has trouble doing anything," Ted replied, his tone a quiet lash. "She's the most capable woman I've ever known." *And her heart is as beautiful as her face,* he might have added. But he was not about to share his potent feelings for Robbin with Kent Hawthorne.

He was familiar with Kent's cavalier attitude toward women; it was one of the reasons they'd drifted apart in recent months. They'd met in February when Kent had taken over as fire safety inspector for this end of the county. He was in charge of any flammable substance or equipment above ground. Ted, on the other hand, worked out of Environmental Health and supervised any hazardous waste removal procedures. Red Rock required both kinds of clearance.

"Let's forget Robbin for the moment and concentrate on the task at hand, shall we?" he suggested, his voice more strained than he'd intended. The trouble at Red Rock wasn't the only burden he was carrying this morning. The look on Robbin's face when Kent had handed her the cat had left Ted more than a little uneasy, as did Kent's nonchalance about the explosion. Ted couldn't pin down his concern, but his instincts told him that Kent should have been more shocked, more upset, more determined to ferret out what had gone wrong. He also should have been more circumspect with the details of the accident, especially since Ted had been bending over backward to avoid telling Robbin the gruesome story and frightening her. He'd wanted to wait until he could tell her that he'd solved the problem and there was nothing for her to worry about. But thanks to Kent's blundering, Robbin was deeply worried about Red Rock—and rightly so.

At the moment Ted was not inclined to share too many of his private thoughts with Kent, so aloud he simply said, "From what I've heard so far, this may be the worst accident we've had in Coltersville in thirty years."

"I doubt that," Kent replied laconically, his smooth tone implying that Ted was behaving like a bleeding heart. "First reports are always unnecessarily alarming."

Ted didn't bother to reply. Somebody was probably dead or dying, and Kent thought he was overreacting! It was hard to remember what had ever caused him to think that Kent had depth.

In the beginning, Ted had felt a kinship with the other man that went beyond the rigors of the tennis court. They both worked in a profession that assumed a commitment to public concerns. Ted took his responsibility very seriously; at first he'd assumed that Kent, lighthearted and fun-loving though he could be, had felt the same way. But over time, Ted had come to realize that Kent Hawthorne was a man who made a great first impression, oozing warmth and sincerity as he had this morning with Robbin. It was a facade he had to work at, though, and as time went on the veneer had grown a little too thin for Ted's comfort, leading him to conclude that Kent's values were more expedient than unwavering.

Ted was surprised, actually, that Robbin had given the guy so much attention. Even more proof that she was ripe for a new beginning; proof that he was running out of time. "You cleared everything in July, right?" Ted quizzed the other man as they neared the plant. "You saw no major problems at this site?"

Kent nodded indifferently. "I went by the book. They had to fix up a few things, but they cooperated fully." His tone didn't reveal a flicker of feeling. "You read the report."

"Yes, I read it." *But maybe not closely enough.* There were any number of things that could have gone wrong,

Ted reckoned. Oil refineries were hardly known for their track records in terms of safety...and their managers rarely earned awards for integrity. But Ted had always watched Red Rock like a hawk. After all, he only lived three blocks away. Yet a nagging voice in the back of his head reminded him that he hadn't really been giving his best to his job lately. Remodeling the house—and remodeling himself—had taken up all of his spare time, not to mention his concentration. Every carefully executed step was part of the exhaustive campaign he called Operation Cinderella, which would come to fruition tomorrow night.

Ted was about to ask another question when Kent pulled up to the gate and waved to the uniformed guard. The handsome young man grinned at Kent as though the two of them were the best of friends. His friendliness surprised Ted. The guards had rotating shifts, so he rarely saw the same one twice in succession, and he couldn't imagine how Kent had gotten to know one, either. Besides, everybody at the plant knew that Ted and Kent served as the community's environmental policemen, and hence they were never particularly welcomed on the site.

"Mr. Gregory is waiting for you over at the plant, Mr. Hawthorne," the guard announced cordially. "You, too, Mr. Ballard."

Apparently, Kent didn't even have to show any identification. Ted was about to ask Kent how he'd managed to get the grand treatment at Red Rock when the other man quipped, "Gregory must be quaking in his boots to roll out the red carpet for us this morning. Normally he hides in the woodwork till I'm gone."

Ted grimaced. "He used to do that with me, too, but now he has too much fun throwing his violations in my face. He knows I'm going to win the game, but he makes me work for every point."

In the early days of their acquaintance, silver-tongued Lowell Gregory, the plant manager, had done his best to win Ted's friendship and subsequent rubber-stamp approval for everything that went on at the refinery. But ever since Ted had made it clear that he was one hundred percent committed to serving the public and protecting the environment, Gregory had fought him tooth and toenail on almost every issue that had come up. Ted expected minimal cooperation this morning.

"So glad you fellows could make it out here right away!" Gregory gushed when he joined them at the front of the plant a moment later, taking Ted by surprise. The obese foreman's bald head gleamed with perspiration. He gripped Kent's hand, then turned to Ted. "I don't think you'll find anything out here to worry your people, Ted, but if you think there's any danger, you just give me the word."

Before Ted could answer, Kent said calmly, "Oh, I don't imagine there's anything to get all hot and bothered about. Were you on duty when the explosion took place?"

Gregory shook his head. "Nope." He began to walk toward the tanks and they followed. "I generally get here at seven. Howard Caldwell's in charge of the night shift; he can fill you in on the details." He flashed Ted a reassuring grin. "All I can tell you is that one of the ammonia valves in the urea unit ripped open—"

"I could have figured that out for myself," Ted snapped, unable to conceal his irritation with the plant manager's false ebullience. "That stench could gag a horse."

"That stench could also save your life," Gregory reminded him with a forced grin that clearly revealed the gap between his buck teeth. "We have to put an odor into natural gas so people will know when they're in trouble. But ammonia smells so ghastly that you don't have to tell anybody when it's time to get out of the way."

"Sometimes people don't have time to get out of the way, Gregory," Ted ground out, his own concern aggravated by Kent's indifference and Gregory's inappropriate cheer. "I realize you don't give a damn about the locals, but from what I hear, some of your own men are in pretty bad shape."

To Ted's surprise, the jovial grin slipped off Gregory's face; his eyes grew dark as he licked his lips. *My God, a heart really does lurk inside this slippery showman,* Ted thought, heartened somehow by the unexpected discovery.

"I—I honestly don't know what happened out here last night," Gregory forced out apologetically, his demeanor more subdued. "You and I haggle a lot, Ballard, but . . . you know I run a clean operation out here. If anything were wrong you would have nailed my hide to the barn door." He studied Ted for a moment, then shifted his gaze to Kent. "You cleared everything just last month, Hawthorne! None of this makes any sense to me."

It didn't make much sense to Ted, either. He'd have to go over every possible angle of the explosion . . . not just the areas that were in his domain, but those that normally fell within the boundaries of Kent's jurisdiction.

"Doesn't make much sense to me, either, Lowell," Kent tossed out nonchalantly, apparently indifferent to the subtle change in Gregory's tone. "Why don't you give us a rundown while we check out the urea unit?" He started toward the back of the plant without waiting for Ted and Gregory to join him. "We know there was an explosion out here. That's about it."

"So far we don't know much more than that," Gregory replied, brushing his damp head with a handkerchief as he took a few quick steps to catch up with Kent.

Ted wasn't about to hurry on Kent's behalf, but with his long legs, he didn't have to. He'd just spotted the mangled cylinder in the distance when Gregory said, "Around 5:00 a.m. one of the ammonia manufacturing tanks blew."

Ted recalled that the tank had once been about eight feet tall and twenty feet long. Now the round end lay in three jagged pieces on the ground. Nearby towers and rails were spattered with an oily liquid.

"There's nothing special about this urea tank," the heavy, squat man continued. "It was already in cool-down. A seam might have given way, or a pressure-release valve could have been set too low or gotten jammed with sludge."

Kent studied the wreckage before him and added quietly, "Or the valve might have been defective."

For just a moment Ted's eyes met Kent's, and he knew they were thinking alike, just as they had in the old days. There were a lot of reasons for a valve to malfunction: sometimes it just got jammed, sometimes it was bad to begin with, and sometimes it was refurbished when it should have been replaced.

"Not a chance," Gregory interjected before Ted could speak. "We replaced every one this summer according to your regulations. Remember, Kent? We debated whether we could risk the economy brand and you talked me into spending the big bucks to do it up right." His dark eyes flicked nervously from Kent to Ted. "You're always telling me that it's not enough just to comply with minimum safety standards, Ballard. Well, this is one time I did the right thing, and it sure didn't help me much." His voice wavered just slightly as he added, "It sure as hell didn't help our three guys in Intensive Care."

Unobtrusively, Ted laid a hand on Gregory's shoulder, who jerked his head up in surprise. Even Ted was startled by his instinctive act of compassion; he didn't have much use for the plant manager, but it went against his grain to kick a man when he was down. "There's always a chance that you got a bad valve in that new batch," Ted suggested more gently, withdrawing his hand. "We'll need to run a test for leaks on the other valves."

"What good would that do?" Kent asked, earning a sharp glance of reproach from Ted.

"It would tell us whether or not anybody else is in danger," Ted growled, wondering how Kent could possibly be so dense. He met the other man's eyes with banked fury, but Kent turned away.

"A helluva lot of good that'll do the men who just took a bath in one hundred proof ammonia!" he exclaimed bitterly. For a moment he just stared at the tank, his jaw set in anger.

Ted was startled by Kent's abrupt explosion. But he'd learned over the months that Kent preferred to mask his emotions; perhaps this morning's earlier display of heartlessness was simply a cover for what the man was really feeling. If Ted felt somewhat responsible for the accident, might not Kent feel the same way? The tank in question was not part of a hazardous waste removal system, so technically it was Kent's job to approve any change in the equipment, not Ted's.

"I think we ought to talk to the men who were on duty and check out the equipment before we come to any hasty conclusions," Kent suggested, his tone more sober now. "Is your night-crew chief still here, Lowell?"

The gap-toothed man nodded. "Probably over in the main switch house."

"Good. I'll go talk to him." Kent tossed a quick glance at Ted, but didn't ask for his opinion. "Let's compare notes later."

Before Ted could answer, one of the workers trotted up to give Gregory a message. "The school principal phoned," he reported glumly. "Wants to talk to you about the explosion. School starts in a couple of weeks, and he's not sure if it's safe for the kids."

Gregory rolled his eyes. "That's all I need. He's going to want answers, and I just don't have any right now."

"Neither do I," Ted admitted, his eyes haunted as he studied the wrecked urea tank. His gaze challenged Gregory for just a second. "But you can be damn sure that I will before school opens in September."

When his glance met Kent's he was surprised to read the same determination on his face.

"I'm going to talk to Caldwell," Kent repeated firmly, giving Ted a nod by way of farewell. "Can you help me find him, Lowell?"

"Sure thing, Hawthorne," Gregory agreed, trotting off next to Kent.

Ted had intended to talk to the night-crew chief himself, but at the moment he was more interested in the wrecked tank before him. He knelt down to examine every inch of the mangled metal, especially the new valve. Diligently he sifted through the evidence, hoping to find something that would explain the explosion—and help prevent another one.

Like a bulldog digging for a bone, Ted spent an hour prowling around the Red Rock plant checking assorted pipes and valves before he started asking searching questions of workers.

Eventually he found Howard Caldwell lounging in the main office, guzzling black coffee and smoking a fierce-smelling cigar. He was a huge man. Heavy jawbones and the dark hair on his arms gave him a simian look. Normally he was as closemouthed as Gregory was chatty, but Ted was in no mood to play games.

"I already told everything to Hawthorne," Caldwell grumped when Ted cornered him near the door. "My shift is over and I'm going home."

"Red Rock had an explosion on your shift and my report could find you personally responsible," Ted answered bluntly, thinking that if the man had shown Kent the same cooperation he was offering Ted, it would take both of them working in tandem to pry the information out of him. "Just tell me what happened—it won't take as long that way."

The apelike man glared at Ted, then his expression grew sly and vaguely triumphant as Kent and Gregory stomped through the door.

"Well, I guess that about does it," Gregory declared, plopping down at his desk.

"Guess so," Kent agreed indifferently. "I'm hungry, Ted. Didn't take time for breakfast. Let's wrap up here and go grab a bite before we crank up your old car."

Ted wasn't sure what to say; the concern he'd observed an hour ago had completely vanished from Kent's expression. "I need to talk to Caldwell first," he announced, feeling like a lone sheep among a pack of wolves. "Shouldn't take more than a few minutes."

Kent tossed up a hand in a beckoning gesture. "I already talked to him. He saw less than some of the other guys. Let's go."

His impatience irritated Ted. He'd questioned every worker on the premises who'd been on duty last night, and he saw no reason to skip the man in charge. "I'll meet you at the car in ten minutes," Ted declared, his voice still low, but his determination unmistakable.

"Come on, Ted!" There was no denying Kent's aggravation now. "I'm perfectly capable of conducting a simple interview! What do you think you're going to find out that I missed?"

This time it was Gregory who interceded, favoring Ted with another one of his phony smiles. "Now, boys, you just ask whatever you want. Howard, just tell them what you saw, all righty?"

A sullen grimace flickered across Caldwell's face, but he followed his boss's orders. "It was an ordinary night," he growled, leaning against the wall with his arms crossed defiantly across the chest. "Nothing strange happened. The tank just blew. I ran into the main switch house to turn off the automatic valve. Once Ben Jackson saw that we had three men down, he called the hospital in Morgantown for an ambulance."

"Did you tell Ben to do that?" Ted asked.

"I didn't have to. We all have our assigned jobs in an emergency. Mine is to shut down whatever system's gone haywire before anybody gets hurt."

"Funny thing," Ted replied grimly. "That's my job description, too."

IT WAS A BUSY MORNING for Robbin. After just two months as a realtor, she still treated every phone call as though it were a certain sale and read each contract as if it contained some secret code. She was the newest member of a very small firm, and at times the office intimacy grew a bit tiring. It was a relief to break free just before lunch to show her favorite house on the top of Crescent Heights Lane.

As she drove her spiffy black Buick up the hill that overlooked sleepy Coltersville and the uncluttered valley beyond, she noticed that the air was brisk and clear in this part of town; no trace of the odoriferous deadly gas had spread this far. Her thought slipped back to the unusual way she'd started the day. A blur of images flowed together in her mind: golden sun, golden man; cloud of ammonia, cloud of fear. Shadows of uncertainty surrounding Ted, painting strange lines of tension on his beloved face. New clothes, new car, new image. New Ted. *Why?* she found herself asking. *The old one was fine with me.*

Glancing down at her own ruffled bodice, Robbin wondered if Ted was the only one who had changed. In the past year she'd worked hard to improve her looks and build up her self-image. Fourteen years ago, Doug would have whistled if she'd sashayed in wearing this attractive turquoise number; but the time had come when Robbin, his cherished high-school sweetheart, had ceased to fulfill his needs. Oh, he couldn't have been more apologetic about "outgrowing" her and, considering the circumstances, he really had tried to be kind. But when he'd quickly remarried a stunning twenty-two-year-old, the facts had spoken for themselves.

Ted had assured Robbin that she wasn't getting older, she was getting better. And, to prove it, he'd promised to give her the snazziest birthday party ever when she turned thirty-five in October. She was looking forward to it, and she certainly appreciated Ted's loyal defense of her looks.

But it was one thing to have good old Ted tell her she still looked okay; it was something else altogether to see approbation—maybe even desire—in Kent Hawthorne's eyes. It wasn't just because Kent was so good-looking; the simple truth was, Ted would have thought Robbin looked marvelous in a paper bag. It was a comforting thought, but not a terribly exciting one. And at this point in her life—with Doug's departure so fresh in her memory—flattery and feminine pride mattered to Robbin a great deal.

Climbing out of the Buick, Robbin pushed away her memories and gave some thought to the task at hand. Always the early bird, she had made sure she would arrive before the Hawleys, a busy young couple who'd decided to use their lunch hour to explore this wondrous house.

And it *was* wondrous, as far as Robbin was concerned: old-fashioned without looking old, stately and full of grace . . . it reminded her of the ancient redwoods that grew over the coast. She would have given her right arm to move into it tomorrow.

"You're daydreaming again, Robbin," a familiar voice greeted her. She glanced sideways to see the softly wrinkled face of Jane Davidson, an elderly realtor from the firm that held the listing for the house. She'd arranged to meet Robbin and the Hawleys here at noon. "You're here to show the house, not buy it," she teased her.

They'd been friends for years, and Jane knew what a homebody Robbin was. Going to work had been the last thing she'd wanted to do while the kids were still in school, but after the divorce the money just hadn't stretched the way it used to. With Jane's inspiration and Ted's encouragement, Robbin had decided that selling houses might be a reasonable use of her talents. She also liked the generous commissions and flexible hours. Of course, without Ted living next door she never would have taken a job that involved going out at night, but Robbin felt secure leaving her eldest, Ruth, in charge when Ted was just a backyard away.

"You can't blame me, Jane. I've loved this house for years. Even when Doug and I were married, I used to drive by here sometimes and think, Someday..."

Jane straightened her fashionable blue blazer and gave Robbin an encouraging smile. "Where would we be without our dreams, Robbin? Maybe someday you'll own a house like this one."

"Not a chance," Robbin murmured, "but it's kind of you to say so." She often wished she worked with Jane instead of Lila Henderson, who tended to be flighty and a bit *too* outgoing. Her other associate was Frank Swanson, a rather brusque character who managed to find fault with almost everything and everybody. She knew she could expect a rather long sermon on the inefficiency of local government when he found out about the latest trouble at Red Rock.

"Jane, what do you know about Red Rock Refinery?" she asked, abruptly shifting gears as the memory slipped back into her mind. "I've never tried to sell a house very close to the plant, but after what happened this morning, I—"

"What happened this morning?" Jane queried. "I haven't heard anything."

Robbin was surprised. "There was an explosion... so loud it woke me up. You could smell the ammonia clear over at my house."

Alarm filled the older woman's eyes. "That's not good, Robb. The last time we had trouble out there—I mean real trouble—was in 1952. It happened just before

Christmas; my youngest daughter was four. I don't remember all the technical details, but somebody made some major miscalculation and mixed the wrong two chemicals together . . . or something like that. A cloud of poisonous gas spread all over Coltersville. Dozens of people died and hundreds more were hospitalized. They had to evacuate the whole area, and property values crashed overnight." Jane shook her head, awed by the memory. "A major subdivision had been planned in that end of town, but after the disaster nobody was about to buy a house out there. The developers were local people; they took a staggering loss. And it took the rest of us years to make good sales near the school again."

Suddenly Robbin's throat constricted. "My kids go to Red Rock School, Jane! I only live three blocks away!"

Jane patted Robbin's arm. "Take it easy, Robbie. I don't have any idea how serious it is or what problems are involved. If it's anything really major they'll probably hold a town meeting to bring us up-to-date. That's what they did before."

Before Robbin could ask any more questions, the Hawleys arrived. She hopped out of the car and made the introductions, all the while studying Sandra Hawley's face for some sign that she was falling under the spell of the vintage home.

"This is a very old house, but it's been beautifully maintained," Jane told the Hawleys as they followed her up the cobbled path. "The seller is a widow who's lived here for nearly fifty years and truly hates to give up this home. She wants to sell it to somebody who loves it as much as she does." Jane couldn't resist a smile in Robbin's direction, knowing full well that nobody would ever love it more than Robbin did. "This is real oak—" she pointed to the massive beams as they followed her inside

"—and the original tile here in the hallway." She went on to point out several other features before the Hawleys decided to look around on their own.

"How serious is this couple?" Jane asked her when the newlyweds were out of earshot. "They don't look wealthy enough to buy a house like this."

Robbin shrugged. "They probably aren't. But they're such a pair of dreamers that I just couldn't resist showing it to them."

"Robbin, you can't resist showing it to *anybody*," Jane reproached her gently. "You just look for excuses to come up here."

She couldn't really refute that. Two-twenty-six Crescent Heights Lane was everything she'd ever wanted in a home, and she longed to find a way to live here. There were nooks and crannies everywhere for all her knickknacks and potted plants, lovely oak panels, windows that gave witness to the rustic valley and the distant hills, and bedrooms for each of her kids, with two left over for sewing and guests. Even the wallpaper spoke to her. It was a near duplicate of the yellow rosebud print she'd chosen for her own kitchen. And the kitchen itself...oh, what a joy! A thousand carved oak cupboards, two ovens, a microwave and a charcoal grill....

"Robbin, are you sure you can't find a way to buy this house?" Jane asked her. They'd had this discussion several times before, but always they came back to the same subject when they were alone. "You know you'll die of a broken heart if you ever do manage to sell it."

Robbin sighed. "I know. But even if I could afford it, I'd never want to live here alone."

Jane could have said that living with three children hardly constituted solitude, but she refrained. A widow herself for a dozen years until last September, she knew what Robbin meant. "Doug's been gone a year now, Robb. Maybe it's time for a white knight to ride up to your front door."

"Funny you should say that," Robbin replied with a grin. "A man fitting that description showed up there this morning."

"Oh?"

"Well, probably not. Actually, I don't know a thing about him except that he's painfully good-looking. He's got a smile that would keep me warm in Antarctica."

Jane smiled indulgently. "Good looks are a dime a dozen, Robbin. You've been alone long enough for any healthy specimen to look inviting. But take it from one who knows: what you need now is a man with character."

"Oh, he's got that, too, Jane." Suddenly Robbin realized why she'd tossed aside her normal caution so quickly with Kent. "He's a friend of Ted's. That's a fourteen-carat character reference as far as I'm concerned."

"Ted? Your next-door neighbor?"

"Yes." Warmth suffused her just thinking of her dear friend. Who else would actually try to find a man for her? "Ted tried to set me up on a blind date with Kent, and he would never steer me toward a fellow he didn't think was perfect for me. And nobody on the face of this earth knows me better than Ted."

Jane shook her head. "Honestly, Robbin, I often wonder why you don't just marry that man and be done with it."

Robbin laughed. "Oh, Jane, I know we act like an old married couple sometimes, but we're just . . . well, too different to live together. I like everything as nice as it can be—Ted says I'm downright prissy at times—and he wouldn't notice a mess unless he had to shovel his way out to go to a ball game. Besides, we talked about getting married once, and Ted said it was a lousy idea."

"He did?"

"Well, everything's a joke with Ted, so it's hard to tell just what he meant. But right after Doug left, I was feeling so down that I couldn't bear to be alone; Ted was bringing over hamburgers and tacos every night. I told him it would be easier if he just moved in, and he told me that the last time he'd snapped up a girl on the rebound, she'd walked out on him six months later when she'd come to her senses. He said it was a risk he wouldn't take again."

"And you think he was kidding?"

"About the girl?" Robbin shook her head. "No. Ellen told me about her once. He fell in love with her during his senior year in high school and took their breakup pretty hard. He didn't get serious about anybody for years . . . until Ellen came along, and even then all he did was make jokes for the first half a dozen times they went out together. Later on, he was so slow to ask Ellen to marry him that she almost gave up on him altogether." She paused thoughtfully. "I'm sure glad she didn't, Jane. I wish they'd had more time together, but while Ellen was alive Ted Ballard was the happiest man on the face of this earth. I think that's why he's never married again. Nobody could measure up to his memory of Ellen. She was a jewel."

Jane, whose memories of loss were not too far behind her, responded soberly. "You don't ever . . . forget someone you've given your love to, Robbin. But if your memory is sweet, the time comes when you want to share your life again. Eventually it happened to me. I suspect the time will come when it happens to Ted."

Robbin felt a mist in her eyes, then pushed away the ridiculous burst of sentiment. Why should the idea of Ted's future remarriage touch her so deeply? She remembered his unaccountable tenderness this morning—juxtaposed against his short temper with Kent—and tried to figure out what was troubling him about the plant. Was it just the danger? She didn't think so. She had an inexplicable feeling that he knew something he didn't want to tell her... at least, not in front of Kent.

Robbin didn't want to think about the explosion anymore, so she deftly changed the subject. "You know, Jane, the first time I took a lady to look at this house, I went home and told Ted all about it. I was in such a silly mood. I'd spent the afternoon daydreaming of an irresistible hunk with a bushy mustache and a white tuxedo." She chuckled at the recollection. "He'd appear on my doorstep, whisk me away to The Old Mansion in Morgantown for dinner—Doug never would spend the money, you know—then cap off the evening with a drive up here to see the view. We'd sit in front of the house, looking out over the valley, and he'd tell me that he'd sold everything he'd owned to buy this marvelous home for me, his precious new wife..." Suddenly embarrassed, she turned back to Jane with a sheepish grin. "I get a bit carried away at times."

"I'll say," Jane answered gently. "What did good old Ted say to all this?"

Robbin's smile widened. "He said he hoped it would happen that way for me someday. Doug would have laughed himself silly, but Ted didn't make fun of me at all." She turned at the sound of the young couple approaching them, and prepared to put her professional cap back on. "Ted is so good to me, Jane," she finished just before they reached her. She felt wrapped in warmth, as sure of Ted's friendship as she'd ever been of anything in her life. "I just don't know what I'd do without him."

Jane greeted the Hawleys before she answered softly, "I hope you don't ever have to find out."

CHAPTER THREE

"CAN YOU STAY FOR DINNER?" Martha Ballard asked her only son as he followed Larry and Tina up the walk. "I can have it ready in half an hour."

Ted shook his head. "Sorry, Mom. I've got an emergency meeting tonight and I've got to go over some things first. I'll probably grab a hamburger on the run."

"You haven't been eating right lately," Martha clucked, her own generous bulk mute testimony to her love of food. "Look at you! Skinny as a rail."

Ted laughed, his tenderness for his mother clearly written in his warm gaze. "Come on, Mom. I *wanted* to lose weight, remember? Robbin said I was getting a paunch."

The elderly woman frowned for just a moment, pursing her lips as though she were about to speak. Then she stooped down to give each of her grandchildren a hug and a kiss. "I made some cookies this afternoon, Larry. If you eat all your asparagus I'll let you have an extra one."

Larry made a face, since it was expected of him, then gave his grandma a heartwarming smile. "Are they chocolate chip?"

"Would I make any other kind for my favorite grandson?" Larry was her *only* grandson, but Ted suspected that the boy would have been her favorite anyway.

Larry grinned and wriggled like a puppy before he asked, "Am I *really* your favorite? Do you *really* like me better than Jarrod?" The child had been told more than once that Robbin's kids were not related to him, let alone to his grandma, but he'd never fully grasped that fact. He'd been less than a year old when his mother had died, and as far as he was concerned, Robbin was his mom. She'd spent almost as much time feeding him, changing him and rocking him to sleep as his father had, and no maternal figure walked nearer to his heart. Not even his beloved grandma.

In those dark years right after Ellen had died, Martha Ballard had been too busy coping with her invalid husband to give her son all the help she'd longed to offer. She and Ted both knew that if Robbin had been a different kind of woman, Tina and Larry would have been raised by a series of housekeepers.

"When you called this afternoon, you didn't tell me why you wanted to bring the kids over a day early," Martha asked. She lived about thirty minutes away from Coltersville in Morgantown, the county seat. Since Ted worked nearby, it was easy for him to drop by as often as he liked, but he always had to make a round trip back to Coltersville if he wanted to bring the children. "I thought Operation Cinderella was tomorrow night."

"It is," Ted admitted, unable to repress a smile of anticipation.

"Watch it, Ted, you're wearing your embarrassed grin," his mother teased him. "When you were little I always knew who'd raided the cookie jar or tracked in the mud. Now I can tell—"

"All right, all right," he cut her off good-naturedly. "I get the picture." He hadn't told Martha very much about his plans for Friday night, but she was his mother, after all, and she knew how much this date with Robbin meant to him. He hoped the trouble at the refinery wouldn't interfere with his plans, but the timing couldn't have been worse. He was already feeling guilty about the explosion; if he'd spent more time worrying about his job and less time worrying about Robbin, he might have been able to prevent the accident at Red Rock.

Ted waited until Larry was out of earshot before he answered his mother's question. "There's been an explosion at the Red Rock Refinery, Mom."

Martha raised her eyebrows. "Why didn't you bring Jarrod and the girls?" She'd taken care of all five kids so often that her concern was instinctive.

"They're still with their dad. Robb expects them back Saturday, but I called Doug today and asked him to come up with some reason to keep them a little longer. I don't want to frighten Robbin, but I don't want the kids that close till I figure out what's going on."

Concern lined the widow's face. "If it's dangerous, Ted, should you and Robbin be living there? Why don't you just close down the plant? You have the power to do that, don't you?"

He nodded uneasily. "I'd close it down right now if I had one shred of hard evidence that it's still unsafe. On paper everything looks hunky-dory. It's just—" he paused and bit his lower lip "—it's just a feeling I have. I can't really put my finger on it." Martha Ballard was a great believer in the sixth sense; Ted knew she would understand his intuitive apprehension.

"There must be something bothering you, Ted."

"There are a lot of things, actually." He ticked them off on one hand. "The guy who runs the plant is usually a real hard-nose, and today he just about tripped over his own bootlaces trying to be helpful. First he was cheerful and when I made it clear that that wouldn't wash, he got downright sentimental over the workmen who got hurt. At the time he seemed genuinely concerned, but the more I think about it, I really...well, I just don't trust the man. He's always taken some perverse delight in opposing me. It's possible that he realizes how close I am to shutting him down and just wants to buy some time, but...he could have some reason."

"And?"

Ted fiddled with his tie. "Then there's Kent."

"The young man you play tennis with?"

"*Used* to play tennis with. He always beat me six ways from Sunday no matter how much I hustled. But the last few times we played, he kept missing gutter shots, fouling his own serves, practically falling asleep in between points. He never acted like he cared about winning before, but all of a sudden he'd go off the deep end if he lost a game. I don't know if he's into some late night racket or taking too much of something, but lately his moods have sure been unpredictable, and his perception on the court is way off."

"So?" she prodded, clearly waiting for more information.

"Kent approved the part of the plant where the explosion occurred, Mom, but he doesn't seem the least bit concerned about the accident, or interested in protecting the public...most of the time, at least. For a while there I thought he was going to say that we didn't even need to investigate." He paused as the memory returned. Kent's behavior at the refinery had been...well, puzzling as well as irritating. How could a man act defiant, friendly, indifferent and deeply concerned all at the same time? "Once we got started, I caught a few tiny irregularities that he should have noticed. I just wonder what else he missed in his current condition."

"So that's it?" Martha saw too much; Ted knew she could tell that he was holding something back. "One man who's usually nice to you isn't, and one man who's usually grouchy is nice?"

"No, it's more than that." For a moment he debated whether or not to tell her the rest. Ted didn't want to alarm his mother, but he really needed to think out loud with somebody he could trust. He was used to bouncing his ideas off of Robbin every night while the kids watched TV—a luxury he'd had to sacrifice lately as part of his courtship plan.

He decided to confide in Martha. "What really bothers me, Mom, is that the whole section of this urea unit where the explosion took place had all new equipment installed this summer: valves, pipes, tanks, everything. Cost a fortune. So much, in fact, that I wonder if somebody tried to cut the cost somehow. Gregory's such a cheapskate that I'm surprised he agreed to such an overhaul."

"And you think he might have... done one thing on paper and something else in fact?" she asked shrewdly.

Reluctantly, Ted nodded. "It's just a theory. One of many possibilities. But I don't have any reason to believe that's what happened... yet."

Martha leaned back against her chair and asked softly, "But Ted, surely you've approved all the equipment out there. Isn't that what your job is all about?"

Ted shook his head uneasily. "Not exactly. I'm in charge of hazardous waste removal procedures. New valves above ground would be subject to Fire Department approval."

He didn't explain further, and she didn't press him. He needed to ask Kent about the valves he'd approved in July, but he couldn't think of a way to do that without implying that somebody—Kent, for instance—had failed to notice some irregularity. Kent was so touchy these days he'd be likely to fly off the handle, and then it would be impossible for them to work together on this project. And they *had* to work together because this wasn't a matter that could be left in limbo. Not when Robbin and the five children were involved.

"I really don't have any reason to believe that somebody's violated regulations," Ted repeated, trying to concentrate on the more likely causes of the explosion. "I've been hearing a lot about faulty pipes lately, even when they're brand new. Gregory says he upgraded everything, but even so, if he tried to save money by buying second-rate material, they might not be strong enough to withstand the pressure. If that's true, then today's problem could be symptomatic of something larger. It's not a very comforting thought."

"Daddy!" Tina's gay voice interrupted them. She bounced out the front door and snuggled up against her father, her silver braces gleaming in the sun. "Don't forget to feed Captain while I'm gone. I usually give him an extra can in the afternoon before you get home, so he'll be really hungry by six o'clock."

Ted smiled at his daughter, then reached out to tousle her hair. "I'll feed your silly cat, sweetheart. But who's going to feed me?"

"Aunt Robbin will," she promised, then stopped and corrected herself. "Robbin, I mean. Why aren't we supposed to call her 'aunt' anymore?"

Ted swallowed hard but didn't answer right away. He gave his daughter a hug, then kissed her gently on the cheek. "I'll explain that to you when I pick you up next week. Okay?"

"Okay." She reached up to give him a mighty hug. "Don't forget to ask her about Yosemite."

"I won't." The two families always camped at Yosemite over Labor Day weekend; the scheduled vacation was one reason Ted felt that he had to resolve things with Robbin in the next few days. If things didn't turn out the way he hoped—Lord help him!—there was no way on earth he'd be able to handle a camping trip with Robbin ten days from now.

Ted called goodbye to Larry, who was inside watching television, then thanked his mother again and headed out toward the tired old Volkswagen. Somehow he and Kent had gotten the beast rolling after lunch. By tomorrow at this time he'd be driving a spanking new Dodge van big enough to accommodate a wife and five kids.

Ted slid in behind the wheel and his mother leaned in through the window.

"Ted, I know it's none of my business, but . . ."

"Yes?"

"About tomorrow night."

"Umm?"

"Have you . . . have you prepared yourself for the possibility—no matter how small—that Robbin might—"

"—say no?" he finished for her.

"Well, yes," she admitted sheepishly.

They'd gone over this before, and Ted didn't really want to explain it all again. But he knew his mother's concerns were genuine, and they were too realistic for him to set aside.

"Mom, I know there's a chance. Of course there's a chance." There were times—late at night when nobody was awake on the whole block but Captain—when Ted would prowl through the house, talking to the cat, absolutely certain that Robbin would turn him down flat. She might be embarrassed when she figured out all he'd done to win her love...or worse yet, amused.

Oh, he could tell her that lately he'd been feeling bold and impatient and ready for a change; that much was certainly true. Any fool could see that he needed a serviceable car and was long overdue for a new wardrobe. And Ted had to admit that he liked the way other women were responding to his new image. At dark moments he comforted himself with the knowledge that if Robbin didn't want him, there were a host of other attractive females who did. He'd actually turned down several dates lately—some from women he'd just met, and others from women who'd ignored him for years.

It would be harder to pass off the changes he'd made in the house. Despite Robbin's valiant efforts over the years to persuade Ted to replace the stained carpet, chipped tile and peeling paint, this was the first time he'd done any redecorating since Ellen's death. In the past few months, he'd implemented all of Robbin's recommendations, hoping to make the place gracious enough for her to live in—or to sell, if she preferred to start over somewhere fresh when they moved in together. Ted had even considered presenting her with the title to her dream house on Crescent Heights Lane as a wedding present, even though he thought the house was too big, too showy and too expensive. In the end, though, it wasn't the money that had deterred him. It just seemed like too grand a gesture for good old Ted Ballard, and he didn't want to end up with egg on his face if she turned him down. Besides, Ted didn't want Robbin to marry him just because he could take care of her. He already did that quite well. He wanted her to ache for him as a lover, to tingle when he breathed her name, to grow warm inside when she felt his lips on her own.

She has to feel that way! How can she not? a part of him roared in confidence and yearning. But another voice, the more familiar voice of reason and practicality, warned him, *She loves you, pal, but just as a friend. And after tomorrow night, she'll never be quite the same friend again.*

"I know you've never really understood how Robbin and I could be so close when we're . . . just friends," Ted finally conceded to his mother. "But I know that nobody's more important to her than I am...except for the kids. She just needed some time to make the jump from friend to lover, that's all."

Martha shook her head. "That's just my point, Ted. That shouldn't be a jump engineered by you. You shouldn't *have* to spend money on clothes or a car to impress a woman who knows you as well as Robbin does. Either she loves you the way you are, or she doesn't. That's all."

Ted couldn't disagree with her logic, but he couldn't concede her point without admitting the folly of his plans. "She loves me, Mom," he persisted quietly. "I just don't think she knows it yet."

"And you think she'll figure it out just because you ask her to marry you?" Martha's voice broke with frustration. "If it were meant to be, honey, don't you think it would have happened all by itself after all this time?"

"No!" he insisted, more confident now. "Not when I've done everything in my power to make sure it *didn't* happen! Right after Doug left, Robbin was easy prey for anybody who'd make her feel like a woman. She would have married me on the rebound if I'd asked her; she practically proposed to me once! But I didn't want her that way, Mom. I didn't want to take advantage of her misery, and I wanted to make sure I was there for her as long as she needed me—in whatever way she needed me." He paused and took firm control of his turbulent feelings. "But she's moved through that gray cloud of pain now. She's ready to meet a man and fall in love. If it's not me, it's going to be somebody else. I can feel the change in her; I'm running out of time. If I don't overwhelm her completely—convince her that this isn't just an idea I had over pizza, a convenient way to deal with baby-sitting and keeping house—I'll lose her forever."

Tears lurked in Martha's maternal eyes. "But Ted, don't you realize that if she says no, you'll lose her anyway? It'll never be the same between you."

It was true. He couldn't deny it. But he also knew he couldn't go on another day the way things were. He ached for Robbin so much it hurt. It was impossible to stay away from her and agony to stay close by. He wanted to run his fingers through her long black hair; he wanted to make her quiver for him, cry out for him as a man instead of a brother. It took all of his self-control to keep from doing something rash that broke all the rules—like devouring her with the deepest of hungry kisses in a quiet moment when they were alone or seeking the softness of her bare skin beneath her nightgown. Robbin would never forgive him if he violated her trust in him and he would never forgive himself.

He studied his mother for a long thoughtful moment, then replied with quiet strength, "I know it's a risk, Mom. But it's one I've just got to take."

ROBBIN GOT TO THE SCHOOL EARLY for the meeting, eager to learn about the explosion, and relieved that Doug had asked to keep the kids for the whole weekend. He hadn't explained his reasons, but Robbin hadn't argued with him. Although she missed her children terribly, she didn't want them to come home until Ted had time to straighten everything out at Red Rock.

Over the summer she'd talked to all three of them at least once a week. Surprisingly, it was Ruth who called most often, usually with some concern about one of the other two. She had always taken her role as big sister very seriously, but in the last few months it seemed to Robbin that she'd grown up a great deal and was more determined than ever to buoy her family with love. She asked Robbin about the Ballards every time they talked, and although she insisted that she was happy as a clam with her father, Robbin could sense that she was eager to come home.

Waiting for Lila and Frank in the back of the room, Robbin watched impatiently as other people began to arrive—school personnel, Red Rock staff, local realtors, business people, irate parents and neighbors. One woman in a brisk, black suit and high heels—a dead giveaway that she was an outsider—carried a notepad and wrote in it steadily as she waited for the meeting to begin. For a last minute emergency meeting, Robbin thought the turnout was impressive; the cafeteria had never been this full for the P.T.A.

A hint of some heady male cologne that reminded her of sunrise on a mountain trail was Robbin's only warning before she felt an unexpected touch on her shoulder. She was surprised by the quick rush of desire that surged through her body; even more surprised when Ted's familiar smile greeted her from beneath the still unfamiliar mustache.

"Hi, Robbs. I didn't expect to see you here tonight," Ted greeted her, his tone unexpectedly gentle as he took in the showy ruffles of her turquoise dress. "I promised to tell you all about it tomorrow."

"Tomorrow?" she echoed, less puzzled by Ted's words than by her inexplicable response to his touch. But Ted's sober expression reminded her that she'd already forgotten his Friday night plans once today, and he wasn't at all happy that she'd forgotten again. Instinctively seeking a way to soothe him, Robbin reached up to straighten his perfectly straight tie and dust some imaginary lint off of his spotless collar. "Of course, Teddy," she assured him. "Tomorrow."

But her efforts to placate Ted failed entirely. He took hold of Robbin's fingers as they brushed his lapel, and a strange expression—half-pleased, half-angry—flitted across his face. "I'm not your kid brother on his way to the prom, Robbin," he told her tersely. "I'm here representing the county. *Professionally*," he added for emphasis.

Robbin took a step back, chagrined, but still a bit peeved by his hard words. "I'm sorry, Ted. I just wanted you to look your best."

"I'm a grown man, Robbin. I can get dressed all by myself."

This time her cheeks flushed. "Teddy! I didn't mean—"

"Shh." His eyes were still grave, but his tone was warm again. "I know you just wanted to help. This isn't the time or the place. Do you understand?"

Quietly Robbin looked at Ted, really looked at him, trying to understand what she'd done to offend him. One of the things she loved best about him was his unchangeably cheerful disposition. Of course, after Ellen died he'd been pretty irascible for a while, but usually Ted lost his temper only about once a year, and even then he yelled at Captain or one of the kids. Clearly he was having a very difficult day; it was Robbin's turn to buck him up. What else were friends for?

"I truly am sorry, Ted." He seemed to sense that her apology was sincere; the tension around his mouth eased perceptibly. "You look—you look just perfect. I really like the mustache. It makes you look . . . older."

"Older?" Now he seemed amused. Robbin was a bit embarrassed, but happy to see the dark cloud passing.

"Well, maybe more mature. Not that I ever thought you weren't, but..." She sighed in exasperation and gave up the struggle. "Oh, never mind."

Suddenly Ted grinned. "Robbin Jean Walker, I do believe this is the first time in the thirteen years I've known you that you just plain ran out of words to say!" Despite Ted's disclaimers about his role as a public servant, he leaned down to brush a kiss across her cheek.

His mustache was thick and wiry, and the stiff ends brushed Robbin's skin in a delightfully sensuous way. *Like a hairbrush on a scalp,* she assured herself, alarmed at the notion that Ted's touch could be anything but comforting. *That's not the same as an erotic response at all.* Satisfied with her analysis, Robbin watched Ted stroll toward the stage, surprised at the barest hint of a swagger as his long, lean legs maneuvered the stairwell.

"Robbin?" The deep voice was insistent, as though the man had called her name more than once before she'd heard him. "When I said maybe we'd meet again, I didn't think it would be so soon."

"Kent!" A lingering hint of blush colored her lovely, heart-shaped face as she turned to face him. "I was hoping you'd be here."

Kent looked just as gorgeous as he had at dawn; his blond hair still shimmered like gold. He'd changed into a pinstriped gray affair that dramatized his blue eyes, which warmed at the sight of her. "I've been shadowing Ted all day," he tossed out casually. "Where he goes, I go."

Robbin laughed. "He's going to 347 Mulberry Lane after the meeting."

Kent smiled a knowing smile that left no doubt as to his interpretation of her casual comment. "Is that an invitation?"

"An invitation?" Robbin repeated, suddenly feeling out of her depth. *It's been so long since I've played this game,* she admitted to herself. *And I was never very good at it to begin with.* "I—I don't know, Kent. You just said . . ." She stopped uncertainly.

Kent studied her for a minute, as though she were a beautiful butterfly he'd just captured and couldn't quite decide whether to pin down or let go. Surely he realized she wasn't in the market for quick flings and complex games! Ted must have told him what she was really like. And Ted, after all, had chosen this man for her. If Kent had as much faith in Ted as Robbin did, he'd see through her uncertain overtures and take the time to get to know her better.

At last he reached out to stroke her face lightly where Ted had kissed her, reminding Robbin that nobody but Ted had kissed her—even as a friend—in over a year. *It's about time, Robbin,* she chastised herself. *You've mourned Doug long enough.*

She couldn't withhold her welcoming smile when Kent murmured quietly, "Let's leave it for now, Robbin; the meeting's about to start and I've got a lot on my mind tonight. But I'll be in touch." His dimpled smile was cautious, gentle . . . and even more promising than his words. "I'll definitely . . . be in touch."

Robbin grinned rapturously as he headed for the stage. She felt silly and sophisticated all at the same time. Hadn't he all but asked her for a date? Granted, she knew that men often said they'd call and never did, but she knew instinctively that Kent Hawthorne had no reason to resort to such games with her. They hardly even knew each other. Their real link was Ted, and Ted—

Robbin's cartwheel feelings careened to a halt as she noticed that Ted was studying her from his post near the podium with an intensity she must have imagined—he simply wasn't capable of such anger. With unspeakable relief, Robbin watched his gaze—and his fury—shift silently to Kent as the other man climbed the stairs. She couldn't imagine why Ted would be so mad at Kent, but it was certainly better than having him mad at her! Why, having Ted upset with her would be like... well, something like having a fight with Doug back when they were married. Every time it happened—more and more toward the end—Robbin had barely been able to eat or sleep or smile at the kids until things were right between them. But she'd never had a real fight with Ted—just a quickly forgiven harsh word or two—and she didn't want to start now.

But Ted seemed to have forgotten Robbin. His eyes were boring into Kent Hawthorne, and anybody who knew Ted as well as she did could read the message emblazoned there.

Match point, his dark eyes warned the other man, *and it's my turn to serve.*

CHAPTER FOUR

"ARE YOU READY FOR THE PRESENTATION?" Ted asked in a low tone as Kent sat down beside him. "Have you...taken care of all the required social pleasantries?"

Kent shrugged, apparently immune to the bite in Ted's voice. "I know you've been doing this sort of thing longer than I have, Ted, but I don't need a wet nurse to get through the meeting. I know what I'm going to say. The pressure explosion is a one-time occurrence that isn't likely to be repeated."

"Right." Ted all but spit out the word. A sudden siege of jealously had racked his body, a new experience that he'd found difficult to handle. He'd seen Kent work on a woman before, and it wasn't hard to read the signs. From Ted's vantage point, it was pretty clear that Kent was moving in on Robbin, and Robbin was falling for him hook, line and sinker.

Don't be stupid, Ballard, Ted ordered himself, knowing he was overreacting to the brief interaction he'd witnessed. *Kent simply had a few minutes to kill before the meeting...just as he had a few minutes to kill at dawn. He's playing a game, and Robbin's too smart to fall for it.* He repeated the hollow assurance to himself several times. Of course, by the time Kent got around to asking Robbin out, she would already belong to Ted. Twenty-four hours until Operation Cinderella began; twenty-four hours until he'd ask Robbin to be his wife.

Oblivious to the thoughts in his colleague's mind, Kent glanced up at Ted and asked with casual interest, "Did you notice how eager Gregory was to help us today, Ballard?"

Taken aback by this display of professional camaraderie between them—sorely lacking in recent months—Ted pushed aside his personal distress and confessed, "Yes, Kent. It bothered me a lot."

Kent shrugged. "Well, he's probably just having second thoughts about giving us so much trouble in the past. We could shut him down in a second, and he knows it."

Surprised, but encouraged that Kent had given this possibility some thought, Ted asked, "Do you think that's something we should discuss?"

The other man appeared to consider the proposition for a moment, then replied, "I don't think so. It could be years before another valve gives out—it was just a freak accident. There's no reason to frighten everybody with the other violations we found there. They're all minor and easy enough to repair."

"And they're all in your jurisdiction, Hawthorne," Ted pointed out, trying not to sound accusatory.

But Kent read his message clearly. He responded in a low tone, "I know how to do my job, Ted."

Ted didn't flinch. "Glad to hear it."

"The way you ran over me out there today, I was beginning to wonder."

"The way *I* ran over *you*?" Ted echoed. "As I recall, you were the one who kept trying to block my path."

Kent leaned back comfortably, master of the situation. "Are you still talking about this morning at the refinery, Ted?" he asked in a casual tone, "Or am I running a length ahead in some other competition?" His gaze drifted purposefully toward Robbin, who gave Kent a grin that could have melted a snowman. Her look was an implied invitation for which Ted would have sold his soul. But Robbin had clearly forgotten him altogether; her radiant eyes were trained on the golden Lochinvar who sat beside him.

Dear God, I'm in trouble, Ted gasped inwardly, struggling to keep his composure. Twenty-four hours might be too long to wait; Operation Cinderella might not be enough to turn the tide. His mother's warnings flashed through his mind, and all the other ideas he'd pondered and discarded galloped across his memory.

Desperately he studied Robbin, then noticed the well-heeled young blonde sitting next to her. Surely that was Lila, the romantic airhead he'd heard so much about. Robbin was fond of the young woman despite her foibles. If Lila cared for Robbin, too, maybe she'd be willing to help Ted.... He couldn't possibly go into escrow on the Crescent Heights house before tomorrow night, but if he could get the ball rolling, it might be enough to make a dramatic statement to Robbin. And Ted realized with a sinking apprehension that left him all but numb, that he was going to need a great deal of drama to counteract the spell Kent Hawthorne was weaving over Robbin tonight.

As the school principal tried to bring the meeting to order, Kent broke off his provocative study of Robbin's flushed face and showy new dress. Ever so casually he turned to Ted and murmured, "I think it's only fair to warn you, Ballard, that I never enter a tournament unless I plan to win."

"ROBBIN, DO YOU ACTUALLY KNOW THAT GORGEOUS HUNK?" Lila Henderson asked her co-worker, gesturing toward the stage. Dressed in an oversize blouse, tight purple pants and a wide, black belt that hugged her round hips, Lila looked more like a teenager than a very experienced twenty-five-year-old. Her boundless enthusiasm—for life in general and men in specific—was a source of wonder to Robbin. "Can you introduce me?"

An unfamiliar wave of pride swept over Robbin as she considered Lila's request. Lila, the office butterfly, had so many boyfriends that Frank often said she ought to assign them numbers because he couldn't remember all their names. To have such a popular woman sound envious of a man who was interested in Robbin was a feather in her cap; no doubt about it. "Well, I don't know why not," she answered. "Even though he looks like Robert Redford, Kent is really very easy to talk to. He—"

"I don't mean the showboat," the other woman corrected her. To Robbin's amazement, she was pointing to Ted. "I mean the real man... the one who doesn't need to tug on his lapels to prove how hot he is." She sighed dramatically, lifting her petite shoulders as she placed a hand on her heart. "I don't see a wedding ring, but I can't believe a guy like that is still single. Looks, charisma, integrity oozing out of every pore! If he were free, you would have snatched him up by now, right?"

Positively glowing, Lila turned to Robbin and waited for an answer. Robbin didn't have one. Was it possible they were looking at the same man? Certainly Ted was the salt of the earth, but... gorgeous? A man among men? A *hunk*? He *was* wearing that classy beige ensemble that Robbin couldn't recall picking out for him, and the mustache had added character to his boyish good looks. Granted, he didn't look much like the real Ted, but he did look rather appealing. A bit tense, perhaps, but under the circumstances that was certainly understandable. Wordlessly, she studied him, trying to decide what to say to Lila.

"Well, actually, Lila, he's a widow with two sweet kids," she finally admitted. "He lives next door to me, and he *is* the nicest guy in the world."

Lila beamed.

"But I wouldn't get your hopes up. Ted doesn't date much. I'm not sure that—" she broke off. She couldn't bear to discourage such a nice woman from interest in Ted. It would be so good for him to have a lady friend! But Ted wasn't, well, Lila's idea of a date. She liked French cuisine and opera and gentlemen who made arrangements two weeks in advance. She had no idea that Ted only looked that good when the moon was full, and she'd surely faint dead away if she ever saw his living room right after the World Series. But how did you tell a drooling blond beauty that your best friend was a spectacular neighbor, but a washout as a date?

It was different, of course, when *Robbin* went out with Ted. But nobody would ever call that dating! If she and Ted were any closer, they'd be brother and sister. Come to think of it, Ted was the best brother that Robbin had ever had . . . and she'd grown up with three of them who weren't half bad. *And I never straightened their ties at a public meeting,* she recalled defensively, still unsure why that affectionate gesture had irritated Ted.

"Lila, I'll introduce you after the meeting if you like. Just keep in mind that Ted is . . . well, a very casual sort of guy. He's all dressed up for the meeting, but he'll probably have his tie off before he gets out the door."

Unless he spills catsup on it first, she might have added. Instead, she turned her eyes back to the stage.

Besides Ted, Kent and the school principal, there were half a dozen men up there whom Robbin had never seen before. They were all lumberjack-sized and gave off an aura of strength that was rather intimidating. One of them was so rotund that he reminded her of a hard-boiled egg—especially with that smooth scalp framed with a halo of short white hairs. The rest of the oilmen looked pretty much the same, all in jeans, plaid shirts, and heavy work boots. They all wore tense expressions on their faces.

"They say there's nothing new under the sun," Frank Swanson grumbled, studying the array of oilmen. "We've been through all this before."

Robbin stared at her dour boss. He liked to think of himself as a cowboy and was dressed in a Western-style leisure suit, pointed boots, and a big felt Stetson. "I beg your pardon?" she said, confused.

He snorted without humor. Frank did everything without humor except close a sale. "When we had that disaster back in the fifties, a whole clump of them strolled in here, sat right up there on that same stage, and made us a bunch of promises like they're going to make tonight."

"Such as?" Robbin asked, suddenly wishing she'd taken more time at noon to discuss the historical accident with Jane instead of mooning over her dream house.

"Such as, there's nothing to worry about. No danger to kids, to neighbors, to—"

"—people who own land nearby," Lila finished for him. The earlier sparkle in her eyes was replaced by a hard glitter that Robbin had never seen before. "They'll tell us that real estate won't be affected, and whatever happened will never happen again."

Her bitterness surprised Robbin, but Frank nodded as though the two had discussed this many times before. "We can't let them get away with it this time. Too much is at stake here."

"*Way* too much," Lila repeated.

Robbin couldn't help but stare at her, surprised and troubled by her vehemence. Frank was always grumpy; that was his nature. But Lila was so saccharine-sweet it was nauseating at times. Her sudden anger was disconcerting to Robbin.

But when Lila glanced up at Robbin and read the uneasiness on her face, she immediately whipped out her compact and touched up her lipstick. After a moment spent basking in the glow of her reflection, she winked at Robbin, her good humor apparently restored.

"Show time," she said in a bubbly tone, looking at Ted again.

Nobody was paying much attention to the principal who'd been trying to call the meeting to order. Then Ted stood up, looking terribly grave and official, and asked if everyone could take their seats so the meeting could get underway. The principal flashed him a grateful look as he reclaimed the podium. After a brief rundown of the agenda, he turned the floor over to the oil people.

"Good evening, everybody," the man who looked like Humpty Dumpty began. "My name is Lowell Gregory and I'm the plant manager of Red Rock Refinery here in back of the school." His gap-toothed smile embraced them. "I know you're all concerned about what happened out here this morning. Believe me, so are we. Last we heard it looks like all of our injured men are going to make it. Bless the good Lord for that."

"I can see why they chose him for this assignment," Frank muttered to her left. "I bet he hires himself out to politicians for baby kissing on the weekends."

Robbin didn't answer. She thought the man seemed genuinely concerned about his employees, but then again, she tended to look on the bright side of things.

"We've had our own people checking into this all day, ably assisted by Ted Ballard from Environmental Health—" he nodded toward Ted "—and his counterpart from the Fire Department, Kent Hawthorne." Much to Robbin's surprise, the grin Kent offered the crowd was almost identical to the one with which he'd favored her a few minutes ago. She'd been warmed by those pearly whites more than once today, but she'd assumed that Kent's smile had been spontaneous, intimate...a special gift for her.

"We're all in agreement that the explosion is the result of a rupture of one of the ammonia processing tanks on the north side of the plant." He pointed to the map over the chalkboard. It was a maze of circles, squares and bullet shapes, none of which had any meaning for Robbin. "What we're not sure of yet is what caused this to happen. There are several possible explanations. Mr. Hawthorne will go over them with you."

Kent stood up, his smile inspiring confidence even in the dark, uneven light of the cafeteria. He looked devastatingly handsome to Robbin; she still couldn't believe he was interested in *her*. That look they'd shared while waiting for the meeting to start had been so intimate, she'd been embarrassed to have Ted in the same room! She knew he'd tease her mercilessly if he found out she was falling for his friend. Of course, Ted had brought the two of them together and he was always encouraging her to go out more. Maybe he'd be kind enough to spare her the ribbing this time. When the chips were down, Ted really could be a pretty sensitive guy.

Robbin was surprised when Frank nodded toward Kent and cracked, "So what does this guy do in his spare time besides pose for *Gentleman's Quarterly*?"

"Don't you like anybody, Frank?" Robbin countered, irritated with her colleague's ongoing attacks on the presenters. "Why don't you let the man talk before you dump on him?"

Frank glared at her but made no reply.

"Hazards at an oil refinery of this type fall into three basic categories," Kent began, sounding like a bored lecturer in spite of his Ivy League smile. "Fire, explosion, and other environmental dangers. My department deals with prevention of the first two, which obviously can be interrelated."

"He makes it sound as though your neighbor's job is inconsequential," Lila complained, her eyes still on Ted. "And he's the one who'll decide whether or not to close down the plant. How often do you hear about a fire at a refinery, anyway? It's all those leaks and spills that are dangerous."

Robbin consciously shut out Lila's prattle: she wanted to listen to Kent.

"There are three likely explanations for what happened at Red Rock today, none of which pose any health hazard to people living in the area," Kent continued, sounding vaguely like a robot. *Is it that unimportant to him?* Robbin wondered. *Has he gone over this so many times that he's sick of it? Or is it tiring for him to explain it in simple layman's terms?*

"First of all, you need to understand what happens during the manufacture of urea fertilizer pellets. During the production process, several chemicals are blended in a tank under tremendous pressure. Safety relief valves are designed to relieve this pressure before it reaches a danger point. During one part of the process, the ammonia mixture must be rapidly cooled, and during this time a semi-solid sludge occurs, which can seep into a valve and temporarily block it."

Robbin wasn't at all sure she understood him. It sounded simple, but chemistry had hardly been her best subject in school! She made a mental note to ask Ted about it later. He was always so good at explaining things. If it weren't for his patient tutoring, Ruth would have gotten a D in algebra last year.

"Problems also can occur with the tanks themselves. Metal fatigue due to age, corrosion, or poor rewelding can weaken some portion of the tank sufficiently to make it give way under pressure." Cockily, he slipped one hand in his pocket and went on a bit more quickly. "Finally, human error may be a contributing factor. If a relief valve is set too high, it won't kick open in time to relieve the pressure. Again, too much pressure is what brings about the explosion."

The audience was stone silent, and Robbin wondered if they were as confused as she was. Of course, they probably hadn't been drooling over the man instead of trying to follow his discourse.

When a man near the back asked Kent to explain the process of making fertilizer pellets again, Ted stood up and moved leisurely to the front of the stage.

"If I may...intervene, Mr. Hawthorne," he said smoothly, "I think a simple comparison to kitchen cooking may be in order here. Years ago, when I first tried to boil potatoes in a pressure cooker, I forgot to leave the relief valve open, even though the kind lady who taught me how to cook made it very clear what would happen if the steam couldn't escape." For a moment he looked straight at Robbin, clearly remembering those days as poignantly as she did. Then his glance shifted to Lila, and his expression softened, reminding Robbin of the way he used to look at Ellen. How long had it been! And now Lila wanted to get to know Ted better. Perhaps the feeling was mutual. He had a right, didn't he? Then why did she feel so . . . resistant?

Oblivious to Robbin's train of thought, Ted was still speaking. "Well, now, an ammonia processing tank is a lot like a pressure cooker . . . with one hundred times the pressure. If the steam can't escape, something's going to give."

"Thank you," the man in the back said gratefully. "That makes it very clear."

Ted nodded—more at Kent than at the man in the audience—and returned to his seat. Despite his smile for the crowd, his eyes looked dark and angry when he gazed at Kent. Robbin couldn't help but be puzzled by the contrast in his brief but warm glance at her. Kent's jaw seemed to tighten as Ted sat down, but he turned back to the audience with a polished smile.

"Mr. Hawthorne, in your opinion, which one of the reasons you mentioned is the most likely cause of the accident, and how can you be sure it won't happen again?" asked the woman in the black suit and heels. Her pencil stood poised over her notepad like a weapon. Robbin decided she was probably a reporter from the Morgantown rag.

Kent took a deep breath before he answered. "We're still looking into that, but regardless of the cause of the accident, there is no reason for the public to be alarmed. The chance of any one of the three problems being repeated is very small."

"I bet your buddy would tell a different story," Lila murmured, her eyes still on Ted. "He looks like a rattler ready to strike."

Robbin followed her gaze. Ted still looked terribly tense, but not even on his darkest day would she ever have compared him to a serpent. She decided that Lila's senses were working overtime where Ted was concerned, just as she was imagining that she knew what Kent's inner feelings were. "Lila, you've got the wrong animal. Ted does lose his temper now and then, but most of the time he's just a teddy bear." She smiled. "In fact, that's his nickname."

"His *nickname*?" Lila was dumbstruck. "People actually call him Teddy Bear Ballard?"

For some reason Robbin was embarrassed. "Well, not *people* exactly. Just me." She shrugged uncomfortably. "I always thought it suited him."

She didn't realize Frank was listening until a male voice on her left said, "If my wife called me 'teddy bear' in public I'd feed her to the sharks. I'm surprised this neighbor of yours puts up with it. He doesn't look like a pushover."

Robbin couldn't answer that. She couldn't remember calling Ted anything frivolous in front of other people, nor could she remember any time he'd complained about her cutesy nickname for him. But she never would have expected him to object to her straightening his tie, either. She wouldn't have offended Ted for the world! Frank's opinion didn't matter to her; after all, he was such a grouch. But if Lila, who knew so many men and thought Ted was so appealing, found her nickname condescending....

Robbin didn't have much time to dwell on the matter, though, because Ted was standing up again, courteously but confidently correcting Kent.

"Excuse me, Mr. Hawthorne, but we've discussed another possibility that seems to have slipped your mind." He faced the audience, looking calm and poised. "While the fire inspector is entirely correct about the dangers of sludge clogging a valve when urea is cooling, a faulty relief valve can jam all by itself. When this happens, the automatic release systems become useless. Only a worker at the plant who is prepared for such an emergency can remain in the atmosphere of deadly gas long enough to operate the backup valve manually."

A woman in the back row asked, "And are Red Rock workers well prepared for such emergencies?"

"Let me field this one, Mr. Ballard," said Lowell Gregory. A vibrant smile split his round face as he declared, "Safety regulations required by the state and the feds are strictly observed at our site. One of those regulations is that protective gear—Tyvex safety suit, gas mask, and oxygen—must be strategically placed for easy access of assigned personnel in the event of an emergency. Once the crew chief slips on this equipment, he can quickly gain access to the manual valve."

"Gas mask?" the woman repeated, looking back at Ted. "If workers at the plant need gas masks, what kind of air are we breathing a few blocks away? My kids go to school here and—"

"So do mine," Ted answered, his expression turning grim, "and I assure you that if I had one shred of evidence that this plant posed the slightest danger to my children, I'd move heaven and earth to close it down." For a moment the rumble in the room grew silent. Everybody knew that closing down the plant would leave half the men in Coltersville unemployed; safety wasn't the only community factor involved. Then Ted added, "But if the explosion was caused by any of the things Mr. Hawthorne mentioned, it's not likely to be repeated."

"What if it was caused by a faulty valve? Didn't you just say that could happen?"

Ted nodded. "If that's the problem, it's still a freak occurrence. Statistically, a man is more likely to get hurt driving to work in the morning than he is working at Red Rock or any other refinery in this state."

This time it was crusty Frank who stood up to ask, "But if one valve is faulty, couldn't another one go bad, too? I mean, that refinery has been here for at least thirty years. Aren't the pipes and valves starting to wear out?"

"You've presented a very valid concern, sir. But the specs require new valves every fifteen years. Mr. Gregory assures me that every ammonia manufacturing valve at the Red Rock site was recently replaced with top quality material, at great expense to the company, I might add."

"Then why did one of them go bad?" somebody else questioned.

This time Kent took over the podium again, anxious, it seemed to Robbin, to put everyone's fears to rest after the hornet's nest that Ted had stirred up. "We have no reason to believe that any of the valves went bad. Mr. Ballard was merely presenting an additional possibility—a highly unlikely possibility—just to make sure we cover all the bases." He glared at Ted. "Isn't that right, Mr. Ballard?"

Ted met his gaze squarely, and Robbin wondered if a stranger could have seen the hostility that sparked between the two men. But Ted, ever the genial one, turned back to the people and said warmly, "Of course. We just want to keep everyone informed. If those Red Rock valves hadn't been replaced last month, we'd have a lot more to worry about. In fact, if I thought we still had fifteen or thirty-year-old valves out there—" his tone held a note of urgency that gave Robbin goose bumps "—I'd be out of town tonight before the clock struck twelve."

CHAPTER FIVE

FOR TWO HOURS the local citizens and the oil people discussed the potential danger to the community posed by the Red Rock Refinery. At one point, Lowell Gregory invited all interested parties to come visit the plant on Saturday morning, insisting that an informative tour would lay everybody's fears to rest. Neither Kent nor Ted looked particularly pleased by his suggestion. It was the only point on which they seemed to agree.

When the meeting was finally over, Robbin stood up hurriedly, hoping for a moment with Kent before he disappeared. She'd even prepared a very official-sounding question to ask him. Before she could take a step toward Kent, however, Lila grabbed Robbin's arm.

"Not so fast, dear. You promised."

"What?"

"An introduction. With a glowing recommendation. I'll split my next commission with you."

Robbin wasn't sure if Lila was kidding, but it didn't matter because Ted was heading their way, easing through the crowd like Moses parting the Red Sea. Kent wasn't far behind him.

Robbin gave both men a nervous smile, trying to catch Kent's eye. But he stopped a few feet short of Robbin and Lila when someone pigeonholed him with a barrage of questions. Lila didn't seem to notice; she jabbed Robbin in the ribs as Ted reached her side.

"Teddy, this is Lila Henderson. She works with me."

Ted took Lila's offered hand. "I've heard a lot about you from Robbin, Lila," he greeted her graciously. His brown eyes looked warm and welcoming, almost as though he'd been looking forward to meeting the vivacious blonde. "She's told me more than once what an invaluable help you were when she first went to work for Three Star Realty."

Lila all but wriggled with delight. "You're very kind to say so, Ted. Frank and I are both very fond of your neighbor."

Robbin noticed that she was still clinging to Ted's hand, and he wasn't trying very hard to escape. She looked around for Frank, thinking she ought to introduce him to Ted also, but he'd cornered Lowell Gregory up near the stage.

"I'm very fond of her, too," Ted told Lila, as though Robbin weren't even there. "Did she tell you I helped her study for her license?"

Lila moved closer yet, still gripping Ted's hand. Robbin fought off an inexplicable urge to take hold of their wrists and pull them apart.

"No, she didn't, but I'm not surprised to hear you're a good teacher. The way you explained the troubles at Red Rock was fascinating. I could have listened for hours."

Ted seemed to be eating up Lila's line. "I have lots more information I could have shared with the group. Usually people don't want to hear all the details of what makes an oil refinery dangerous to the surrounding community."

Lila gave him a radiant grin, and Ted smiled back as though his sole purpose in life was to make her happy. He glanced at Robbin for just a second, flashing her one of those embarrassed grins he usually reserved for the times he forgot an appointment, or got caught with mismatched socks. This time, his apologetic expression told her plainly, *I haven't lost my mind, Robbie. I've just got to play along and pretend to like all this gush. Someday I'll tell you why.*

Robbin thought she knew why and, for some reason, that suspicion made her angry. She'd always believed—foolishly, perhaps—that Ted was above the sort of shenanigans that so many single men indulged in. Certainly he had a right to date anyone he wanted, but the fact that he'd even *pretend* to fall for a line like Lila's left a bad taste in Robbin's mouth. Surely he wasn't genuinely intrigued by this saccharine come-on! Did he really want what a woman like Lila had to offer?

No, he doesn't. Not Ted... not my Ted, Robbin assured herself more rationally. *There's got to be some other reason he's trying to placate her.*

Before she could ponder Ted's behavior much longer, Kent escaped from his questioners and made his way to Robbin's side. He didn't look warm and sunny anymore. Robbin wasn't too surprised that he looked a bit worn around the edges; he'd put in a long day.

"I have a feeling this may be a dangerous place to be tonight," he admitted quietly, the heavy vibration of his bass tone now sounding more ominous than exciting. "Before today, I'd only heard the 1952 Coltersville disaster mentioned once or twice. In the past few hours I've heard every local's version of what happened. It's downright eerie."

"Eerie?" she asked.

"The similarities, I mean." It was the first time Robbin had ever seen Kent look less than totally confident. Nervously, he brushed back a couple of strands of blond hair that were hanging limply against his forehead. "There was a pressure leak explosion the summer before the big disaster of '52, Robbin. Two workers were injured, but they recovered and everybody thought everything would be all right. The plant went back to full operation and the kids went back to school. Even the chief muckraker at the Morgantown newspaper stopped pointing fingers and asking questions. Construction was started on a new subdivision nearby."

Robbin shivered despite the stuffy air in the school cafeteria; she wished she'd paid more attention to Jane's story at noon. "And then?"

Kent shook his head. His blue eyes, to her surprise, looked more than a little haunted. "Four months later the whole place blew up. A hundred and seventeen people died."

A fresh surge of panic gripped Robbin as she digested Kent's words and considered their implications. Instinctively, she turned back to Ted. Surely he would tell her that the two situations were entirely different, and she had nothing to worry about. But Ted was already so far away that Robbin only caught a glimpse of his arm at Lila's back as he ushered her out the cafeteria door. Lila's abundant laughter, light and carefree, was jarring after Kent's awesome story.

Slowly Robbin turned back to Kent, trying to remember the brilliant question she'd thought up to ask him. But all she could remember was the feel of Ted's mustache as it had brushed her cheek an hour ago. Robbin couldn't help but wonder if Lila would like the sensation as much as she had.

She realized that the hard lump of ice in her stomach was a response to Kent's grim tale. She knew, too, that a quick hug from Ted would instantly dissolve it. Normally when she felt like this, all she had to do was run next door and Ted would greet her with open arms. The trouble was, Ted's house was empty right now. And since he'd just left the meeting with loquacious Lila, chances were he wouldn't get home for hours. And even then—Robbin balked at the unsettling realization—he might not be alone.

ROBBIN GOT TO WORK A LITTLE LATE the next morning, after a restless night in bed. She hadn't had time for her morning jog, much less a chance to hop next door and ask Ted for reassurance that Red Rock was perfectly safe. And Robbin had really felt the need for some assurance this morning; Kent's disturbing tale had left her more than a little rattled. She had also wanted to ask Ted about his gorgeous friend, who, by an incredible stroke of fate, actually seemed to return some of Robbin's breathless interest in him.

She wasn't sure why Ted had never mentioned Kent to her as a possible date; he'd obviously discussed her with his co-worker. Again Robbin realized that she hadn't been spending much time with Ted in recent months, and she missed him a great deal.

Until this summer, chatting with Ted had been like talking to one of her own kids; all Robbin had to do was slip through the back gate that Ted had built into their mutual fence and knock on his back screen door—two soft taps, then one hard—before zipping inside to ask a question or borrow a cup of sugar. This morning, however, she felt as though a visit with Ted required some preparation. *It's probably just because I haven't seen much of him lately and I'm no longer in the habit of popping in and out of his kitchen,* she assured herself. The possibility that Ted might have company this morning—for the first time in all the years she'd known him—surely couldn't be the cause for her reticence!

Nor could the fact that Lila's office remained determinedly empty have anything to do with the unnerving malaise that had settled over Robbin ever since she'd climbed out of her Buick and noted that the smell of ammonia still lingered in this side of town as well as her own. Suddenly in need of company, Robbin marched down the hall to Frank's office and poked her head inside.

"Well, look what the cat drug in," Frank greeted her gruffly, his square features dramatizing the dark shadows under his eyes. He sat back in his swivel chair with both booted feet up on his desk, twirling his Stetson around the forefinger of his right hand. "Are you starting to take after Lila, Robbin? Bad enough having one woman show up here late every morning. Sure don't need two of you."

"It's nice to see you, too, Frank," Robbin countered with an exaggerated grin.

Frank shrugged apologetically and changed the subject. "Did you notice the weather outside?"

"The weather?" It was summer in northern California, which meant that it was hot as Hades and would be for at least another month. "It's August, Frank."

"Last time Red Rock blew up it was August, too. Smelled the same way. Different set of men came to see us, but they told the same pack of lies."

Ignoring Frank's surly expression, Robbin took a chair by his desk and decided to extend their conversation. Last night she hadn't paid much attention to the man's griping, but after what Kent had told her it seemed prudent now to listen to his laments. "Is it true that...a hundred people died?"

His homely face grew ashen. "At least. Including my sister's husband and another fellow I went to school with."

For the first time since she'd known Frank, Robbin felt a moment's pity for the man. "I'm sorry, Frank. That must have been very hard."

He shrugged off her sympathy as she'd expected he would. "You don't know the half of it, Robbin. They closed down the plant for about a year; the workers who didn't die went on the dole. We had our own mini-depression right here in Coltersville. Some folks never did get over it."

Robbin shivered. "I've heard some talk about . . . real estate problems that lingered after the plant reopened."

Frank slammed his hat down on his desk and glared in Robbin's general direction. "We'd have had better luck trying to sell houses in a leper colony. I knew a man who commuted eighty-five miles to Grass Valley for seven years after that—he couldn't get work here and he couldn't sell his property for love nor money. Lila's dad was in even worse shape. That explosion ruined him."

"Lila's dad?" Robbin queried. "I didn't realize she grew up near the school."

"She didn't—lived up near Crescent Heights. But Jack Henderson owned a hundred and fifty acres adjacent to the refinery. Had a terrific subdivision planned—permits all approved, backers lined up, buyers signing on the dotted line. When Red Rock blew up, he lost his shirt."

The news made Robbin regret her recent catty thoughts about Lila. Despite her cotton-candy personality, Lila was a decent girl who had always treated Robbin like a friend. No wonder she had bitter feelings about Red Rock.

"That's terrible, Frank," Robbin sympathized. "How did he ever sell the land?"

"He didn't, except for a small parcel on the far side he sold for a warehouse years ago. Lately he's started working on plans for another subdivision. But if Red Rock—"

The jangle of the telephone cut him off. He grumbled into the receiver and then punched the Hold button.

"For you, Robbin. Why don't you take it in your office? We can finish our talk a little later."

Robbin, the neophyte at the agency that Frank owned, was in no position to argue. She walked quickly down the hall, enjoying the quiet swish of her white gathered skirt.

She picked up the phone before sitting down. "Good morning, Three Star Realty, Robbin Walker speaking," she told her caller. "May I help you?"

"Robbin, glad I caught you," the deep voice rumbled beguilingly. "This is Kent Hawthorne."

He didn't bother to ask her if she remembered him or to remind her that he'd implied the night before that he might call her. His rich tone indicated that he was certain she'd been waiting for his call. It was clear that he'd been savoring that thought.

"Hello, Kent. I didn't expect to hear from you so soon," Robbin greeted him truthfully as she groped for her chair. Dizzily she tried to imagine his face; all she could remember was that he looked like Robert Redford, and Captain had purred in his hands. Granted, Robbin had hoped that Kent would contact her, but as gorgeous as he was, she hadn't been keeping her fingers crossed.

"I never like to let any grass grow under my feet when it comes to a lovely woman," he answered suavely. It was a pat line, but flattering nonetheless. Yet Robbin found herself wishing that he could have been more original. As if he knew what she were thinking, his next words were straightforward and unadorned. "I really want to see you, Robbin."

The statement was *so* simple, so straightforward, that there was absolutely nothing to tell him but the truth. "I want to see you, too, Kent."

"Tonight at seven?"

"Yes." She didn't give it a moment's thought; you didn't question miracles. "I . . . I'll see you then."

He ended the call as quickly as it had begun, leaving Robbin feeling like a tumbleweed in a Texas sandstorm.

Suddenly it smelled like roses outside, not ammonia. It was going to be a beautiful, beautiful day.

"Who was that?" Lila's cheerful voice sailed in from the doorway. She looked exceptionally pretty this morning: her matching fuchsia earrings, dress and sandals positively shouted "available." "That sounded personal, Robbin. Who's the lucky guy?"

"Robert Redford," she answered smugly, delighted that for once she had a social calendar to match the blonde's. "Where have you been all morning?"

"At the library. Where else?"

Robbin wasn't sure what she'd done to earn such a flip response, but she didn't get a chance to pursue the matter before Frank rolled into the room.

"There you are, Lila. Call just came in for you from that fellow at the meeting last night."

"No, that was *my* call, Frank," Robbin interjected.

He looked puzzled. "Uh-uh. This message—" he checked the little pink note to be sure "—is from Ted Ballard, for Lila."

"For Lila?" Robbin blurted out, hurt shadowing the surprise in her tone. "Are you sure?"

Frank gave her an impatient "how stupid do you think I am" kind of look, while Lila grinned in triumph.

"Now, Robbin, you do remember that you assured me you didn't want him for yourself. It's too late now for second thoughts."

Robbin's cheeks grew so hot she could have sworn she was blushing. "Don't be silly, Lila. I just meant . . . well, I was surprised. Ted always calls me here." Mentally she added, *Or at least, he always used to.* "I just assumed he was trying to reach . . . me."

Lila studied her pensively for a moment, and Robbin felt her face grow hotter.

"Well, you're out of luck this time, partner," Lila finally declared. "Besides, you can't hog all the good ones. If you've got the flashy one on your line, you don't have time to bait Ted's hook anyway."

"May I assume," Frank interrupted with a note of irritation, "that this . . . female chatter has nothing to do with any real estate business?"

Lila laughed. "Not exactly, Frank."

"Good." He glanced at Robbin as though waiting for similar reassurance. "Now, what were we—"

The phone rang again; Robbin answered it, but this time it was for Frank.

As he turned away the front door opened and a young woman walked in and asked how to get to the main highway.

"Why don't you help her, Robbin?" Lila suggested before she floated down the hall. "I've got to call my 'teddy bear' and confirm our date for lunch."

You can't call him that, Robbin wanted to cry out. *He's my teddy bear.* But the sentiment sounded ridiculous, even to herself.

After the girl seeking directions had gone, Robbin found it necessary to close her own office door so she wouldn't eavesdrop on Lila's call. But concentration was a major challenge with Lila's rich, sultry tones and heady laughter filtering through the walls.

Robbin told herself that she wasn't listening, and what Lila had to say to Ted was no concern of hers anyway. Furthermore, it was pure coincidence that she had to change the figures on the Arnolds's offer three separate times that morning, that she finally had to shred the bid and start all over again when she saw Lila flounce off gaily to lunch. . . .

CHAPTER SIX

TED STOOD UP as Lila reached his table, careful not to spill the glass of water he'd left teetering near the edge. He wasn't used to pulling out a chair for a lady—especially in a carnival-colored coffee shop—but he knew it was a gesture that Robbin would appreciate when he took her to The Old Mansion, and he needed the practice. The last thing he wanted to do tonight was send a gravy boat clattering into her lap half an hour after he pinned on the exorbitantly priced orchid corsage he'd ordered for delivery within the next few hours. After all his meticulous planning and effort, he couldn't afford any gaffes on this date, any accidental reversions to his time-honored role as neighborhood clown. This evening he would play the part of knight in shining armor according to Robbin's romantic vision; he'd done everything but rent a white horse.

"Thanks for working me into your schedule," Ted said to Lila by way of greeting. "It was a stroke of luck that Frank answered the phone since you were out. I was afraid I might have to do some fancy footwork to get past Robbin."

Lila laughed. "Well, I hope your usual luck is better, Ted. Robbin overheard Frank telling me you'd called, and she gave him the third degree. She was sure he'd made a mistake."

Ted licked his lips uneasily. "What did you tell her?"

"I told her that she was out of luck. She'd given me the green light last night and now she'd have to live with the consequences. She didn't look too happy when I left her, let me tell you."

Ted had mixed feelings about Lila's report. He rather liked the idea of Robbin feeling a bit possessive of him, but he didn't like to see her unhappy for any reason, nor did he want to win her by some trick of false jealousy. Of course, he hadn't had time to explain all of this to Lila; their conversation in the school parking lot last evening had been little more than a brief exchange in which they'd agreed to swap favors. Lila wanted information on the true state of things at Red Rock; Ted wanted her to help him make an overnight bid on Robbin's dream house. He hadn't had the time—or the inclination—to tell her very much, but it was obvious that she'd read between the lines. Now he asked cautiously, "What do you mean by she 'gave you the green light'? Did you two discuss me?"

Lila couldn't stifle a chuckle. She was pretty when she laughed, Ted noticed, especially in that vibrant pink outfit. He wondered what Robbin would look like in that color. Then again, he thought she looked just as wonderful in her rattiest housecleaning garb as she did in her finest Sunday best, so he rarely commented on her clothes. Now it occurred to him—rather belatedly—that perhaps that was something else he should have been doing these past few months. *There are probably a dozen other things I've done wrong,* he thought glumly, his apprehensions growing with each passing hour. *When push comes to shove, I'm still just "good old Ted." Mom's right; either Robbie loves me or she doesn't, just the way I am.* It wasn't a terribly encouraging thought.

"Ted, surely Robbin's told you enough about me for you to realize that I *never* pass up the chance to make inquiries about a good-looking single man." Her flattering tone made it clear that she included Ted in that description. Since he'd been turning down invitations from attractive women with greater frequency of late, he was not as surprised by her frank appraisal as he would have been a year ago. "Robbin was quick to tell me you were fair game, but she kept coming up with excuses when I pressed her to introduce us. I'm with her every day, Ted. I've heard the way she talks about men."

"How does she talk about men?"

"Relax, Ted. She talks like...well, like a married woman. A looky-loo, as we say in the business. A window-shopper who doesn't want to handle the merchandise."

He was baffled. "Is that good or bad?"

"In your case, a little of both. Until last night I thought she still wasn't ready to take a chance on a fellow. But when I started talking about putting you in my stable, I got the definite feeling that Robbin wanted to tell me you were already wearing her brand."

Ted was so pleased with the possible implications of Robbin's possessiveness that it took him a moment to realize that Lila had inadvertently confessed her own romantic interest in him. Last night he'd put up with her prattle just to keep her talking until Robbin got out of earshot and he could bring up the subject of the house. Now, putting all the pieces together, he said simply, "Lila, when you...gave Robbin the impression that you were, well, interested in me... you were just, well, trying to help me out by making her jealous. Right?"

Smiling provocatively, Lila left him hanging for several seconds before she dropped all subterfuge. Her tone was sincere as she revealed, "Ted Ballard, I think you are a very sexy man. And as a general rule, when I set my sights on a hunk I don't let him escape until I'm tired of him. However—" she grinned at her open confession "—I tend to tire very easily. I also have...three things in my life that mean even more to me than sensuous men."

"Such as?"

Her serious tone surprised him. "My career, my family, and my friends."

Uneasily he answered, "Well, I'd...sort of like to be counted among the latter."

"You are," she assured him. "And so is Robbin. And even if she doesn't know it yet, *I'm* certain that you are just what she needs. That puts Lila Henderson right out of the running as far as I'm concerned. I never date a guy if one of my friends has her sights set on him. Besides, a man of your—" she struggled for the right word "—integrity...would really be wasted on a playgirl like me."

Ted shook his head, suddenly certain that there was far more depth to Lila than she was ever brave enough to show the world. Last night she'd given him just a glimpse of her true priorities when she'd tersely revealed the tragedy that had befallen her dad. More than thirty years had passed since his development had been scrapped in the wake of the Red Rock disaster, but it was an old family wound that still festered. Lila was determined that nothing would get in the way of the subdivision he was planning now. Her loyalty to her father—and to Robbin—had made quite an impression on Ted.

"Now, about the Crescent Heights house," she changed the subject briskly, "I've checked out the other buyers. A bid was just submitted Wednesday morning, which means that dear old Mrs. Ruckson has until tomorrow morning to act on it. The fact that she hasn't accepted it yet probably means it's less than she wants for the house . . . or she doesn't think it's the right family for her beloved home.'' Lila smiled at him. ''Mrs. Ruckson is an elderly widow who's lived in the house for forty-seven years, Ted. She hates to sell it, but it's just too much for her to handle now that her children are grown and her husband is gone. I suspect that if Jane Davidson and I told her the true story behind your interest in the house, she'd be willing to give you a little more time. She'd love the romantic intrigue!''

Ted felt a little silly; it shouldn't take a whole party of realtors and widows to get a woman to marry him! There were times—more times this summer than he'd wanted to admit—when he'd had to fight off the urge to use his key to slip into Robbin's house at midnight, march right into her room and say, ''Robbie, I love you. I want you to be my wife . . . starting right this instant.'' In his dreams, a tousle-haired Robbin would stare at him in shock for a minute or two, then pull back the covers and pat the bed in mute but joyous expectation. . . .

''How much was the other offer?'' he asked tersely, thrusting away his fears and desires.

''I'm not at liberty to disclose that, Ted. . . professional ethics and all,'' Lila responded. ''However—'' her quick wink gave her away ''—I could hazard an intelligent guess.''

Her guess was enough to cut his food budget to bread and water for the next three decades, and signaled instant death to his social life. ''Lila. . . I don't know. Jeez, I don't think I can come within twenty thousand dollars of that figure, let alone top it.''

''If we sit down and work out some financial options, Ted, it might not be as bad as it looks. With Robbin's income on top of yours—''

He shook his head. "I don't want to do it that way, Lila. I mean, what kind of gift is it if she has to pay for half of it?"

Lila met his gaze squarely. "The kind of gift that a wife gives a husband and a husband gives a wife." Before he could offer any further resistance, Lila suggested, "Would it help if you . . . didn't have to pay the full commission?"

He smiled as he refused her generous offer. "Thanks, Lila, but I don't think I could let you do that."

"Well," she persevered, "Robbin wouldn't have to pay, and if it's going to be her house—"

"But if she refuses to marry me, it won't be her house." *If she refuses to marry me, I'll look like an idiot for making a bid in the first place,* he reminded himself.

A pretty middle-aged waitress came to take their order, and then Lila suggested, "Well, you think on it, Ted, and get back to me this afternoon." As a kindness to him, Ted was certain, she switched topics again before he could fumble for an answer. "I did some more research this morning, Ted. In the places where refineries have been shut down because of public protest, the closings have usually taken place *after* the disaster." Her expression grew determined. "I'd like to reverse that pattern in Coltersville."

Ted took his time before he answered, choosing his words with care. There were certain things he couldn't share with anyone but Robbin and his mother, both of whom had proven time and time again that they could be trusted with sensitive information. To hint to Lila that Kent Hawthorne might have been involved in a kickback scheme would be unforgivable without some kind of evidence. Thus far, the man's only proven crime had been making a move on Robbin Walker—and only Ted considered that a crime.

"I'd like to help you, Lila," he finally decided to say. "But there's only so much I can do right now. Last night you told me some of your personal reasons for hoping I'd shut down the plant. You realize, of course, that *I* have personal reasons for wanting the same thing—five kids and one incredible woman." He lifted his hands in a helpless gesture. "But I can't just cut Lowell Gregory off at the knees without a good reason. Even though I'd like to," he added grimly.

"I understand that, Ted. But I also think that if you dig deep enough, you'll be able to find what you need to bury Red Rock. And I—" she paused for emphasis "—may be able to show you just where to look."

THE DOORBELL RANG at six o'clock. Robbin hadn't even decided what to wear yet, so she hoped Kent hadn't arrived unforgivably early. But a glance through the peephole in the front door revealed a short-haired teenage boy with a gold box in his hand. The truck out front had Coltersville Flower Shop painted on its side. Standing next to the truck, her eyes on the house in rapt interest, stood Mrs. Griswald, the neighborhood busybody who lived down the street. The old woman was perennially dressed in a shabby sweatshirt, ragged jeans and a straw hat with dry flowers sprouting from the top. Under the guise of walking her dachshund, Peppy—at least four times a day—she managed to keep an eye on everybody. Robbin was sure that the florist's delivery would be the highlight of her day.

"Mrs. Robbin Walker?" the boy greeted her cheerfully. "This is for you."

Robbin positively shivered with delight. Flowers from Kent on their first date? *He must have something more in mind than pizza!* she thought with girlish delight.

"Thank you," Robbin managed to say, all but speechless as she gazed at the purple orchid. All her life she'd dreamed of one! It was another luxury that Doug had considered a waste of hard-earned cash, and he was the only person who'd ever taken her out on a formal dress date; he'd taken her to his high school prom. More than once Ted had promised her that someday the right man would send her one. *And you were right, Teddy,* she breathed in wonder. *Thank you for sending me your friend!*

"Sometimes when we don't have a card, it's 'cause the customer ordered flowers so far in advance that somebody lost it," the delivery boy told Robbin apologetically when he saw her check for an envelope. "This time somebody mixed up the address, too. They gave me the number of the house next door by mistake, but there's nobody there. This lady walking her dog said that you lived at 339, not 347, so—"

"It doesn't matter. I know who it's from, and it's absolutely lovely," Robbin assured him, blessing Mrs. Griswald, who still gawked happily from her post by the truck. Robbin waved to the woman, then gave the boy a bright smile as she thanked him again and closed the door. As soon as he was out of earshot, she let out a whoop of glee.

"Can you believe it, Captain?" she bubbled to the smug Siamese, who was perched loftily on the blue tapestry sofa. "Nobody's sent me a corsage in almost twenty years! And I've *never* had an orchid," she added for good measure. Captain was indifferent to her pleasure, but Robbin scratched him behind the ears anyway before she bounced off to dress for the evening.

The corsage cleared up any doubts as to her choice of wardrobe. The only dress she owned that was formal enough for an orchid was a simple black knit that hugged her waist and bodice tightly. It had flutter sleeves and a gored skirt that gave her a flippant, saucy walk. She decided to wrap her hair up on top of her head to add a little height and sophistication; then she added a simple gold chain and hoop earrings for what she hoped could pass for understated elegance.

"Maybe I wasn't so far off the beam when I told Jane that my white knight had just arrived," she told Captain, delighting him with an extra can of his favorite food in honor of the occasion. "If he shows up in a white tuxedo and takes me to The Old Mansion, I'll be sure of it."

Intent on his meal, Captain didn't answer; he didn't even look at Robbin's dress. But she quickly forgot her feline friend's disinterest when the doorbell rang a few minutes later. She was dabbing on some perfume in her bedroom, but otherwise she was ready to go. Taking a deep breath, she sauntered slowly down the hall, trying to control her frantic pulse and her tendency to chatter when she was nervous. She felt just like a sixteen-year-old on her first date.

When she opened the door, Kent didn't say a word, just caressed her with that mesmerizing Robert Redford smile that had thrown her off guard the first moment they'd met. She couldn't seem to find her voice at first, so she just allowed herself to smile right back.

Kent looked terribly dapper in his light summer suit of powder blue, but Robbin couldn't help but wish he'd been wearing her fantasy white. The fact that he wasn't reminded Robbin that she was going on a real date with a real man; this wasn't just another one of her daydreams. The simple truth was that she knew almost nothing about Kent Hawthorne, aside from the fact that she felt girlish and gorgeous when he smiled at her...and that he was handsome, he knew Ted, and he wanted to get to know her better. *And he sent me an orchid corsage on our very first date.* At the moment, that seemed to be more than enough information.

"Good evening, Kent," Robbin finally managed to utter with some semblance of sophistication, clutching the small beaded bag in her hand. *Now if my heart would just stop beating...* "I'm just thrilled with the corsage. Thank you."

His eye fell on the orchid with a twinge of interest—or was it surprise—before he took in the rest of her nicely rounded form, lovingly caressed by the smooth black knit.

"You're looking very chic, Robbie." His heady smile continued to embrace her. "I can hardly wait to see what...other surprises you have in store for me this evening."

His husky tone implied that he was looking forward to discovering just what the dress was hiding, and Robbin was surprised that he made so little effort to conceal his desire. A part of her tingled with pride at his flattery, but another part said, *Whoa, boy, you're moving much too fast.*

Suddenly, Robbin felt a bit uneasy inviting him into the empty house. Since it was already seven, she decided to lock the door and join him on the porch. Mercifully, Mrs. Griswald was nowhere in sight.

Out loud she suggested, "Shall we go?"

"By all means, Robbs," Kent agreed, as though they were leaving at his suggestion rather than hers.

She couldn't stifle a moment's resentment that he'd borrowed Ted's private name for her. Many friends called her "Robbie," but Ted was the only person in the world who had ever called her "Robbs." In fact, she could generally read his moods just by the name he used during any given conversation. He usually called her "Robbie" unless he was feeling particularly warm and close; at times like those, only "Robbs" or "Robbsie" would do. He rarely called her "Robbin" unless he was feeling terribly formal—or just plain mad.

As they strolled to the Mercedes, Kent reached for Robbin's hand as though they'd been friends—or lovers—for years. But the gesture made Robbin uncomfortable; Kent's fingers were soft and smooth, not square and strong like Ted's. She wasn't sure she liked holding hands with a stranger.

You don't waste any time, do you? Robbin wanted to protest. But before she could speak, Kent informed her, "I made reservations at The Old Mansion. I hope that's all right with you."

"All . . . all right?" she stammered, unable to believe her ears. Granted, The Old Mansion was the only restaurant worthy of a corsage for nearly sixty miles in any direction, but it was clear over in Morgantown, and it took about a half an hour to get there. "The Old Mansion? Tonight?"

Kent glanced at her in surprise. "Is there somewhere you'd rather go? There's no place much closer that I'd choose to take a lady to."

Robbin beamed. Maybe there were some advantages to living in an isolated rural town! "The Old Mansion is . . . just fine, Kent. Terrific, in fact. I've heard so much about it, but I've never been there. I hear there's a seven-piece live orchestra and—"

"You've never been there?" He was incredulous. "How long have you lived in this area?"

Robbin slipped in the car as he opened the door for her, regretting her guileless confession. "Well, I've lived in Coltersville for thirteen years, but I usually go out to eat with at least three children. The Old Mansion isn't really the sort of place you can take a family."

Kent frowned. "I once took my daughter there."

He closed the door and came around to the driver's side of the car. Despite the new sobriety on his face as he started up the engine, Robbin asked, "Where does your daughter live, Kent?"

"Colorado." His tone was colorless as he smoothly maneuvered the Mercedes out of the residential neighborhood. "She moved away last fall. Now I see her so rarely that... well, I don't really know her anymore."

For Robbin, who was nearing the end of her first summer without her children, his simple words were especially poignant. "I'm sorry, Kent. My kids have been gone for almost two months now, so I have... well, just an inkling of what you feel."

He turned to face her, blue eyes suddenly haunted. "I doubt it, Robbin," he admitted darkly. "If you had any idea..." His voice trailed off, melancholy, and she marveled at his abrupt change of mood.

For several moments they rode in silence along the two-lane highway. Then, rather briskly, he asked her, "Have you talked to Ted since last night?"

Robbin shook her head. "No. When my kids come home on Sunday I imagine we'll get together. We tend to live like... one big, happy family. When Larry was a baby, Ted even built a little gate to connect our backyard directly with his so I could slip back and forth without fussing with heavy latches."

Kent eyed her curiously. "Are you still...that close?"

A couple of months ago, Robbin would have had no problem with that blunt question. But now she wondered uneasily just how close she and Ted still were. He seemed friendly enough when they were together, but there was . . . well, a distance between them these days. It wasn't just that he didn't seem to have time for her anymore; it was more the sense of separation, the lack of camaraderie, that troubled her now when she was with him.

"Well, he's my best friend, Kent," she answered loyally, pushing away her doubts. "Has been for years . . . even when I was married."

Kent pulled into the parking lot of The Old Mansion, his eyes on Robbin's face. "Then he . . . shares a lot with you. Worries, plans . . . suspicions."

Robbin laughed, too intrigued by the white painted verandas and honeysuckle vines that surrounded the restaurant to think about anything else. "We're not lovers, Kent, if that's what you're asking. Ted's always encouraging me to date more. He'll be delighted that I took you up on your offer this evening."

Kent looked taken aback by her comment, and Robbin wondered if she'd misread the intent of his questions altogether. She also wondered why they were discussing her relationship with Ted instead of concentrating on each other. She comforted herself with the notion that perhaps the restaurant's romantic Old South aura would surround them once they got inside.

The inside of The Old Mansion looked just as she'd imagined it; with pristine ivory lace tablecloths, sparkling chandeliers, and lush carpets running up and down the intricate network of stairs. Each hand carved oak chair was richly padded in carmine velvet; delicate gold fill framed the scalloped edging on every plate. Even the tableware was gold. The lovely young greeters, carrying long-stemmed roses for the female guests, wore dresses that looked like wardrobe costumes for *Gone With the Wind*. Kent's and Robbin's waiter could have passed for Rhett Butler.

"Oh, Kent," she murmured breathlessly as soon as they'd placed their personal order without the restraint of a written price list or menu. "It's lovely. Thank you so much for bringing me here."

She expected a simple "My pleasure, ma'am," but to her surprise Kent crushed the mood by joking, "I imagine I'll get my money's worth before the night is over."

Her enthusiasm crumpled into dust. The first hint of tarnish on her white knight's armor had revealed itself....

Robbin's uneasiness persisted throughout the evening, despite the regal ambience and extraordinary southern cooking. Most of the time Kent talked about his work, filling Robbin in on the technical details of his job and Ted's. He was especially thorough about his responsibilities at Red Rock and questioned her regarding Ted's impressions of Kent's work there.

"I told you, Kent, I haven't had a chance to talk to Ted about Red Rock," she reminded him impatiently the second or third time he brought up the subject. "Could we talk about something else for a while? That refinery trouble gives me the shivers."

Abruptly his manner softened. "I'm sorry, Robbin. I didn't mean to frighten you. I forget, sometimes, how close you live to the plant."

"Well, I can't forget," she answered intently. "My family, my friends, my job—everything that matters to me is tied up in Coltersville. If Ted hadn't promised me that he'd get to the bottom of the mess at Red Rock, I wouldn't be able to sleep at night."

Twin discoveries came on the heels of her words. In the first place, she *hadn't* slept at all well last night. And in the second place, Kent had as much involvement in the investigation as Ted did, yet it had never occurred to her to put her faith in Kent. His eyes revealed that he'd come to the same unflattering conclusion.

"Why don't we dance?" he suggested suddenly, rising to his feet before Robbin could offer protest. "I've never held Scarlett O'Hara in my arms before."

It was another one of those overly dramatic lines that made Robbin decidedly ill at ease. As Kent led her onto the tiny dance floor, she couldn't help but wonder what he had in mind for "dessert."

It wasn't until the orchestra actually started to play the "Gone With the Wind" theme and Kent laughed out loud—dimples dimpling—that Robbin found herself melting toward him again.

Now that's the man I wanted to get to know better, she told herself with relief. *I've only seen glimpses of him this evening, but he's still in there . . . somewhere.*

The evening got better after that. Kent seemed to relax as they danced and chatted about their childhoods, Robbin's work, and the way music had changed over time. It was nearly eleven when Kent paid the exorbitant bill—Robbin didn't see it, but he'd left a twenty for a tip—and escorted her outside into the cool evening air.

He put his arm around Robbin as he walked her to the parking lot, and she felt a little bit like Cinderella after the ball. The gold Mercedes, she noticed, looked vaguely orange in the moonlight; in her mind it had already changed into a pumpkin.

When they reached the car, Kent didn't open the door right away. Instead, he slipped his free arm around Robbin's waist, effectively pinning her against the Mercedes, then lowered his lips to hers.

Robbin wasn't ready for him to kiss her, but it seemed childish to resist if that was all he had in mind. His mouth was warm and smooth, but the slick maneuver was so well executed that it failed to move her. It was obvious that trapping a woman against his car was a trick he'd used before.

What did I expect? To be the first girl he ever courted? Robbin chastised herself. *He's not my high school sweetheart, and I'm a long way past sixteen.*

Still, there was something more she wanted from a man's kiss, and she was relieved when Kent pulled away...and surprised when he asked in a husky tone, "Would you like to stop off at my place for a drink?"

It was a reasonable suggestion; it was early yet, they'd hardly begun to get acquainted, and Kent had mentioned earlier in the evening that he only lived about ten minutes away. But for some reason, Robbin didn't want to go to his apartment. There was something in his tone that said, "My place or yours?"—a question she thought it was much too soon to be asking.

Of course, the rules had changed since she and Doug had dated, and she'd been painfully young and innocent when they'd first met. She was a woman now, with a woman's needs...and Kent's handsome face wasn't likely to help her forget that. It had been a long, long time since she'd been seduced by a man; Ted was the only one who'd even embraced her during the past year, and a hug from Ted definitely fell under the category of fraternal comfort.

Robbin wondered how much he'd "comforted" Lila last night. Yesterday she'd been so pleased that Ted had encouraged Kent to date her; now she suddenly wondered if he had merely grown tired of spending all of his free time with his lonely neighbor. If she were dating steadily, he wouldn't have to feel guilty about gallivanting here and there with gals like Lila...and leaving Robbin on her own.

Even though she knew perfectly well that a flighty woman like Lila could never hold the interest of a solid man like Ted, the sudden vision of them together soured Robbin's mood even further. Pushing away the absurd picture, she tried to focus on her escort, who stood beside her in the moonlight, the breeze ruffling his golden hair.

"Well, Robbs?" Kent asked in his deep, throaty rumble, his body still pressing close to hers. "Shall we go?"

CHAPTER SEVEN

BY EIGHT O'CLOCK, Ted suspected that something was wrong. By ten o'clock he was sure of it. Now, at twenty to twelve, he was all but sweating with fear.

Robbin was nothing if not punctual; it had always been a bone of contention between them. Of course, there was the outside chance that she'd forgotten their date—frustrating to consider, but better than imagining her bleeding to death in a ditch somewhere. But where on earth would she be? The kids were with Doug, so she couldn't have taken them out. Robbin dated very rarely and always told Ted when she did. Besides, she couldn't possibly have made plans to go out with a man this evening because she had a date with *him*. Granted, she'd forgotten that fact once or twice this week, but during their evening stroll with Peppy, Mrs. Griswald had cheerfully informed Ted that somebody had delivered flowers to Robbin in the late afternoon. Once that orchid was in her hand, Ted assured himself, there wasn't much chance that their date would slip her mind again.

The only other possibility that he could think of was that Robbin had gotten held up showing a house on a Friday evening. But her car was in the garage, and she would surely have called if something like that had come up.

"Captain, what would you do if you were me?" he asked the lofty feline who was still miffed because Ted hadn't allowed him to rub his beige fur all over the rented white tuxedo. "If I call the police and she's off having fun somewhere I'll be mortified. But if Robbie's in trouble and I'm too proud to try to help her, I . . ." He closed his eyes against the frightening vision. She *had* to be all right. She had to be!

His heart lurched when he heard the thud of a car door outside. Instantly, he ran to the front window and glanced out onto the street. Nothing there, but there *was* a glimpse of chrome in the visible patch of Robbin's driveway. Someone was bringing her home.

Pride forgotten in his panic, Ted bolted out the front door and scrambled across the lawn just as Robbin and her escort disappeared into the house. Only vaguely did the make of the car register on his consciousness. The instant he trotted up the front steps and threw open the door, however, he remembered who owned the snazzy gold Mercedes. But by then it was too late.

Kent and Robbin stood in the hallway; he couldn't tell whether they were finishing off the evening with a good-night kiss, or exploring the possibility of spending the rest of the night together. He was too confused and outraged to determine much of anything except that Kent was holding Robbin in his arms.

Kent whirled around to meet the intruder, anger and shock spelled out in bold letters on his face. Robbin, on the other hand, gawked at Ted as though she could not imagine what on earth he was doing in her house . . . or what he was doing in his ridiculous white tuxedo.

Ted felt as though he'd barged into the middle of a movie, and everybody else knew what had led up to this climactic scene except for him. Robbin was wearing the corsage he'd sent her—that part made sense. Her black knit dress hugged her curves invitingly, but her upswept hair gave her such a formal, distant look that for a moment he had trouble remembering what she looked like in casual attire. The most bizarre thing of all was that, for the first time in his life, he felt unwelcome in Robbin's house, a place he'd always regarded as a second home.

A muddle of images and feelings gripped him, and only one thing was perfectly clear to Ted: Robbin had completely and totally forgotten him on the most important night of his life. He would have forgiven her for turning him down, maybe even for chuckling softly with surprise and dismay. But to forget him so completely—while she stood in another man's embrace with Ted's extravagant purple orchid pinned to that body-hugging dress—was reprehensible.

"Look, Ballard," Kent growled at him, "I hate to be so blunt, but even you ought to have enough savvy to realize that there are times when three can be a crowd." His tone was hard and husky, laden with possessive desire. "And this is one of them."

It was, in Ted's estimation, the understatement of the century. Of all the foolish things he'd done in his life, barging into Robbin's house tonight was unquestionably the most ludicrous. *No, lying to myself that she'd ever love me was even more absurd,* he thought bitterly. The memory of all his months of careful planning overwhelmed him. His afternoon bid for the Crescent Heights house laughed in his face. Even the white tuxedo now seemed to mock him. He hadn't felt quite so gauche since the first time he'd asked a girl out when he was fifteen. He had adored her, and she'd laughed herself silly when she'd turned him down. Years later, he'd been able to chuckle at the memory, but he didn't think he'd ever see any humor in what Robbin had done to him tonight. After all, she wasn't fifteen, and he certainly wasn't a stranger.

He battled the urge to rush forward and rip the orchid off her dress and he mastered his passionate desire to punch Hawthorne in the nose; he was determined to salvage his dignity.

"Excuse me, Robbin," he forced out almost evenly, ignoring Kent altogether. "You didn't mention that you had...plans...for the evening, so I was...concerned...when you were still out so late."

As a neighbor and close friend, it almost sounded like a reasonable explanation for his unorthodox behavior. But as a man in a rented tuxedo who'd been stood up by this glamorous creature who only vaguely resembled his Robbie, Ted didn't feel like a friend; he felt like a ridiculous child.

Then, quite abruptly, his keen humiliation gave way to wrenching pain. *Dear God, it's over,* he realized in the nadir of despair. *I should have married her when I had the chance and taken the crumbs of her love.* It was suddenly difficult to meet Robbin's eyes; impossible to imagine her ever again slipping through the fence to do his laundry, or water his plants when he was out of town. It was equally impossible to imagine life without her, but Ted knew without question that after tonight, nothing would ever be the same again between them.

Robbsie, he wanted to beg her just once before he left, *can't you see that I love you? Can't you see that I'm what you need?*

Instead, Ted straightened ever so slowly and gave her the tiniest bow; he didn't even glance at Kent. "Goodbye, Robbin," he stated stiffly.

"You mean...good night, Teddy," she blurted out, finding her tongue for the first time.

He forced the faintest ghost of a smile. "Sure, Robbin. Good night." But in his heart, he knew he'd gotten it right the first time.

KENT'S MERCEDES WAS ONLY halfway down the block before Robbin slipped into Ted's backyard through the private gate. She hurried to the kitchen door and knocked—two soft taps, then one hard—and tried to sort out what had happened while she waited.

She would never in her lifetime forget the look on Ted's face five minutes ago when he'd thrown open her front door and found her in Kent's embrace. Nor would she forget the volcanic shock of seeing Ted in a white tuxedo...and remembering that he must have been wearing it in anticipation of their Friday night date.

How could I have forgotten a meal with Teddy? she asked herself again. *Not once did I remember it, even though I thought about him often all through the day.* In a way, her faux pas made sense to Robbin. An evening with Ted was like an evening baking cookies with the kids: something to look forward to, but a comfortable, routine event, hardly an experience on par with dinner at The Old Mansion accompanied by Robert Redford!

Robbin knocked again, wondering why it was taking Ted so long to come to the door. She hoped he was changing out of the shiny tuxedo. He looked so different in the majestic white outfit—handsome and sophisticated—that it was hard to remember he was the same man she'd seen so often in T-shirt and cutoffs. She realized belatedly that Ted's regal demeanor had stricken her dumb as much as the circumstances in which he'd found her had. *And I can explain that, too, Ted, if you'll just answer your door.*

She knocked a third time, then bravely pulled open the screen door and stuck her head inside. "Teddy?" she called out as she had a thousand times before. "Teddy, are you in there?"

Robbin had always teased him about how easy it would be to lose him in his messy house. Once the girls had spent an hour looking for Captain in every nook and cranny of the kitchen so Robbie could take him to the vet. She was trying to formulate an updated version of their old joke in her mind when she realized that she wasn't looking at Ted's ratty old house at all.

No wonder he's not answering the door, she decided as an eerie feeling gripped her. *I must be dreaming; this must be my house, not Ted's.*

And indeed, it could have been. Not just because the floor plans were identical, and not even because of the fresh sandstone paint on the living room walls. But the new blue tapestry couch was just like her own, and the freshly remodeled kitchen looked exactly like hers, too.

A huge double oven and a microwave were enclosed in rich wood cabinets, and spanking new gold-colored tile had replaced the chipped countertop that had come with the house. The wall that faced the backyard, formerly a nondescript shade of gray, was now covered with a tiny yellow rosebud print that matched the wallpaper in Robbin's kitchen. If she had redesigned Ted's kitchen herself, she could not have done a better job.

"It's late, Robbin," Ted growled at her from the hallway that led to his bedroom. "Whatever it is can wait till morning."

He had changed into a brief pair of green swimming trunks that intimately hugged his trim bottom. It had been so long since Robbin had seen Ted's hairy legs that she'd forgotten how firm and muscular his thighs were, how richly brown his body got from the sun. His chest was covered with curly reddish hair, which highlighted his pulsing pectorals. At the moment his arms were so knotted with tension that he looked less likely to swim than to march into combat.

Getting a grip on herself—despite Ted's icy greeting—Robbin slipped inside and walked a few steps toward him. "Ted, I just came over to say I'm sorry. I would never stand you up on purpose; I know we had a date." Robbin had always been totally honest with Ted; she felt better already, having just started her apology. "I just . . . when Kent called and asked me out this morning, I was so surprised and thrilled that I forgot all about our plans."

"Thank you for sharing that with me, Robbin," Ted replied harshly. "I'm deeply comforted by that explanation."

"Teddy!" she cried out. "I feel awful about this, really I do! Don't make it any worse. I sent Kent away the minute you left just so I could come over here to apologize." She could have added that she'd been a bit relieved that Ted had given her an excuse to cut the evening short. Even though she'd convinced Kent to bring her directly home from The Old Mansion—bypassing a drink at his place—he clearly had had more in mind at Robbin's than a simple good-night kiss.

Ted said nothing; his eyes were on her disheveled hair.

"Ted, I've really missed you lately," she stumbled on, determined to ease his anger and her own discomfort. "I've really been looking forward to seeing more of you when the kids get home."

"Yes," he answered coldly. "I can see you were breathless with anticipation."

Robbin moved closer yet, until she was standing before him like a supplicant. If she'd been trying to make amends with anybody but Ted Ballard, she would have been worried by now about her chance of success. But Ted never held a grudge, and he loved her dearly, so she was sure his anger had just about run its course. In a minute or two she would offer to make some popcorn while he found some one-star Japanese dinosaur flick on TV. Captain would join them on the couch until a spate of silly tickling evolved into a wrestling match during the commercials....

"Ted, I love going out for pizza with you, but I do that all the time. Having a date with Kent was like—a trip to Disneyland. Half the time I pretended he was Robert Redford. He took me to The Old Mansion, Ted! He even sent me a corsage!"

Her last words seemed to trigger something deep within Ted; his mouth twisted in a grimace of pain—or was it anger?—as he roughly pushed past her and headed toward the pool. "The last time I checked, Robbin, the Pizza Palace wasn't accepting reservations four days in advance."

Robbin stared dumbly at his retreating back. "I thought...when you mentioned reservations...I thought you were kidding, Teddy. It wasn't until I saw you in that tux that—"

"Well, I *was* kidding, Robbin," he snapped. He stopped at the door, whipping around to face her grimly; his eyes were on the purple flower. "I was kidding myself. Now that we all know that the joke was on me, would you *please* go home so I can take a dip in the pool and then get some rest?"

His eyes were dark and distant; anger had made the solid muscles of his arms and chest into thick cords.

Robbin sought some trace of softening in his eyes, some hint of the Teddy Ballard she so dearly loved. But she couldn't find any trace of him in the sarcastic man before her. A sense of profound loss she could neither describe nor explain wrapped itself around her. She only knew that it began and ended with Ted, her dearest friend.

And then suddenly it was clear; blazing desert-sun clear. Ted had dropped enough clues for her to read, but she'd been too blinded by Kent Hawthorne's diamond dazzle to see the fine print before her eyes. This wasn't good old Ted any longer—her buddy, her brother, her pal. That man had vanished—overnight, it seemed. His replacement needed no help with his children, or his cooking, or his clothes. Nor would he ever again spend hours listening to her deepest joys and woes. Without an explanation—without any warning whatsoever—Ted Ballard had broken all the rules of their special bonding. He'd fallen in love with her. It was awesome, irrevocable, and inescapably clear.

Robbin was flattered; she was proud. But more than that, she was frightened and confused. She loved Ted more than anybody on the face of the earth—except for her kids—and she would cheerfully have died before willfully hurting him. But what else could she do? After the fuss she'd made over Kent, Ted would feel patronized and pitied if she told him she returned his romantic feelings. And she *didn't* return his feelings, as much as she wished she could. She adored Ted, but he didn't make her feel topsy-turvy, inside-out, like a kid on a Ferris wheel. And that was what love was all about, wasn't it? That teeter-totter feeling was what made the difference between liking the boy next door and drooling over the man of one's dreams!

A warning voice reminded her that Kent hadn't exactly turned out to be the man of her dreams. She wasn't even sure if she cared to go out with him again. To have wounded Ted for a man she truly longed for was one thing. To have hurt him for a fellow she wasn't even sure she wanted was nearly unforgivable.

Instinctively, Robbin reached up to put her arms around Ted, longing to give—and receive—the kind of fraternal hug that had always healed wounds between them in the past. But she felt his shoulders stiffen as her fingertips brushed his face. "I'm so very sorry, Teddy Bear," she breathed against his suntanned neck. "I wish—"

"Goddammit, Robbin! I am not your *teddy bear!*" Ted's dagger-sharp tone pierced her heart with each syllable; he stepped back so abruptly that she felt as though he'd slapped her in the face. "I... am... a... *man!*" he thundered at her, his fist clenching the air in a blind, territorial gesture. "And I deserve to be *treated* like one!"

Robbin just gaped at him, too stunned to respond.

"How long did you think it could go on like this, Robbin? How long did you think you could have your cake and eat it, too? Or didn't you ever bother to think of my point of view at all?"

"Ted," she stammered, "you act as though... I cheated on you. As though I've been an unfaithful wife! But we're not married, Teddy. We're not even in love. We're just—"

"Aren't we married, Robbin? Aren't we married in every way that suits you... in every way that really counts?" Before she could even begin to summon up a reply, he rushed on. "Who do you call when your car's in the shop and you need a ride? Who do you call when the sink backs up? When the sprinklers break, or a branch of the poplar tree blows down in the wind?''

She couldn't answer.

''Who do you turn to when the kids are sick? When you need to cry? When you've got good news that just won't keep?'' His nostrils flared as he demanded, ''Who, Robbin Walker?''

Subdued and almost frightened, Robbin whispered, ''You, Ted. I always turn to you.''

''You're damn right you turn to me. And you expect me to be there for you, Robbin. And *I am*. The way I was always there for Ellen. Have you ever stopped to ask yourself why? Do you think it's because I'm such a nice guy...or a pushover...or because it's just become a habit? Do you think I don't have anything else to do, or anybody else I could do it with?''

Robbin shook her head; in spite of herself, she knew she was going to cry.

''I give myself to you because I love you, damn it! I love you the way I loved Ellen, and I've waited a thousand years until the time was right to ask you to marry me!'' Robbin had never imagined that a declaration of love could be proclaimed with so much anger; and she'd never imagined that Ted would holler at her like this for any reason. She wasn't sure which discovery surprised her more. ''But you've never once thought of me as a lover, Robbie, and I'm tired of pretending you ever will. You want to have me handy whenever it's convenient for you, but you've never once considered what *my* needs might be.'' His tone grew husky, deep with feeling. ''Have you, Robbin? Or don't you think I have any needs worthy of your concern?''

The first tears spilled over; Robbin began to tremble. She was afraid, terribly afraid. It wasn't fear of Ted; even in this unprecedented rage, Robbin knew he would never hurt her. But she also knew that she was the cause of his fury, that she had caused her dearest friend this inextinguishable grief. She, in her selfishness, had made their Shangri-la unlivable for Ted. There had to be a way to mend their fences. There just *had* to be a way.

"Teddy," she pleaded through wet, spiky lashes, "tell me what you want from me. I mean—" she realized at once that her choice of words was awful "—tell me what I can do to make things right betw—"

"I want *everything* from you, Robbin!" His brown hands gripped her shoulders as he spelled out his passion in terse, hungry words. "I want you to love me in every way a woman can love a man."

His kiss was neither kind nor gentle, nor was the touch of his hands. Anger, frustration and molten desire melded together in his torrid grip. It was the opposite of Kent's kiss outside The Old Mansion. There was nothing practiced or rehearsed about Ted's passion, no hint of a seasoned lover's plan of seduction. There was only Ted—this Ted who wasn't Teddy—branding her with his fire, pressing her against his virile chest and naked thighs.

Robbin trembled in confusion, too stunned to respond. She said neither yes nor no with her body; no reaction cried out in her heart. This volatile stranger who was crushing her with months of pent-up frustration bore no resemblance to the teddy bear she so dearly loved.

When Ted finally let her go, it was with the same spirit in which he had taken her. His eyes were bleak and full of torment; the fury had subsided, but in its place was naked pain.

"Now for the love of God, get out of here, Robbin," he begged her, "before I do something *else* that you'll regret."

Robbin couldn't move, couldn't answer. She was even too stunned to cry.

"Do you hear me, Robbin?" he shouted, sweat glistening on his hirsute upper half. "Get the hell out of my house this instant if you plan to sleep alone tonight!"

CHAPTER EIGHT

IT WAS MUGGY AND OVERCAST IN THE MORNING, a fitting backdrop for Robbin's mood. A few hours of troubled sleep had done little to ease her pain and bewilderment. Not even her conviction that she and Ted could mend their fences after he had had some time to lick his wounds did much to help. The simple truth was that Robbin's priceless friendship with Ted had taken a beating; compared to that crushing blow, the majesty of The Old Mansion was unimportant. The memory of her date with Kent had faded, like summer wildflowers in a snowbank.

Robbin was hopeful that Ted would feel better now that he'd vented his pent-up frustration, and she was certain that *she'd* feel a lot better once he apologized for that turbulent kiss. It had broken all the rules of their friendship. If she'd ever imagined that Ted would kiss her—and she hadn't—she would have predicted a gentle, tender kiss of promise more in keeping with their long-standing love and respect. Now that he'd broken down the physical barrier between them, Robbin couldn't help but wonder how she might have felt if he'd touched her in a different spirit. Since that man who'd kissed her with such anger had borne little resemblance to her dear friend, she still didn't have any inkling of what it would feel like to be the recipient of Ted's true passion. She felt cheated, in a way; it wasn't fair of Ted to accuse her of never having thought of him as a lover when he'd never given her any warning that the nature of his love for her had changed.

Unfortunately, she realized that didn't alter the fact that her feelings for Ted, powerful though they were, simply weren't sensual in nature. And she was deeply alarmed that his feelings for her had taken such a drastic turn. For so long now, Ted had been Robbin's rudder; in some ways, she'd leaned on him long before Doug had moved out. Any hint of a major change in their relationship threatened the very core of her inner peace. She tried to think of a way to break the ice the next time she saw him; it was important that they heal this breach before her kids came home tomorrow—let alone before all seven of them took off for Yosemite next weekend. Robbin refused to consider the possibility that the break was too great to mend. The love she and Ted had for each other could survive anything. Of that she was certain.

Robbin could have eaten a dozen breakfasts in the time she took to nurse one cup of coffee, but her appetite was nonexistent, and her concentration was dulled by her anxiety about Ted. By the time she remembered that she was supposed to meet Lila and Frank at Red Rock this morning for the realtors' tour of the plant, she was running late and had to rush to get there on time.

In all the years Robbin had lived in Coltersville, she'd never actually been on the refinery grounds . . . nor had she had any desire to be. Now she was curious and concerned . . . but a little uneasy, nonetheless. She wasn't particularly reassured by the sight of the woman reporter sandwiched in among the small coterie of realtors. Robbin didn't like the idea of Red Rock Refinery making the Morgantown news; it meant that the accident was more serious than Lowell Gregory would have them all believe.

"Gives you goose bumps, doesn't it?" Lila greeted Robbin just outside the gate. This morning she was wearing a short, yellow skirt and a black and yellow polka-dot blouse; she looked just as perky as ever. Drawing Robbin's attention to the fence, she read aloud the sign posted there. "'This plant has worked 74 days without a lost-time accident.' Impressive lie, isn't it?"

Robbin didn't know how to reply to that. From the noises beyond the fence, it was apparent that the refinery—or at least some part of it—was still in full swing despite the recent explosion.

"Having this thing blow up in your own backyard must be kind of like finding a skeleton in the basement," Lila continued on a cloudy note.

"I really needed that thought this morning, Lila."

Lila's eyes widened at Robbin's rebuke. "I can see you got up on the wrong side of the bed today. Or maybe you slept in the wrong bed altogether." There was an unusual bite to her words as she asked, "How did things go with Robert Redford?"

"His name is Kent Hawthorne, and he's a human being just like anybody else."

"Umm," Lila murmured. "Real loser, huh?"

"I didn't say that," Robbin countered, suddenly not at all sure how she felt about Kent. There had been moments, after all, when he had been quite charming. He'd just been a bit too eager, too sure of himself. And too quick to tell Ted to get lost when he'd barged in on them so unexpectedly. "I just think it's time to separate fact from fantasy. Kent's not a celebrity; he's just an ordinary guy who happens to look like one."

"So does this guy manning the fort," Lila quipped, gesturing with a toss of her blond head toward the security guard at the gate. He was tall man, somewhere in his mid-twenties, Robbin guessed, with striking dark features and a beguiling grin that was clearly directed at Lila. "But I'd say," she continued casually, "he looks a little bit more like Erik Estrada. What do you say?"

"I say you're welcome to him," Robbin said crabbily. "He's too young for either of us." Even though she suspected that the guard and Lila were about the same age, he didn't look experienced enough to handle her man-hungry friend.

Lila laughed. "They don't make them too young for me, Robbie, girl. Or too old." Suddenly her tone grew hard. "I suspect I could even work up a case for that bald-headed manager if I thought it would help."

"Help with what?" Robbin asked, curious at her friend's meaning. Lowell Gregory was notably lacking in sex appeal; Lila's interest in him had to be professional.

"I want to know what happened up here, Robbin. I want to know how to keep it from happening again. I need to get close to anybody who can give me some answers."

Her bluntness appalled Robbin. "I'm curious, too, Lila. But the last thing I'd ever consider would be sleeping with—" she cut off quickly as another thought hit her. "Is that why you were so interested in meeting Ted the other night? Just because he's the one who has the power to close down this plant?"

Lila smiled provocatively. "Well, I won't deny that his power appeals to me. But it's only one of his many charms."

Robbin wanted to reply, but her normally quick wit was slowed down by an unaccountable surge of jealousy. Before a clever retort could form in her mind, Lila continued.

"Have you spotted Ted, yet, Robbie? When he called me this morning he said he'd be here by ten."

"This morning?" Robbin blanched. Lila and Ted had gone out for lunch together only yesterday, and he'd already called her today? *You sure didn't waste much time, Teddy,* she reproached her absent friend. *And here I was afraid that it might take you a while to get over me.*

"Yes, indeed. He called me at seven. He seemed very eager to chat with me again," Lila added evasively.

Robbin turned away, suddenly too dismal to face Lila's nauseating cheer. Ted was free to see anybody he wanted, but why Lila? He would never be small enough to punish her by using one of her friends, and he wasn't the sort of man who enjoyed playing the game Lila had mastered. There had to be some other reason he wanted to see her, something to do with the plant, perhaps.

"Robbie?"

Robbin turned back to Lila, surprised by the look on her face. It was sober now, almost apologetic. "You know I've done a lot of research on calamities at plants like this. Ted and I have just been comparing notes." She smiled nervously and tugged on a tiny lock of hair. "I know he's special to you, Robbie, and I'd never step on your toes. I just like to tease. You know how I am."

Despite her soothing words, Lila couldn't meet Robbin's eyes. While she was certain that Lila was trying to ease the sting of her earlier implications, Robbin also had the feeling that Lila wasn't telling her the whole truth. But before she could remind Lila that she had no romantic interest in Ted, Lila flitted off in the direction of the handsome security guard.

Frank showed up a moment later, looking even more grumpy than usual. The only person who looked less happy to be there was the giant gorilla of a man who lounged just inside the gate, arms crossed like a wrestler about to enter the ring. Robbin remembered him from the meeting; he'd looked just as sour-faced then. She hoped that somebody else would be conducting the tour.

Somebody else did. When Lowell Gregory arrived to welcome the crowd, he had a ludicrous grin pasted on his face, and his bald head glistened in the sun. Although he looked as friendly as an old shoe, there was a nervous, watchful look in his eyes that belied his surface calm and innocence.

"Good morning, everybody," he greeted them. "Glad to have you with us. Here's the plan. I'm going to give you a brief tour of the plant, then you can feel free to wander around on your own. My boys have all been instructed to answer your questions."

Robbin noticed that he was sweating in the muggy August heat, already intense before high noon. He had large, dark circles under his eyes, and she couldn't help but feel sorry for him. *He probably slept even worse than I did,* she realized, feeling a moment's pity for the man. Frank viewed him as the enemy, but Robbin saw him as a beleaguered general just trying to hold his fortress and protect his men.

The tour was not particularly informative. Beaming falsely throughout the next ten minutes, Gregory led the group through the maze of pipes and ladders, explaining the function of this or that tank, much as Ted and Kent had lectured at the meeting. When he got to the center of the plant, he told the group, "This is the ammonia processing unit where urea pellets are made. Thursday's explosion took place in this section."

"Where did the last explosion take place?" Frank asked loudly. "The one in '52?"

The muscles in Gregory's cheeks twitched as he searched for an answer. "I...haven't been here that long, sir. I'd have to look that up."

"I suppose you'd also have to look up how many people died? How many people were laid off? How many businesses went belly up, and how many developers lost their shirts, too?"

"Frank, please!" Robbin whispered, embarrassed by his display. "Gregory can't do anything about that! It's old business, anyway."

"It's new business, too, Robbin, if you live in Coltersville or own property near this plant," Frank hissed. Then, out loud, he continued brashly, "So what do we tell people who won't buy houses in this end of town? Don't worry about Red Rock Refinery, because after you're dead and gone nobody will remember what happened here?"

Gregory took out a handkerchief and mopped his sweating forehead. He licked his lips as he struggled for a reply.

"I think I can assist this gentleman," another voice called from behind him, and Robbin turned to see Ted join the crowd.

She couldn't believe how much better she felt just hearing the sound of his voice. *As long as Ted's here, everything will be all right,* she realized with a jolt. Instantly the air seemed a little more clear, the sun outside a tiny bit brighter.

"I've been doing research on that very question, Mr. Swanson." Ted soothed her irate boss with an easy smile. "If you'll join me back here in the plant office, maybe I can set your mind at ease."

Gregory offered Ted a stunned, grateful look. Frank looked surprised, but followed Ted without further trouble. In the quick glimpse of Ted's face Robbin had before he turned around, she saw no trace of last night's burning anger. He looked sad and exhausted . . . almost defeated. Not even his dark blue suit—another new one—could do much to brighten his demeanor.

Maybe the sight of Lila will cheer him up, Robbin thought dully. She glanced around for the other woman, but saw no sign of her anywhere. Quickly Robbin decided to tag along after Frank. She was curious about the last explosion and the intense concern that still plagued both of her fellow agents. And, more importantly, she wanted to talk to Ted. The sooner she invited him over, the better he'd surely feel. The presence of a third party—even grumpy Frank—might give them a comforting temporary buffer. She had the feeling they were going to need it.

The office was bare of aesthetic comforts, and Ted's greeting to Robbin had none of the warmth she'd expected, either.

"Good morning, Robbin."

"Hello, Ted." Ignoring his coolness, she forced herself to act normal. "I didn't expect to see you here on a Saturday morning."

He shrugged and tapped his thigh nervously with the yellow notepad he was carrying. "Refineries operate twenty-four hours a day. Trouble can occur at any time. I need answers that can't wait till Monday."

So do I, Ted, she longed to tell him. *I need to know that everything's all right between us. I need to know that you forgive me for forgetting our date.* She knew that greater wounds stood between them, but she had to believe that their years of caring would overrule her thoughtlessness and Ted's explosion the night before.

Ignoring Robbin, Ted motioned for Frank to sit down. But Ted remained standing, as did Robbin, while he quickly outlined his thoughts to the other man. "Mr. Swanson, I know that you've got a very legitimate concern about the trouble up here. So do I. But believe me, there's nothing any of us can gain by a... well, a personal vendetta."

Frank thrust out his booted feet in silent rebellion, but made no comment.

Ted continued. "This refinery has changed hands three different times since '52. None of the same top brass work here or garner income from Red Rock's operation. The cause of the incident in '52 was the inadvertent mixture of two chemicals in a refining process that is no longer used in this state—precisely because of the accident in Coltersville and others like it." Ted's tone was calm but determined. "I'm going to find out what happened up here, sir, and I'm going to make sure it doesn't happen again. Don't forget that I've got a vested interest in Red Rock's safety that goes far beyond my job. But I've also got the training—and the authorization—to pursue this inquiry using scientific and legal means. The more I can cultivate Lowell Gregory's cooperation, the better chance I have of getting to the bottom of this. Right now he's pretending to be helpful. If he gets his back up, it'll only make my job that much harder. Do you understand?"

To Robbin's surprise, Frank nodded without complaints or nasty comments. "Lila says we can count on you, Ballard," he admitted gruffly. "That's good enough for me."

Robbin almost squawked, but she bit her tongue. *Ted's my special friend, not Lila's!* she wanted to holler. *I told you at the meeting we could all trust Ted. So when does Lila—*

"I'm grateful for your confidence, sir, and for Lila's. I promise you I'll do my best."

Frank grunted, then held out his hand to Ted. Ted shook it, then turned to leave the office. Frank followed him for a few paces, then took off in the direction of the urea processing unit. Robbin, ignored by both men, trotted briskly to catch up with Ted.

"Teddy—uh, Ted," she called out uneasily. "Do you have a minute?" Robbin knew it wasn't the best time to try to straighten things out between them, but she was certain she couldn't bear another hour with Ted being so cold and distant.

Ted stopped and glanced in her direction, but he didn't turn around. His eyes looked blank—no, haunted—as he studied a broken pipe on the ground.

"I'm here to do a job, Robbin, which is hard enough without a herd of realtors traipsing around."

She took his rebuke in silence, then said softly, "I just wanted to say I'm sorry, Ted."

No color laced his tone. "You said that last night. I imagine you'd like an apology from me, too, so let's call it even."

Again he started to walk away.

"Ted—" she had to stop him "—you're not still mad at me, are you? I mean everything's okay now that you're done blowing off steam?" She'd planned to have this conversation a few hours later, when he'd had most of the day to heal his wounds. But Robbin realized that she could hardly function another minute with the cloud of Ted's anger hanging over her. She waited tensely while he stopped once more and slowly turned again to face her. Vaguely she realized she was chewing on her lower lip, but she couldn't seem to stop.

"Does it matter, Robbin? I assure you I won't be bothering you anymore."

"Bothering me?" she burst out, then took a few steps closer to her friend. "Teddy, you've never been a bother. I told you last night that I hardly see enough of you these days." A vague idea that had been forming in the back of her mind now crystallized as she suggested, "The kids are due home tomorrow night, so I thought we'd have a backyard barbecue to celebrate. They haven't seen Larry or Tina for almost two months."

Ted's mustache seemed to accentuate the firm lines of his mouth. "That's a nice thought, Robbin, but we've got plans for tomorrow. I'm sure Tina and Larry will be over first thing Monday morning to play."

He glanced at a tower about thirty feet away, then scribbled a few notes on his yellow pad. His stance told her the conversation had ended, but Robbin was not so easily deterred.

"We can make it some other time, Ted. Monday night would be fine, or even Tuesday. We need to sit down and work out a packing list for Yosemite, anyway." When he didn't answer at once, she tacked on nervously, "It won't be much of a homecoming, Ted, if half the family isn't there."

This time he dropped the pretense of concentrating on his work. For the first time since he'd seen her this morning, he looked Robbin straight in the eye.

"Robbin, I didn't want to have to say this outright, but you're being just a bit obtuse. I won't be joining you and your kids for a barbecue this weekend. I won't be joining you for Friday night pizzas or late night TV. And I'm certainly not going to spend Labor Day weekend at Yosemite with you."

Robbin stared at him as the terrible words fell like rocks in a landslide; his gentle tone did nothing to ease her pain.

"If we're not married, then we're not one big happy family," he concluded firmly, as though this justified all of his previous declarations. His voice was perfectly even—neither kind nor cruel—as he told her, "Robbin, you are no longer going to be the center of my life."

Last night he'd said some awful things, but he'd been hurt and angry. This morning he was so calm, so deadly still, that it was impossible to pretend he was in the grip of some ravenous passion that would soon subside. Robbin felt her hands begin to tremble; she bit her lip so hard she drew a little blood.

"Teddy," she beseeched him, "I'm not asking to be the center of your life. I just want to make sure that we're still special friends."

His eyes swept over her troubled features, her brimming eyes, her flowing hair. For a moment she was sure that he'd reach out to touch her and end this madness; that he would shake her awake from this nightmare.

Instead, he slipped his free hand securely in his pocket and spoke with calm intent. "I thought I made myself clear last night, Robbin, but I'm going to repeat everything just once to make sure that there are no misunderstandings between us." His tone became even more dry. "We grew as close as a man and woman can get without becoming lovers. There was only one step left to take before our love could be complete. I wanted to take that step with you. You didn't want to. That's your prerogative; I don't begrudge you your feelings." The resignation in his voice made Robbin ache for him; she would have done almost anything to give him the love he wanted. "But I can't pretend that last night never happened; I can't change the way I feel. I can't go back to that platonic bliss we used to share, Robbin, and I can't pretend that I'm not battling with some very potent needs." His tone offered no apology for his confession of manly desire. "I'm a survivor, not a masochist. To spend a lot of time with you right now would be counterproductive for me and—" for the first time his tone quaked with feeling "—also very hard."

Robbin couldn't answer. She felt nauseous and faint. Maybe she had broken his heart, but it wasn't something she'd done on purpose. Now he stood before her, calmly talking about cutting her out of his life as though she were a chunk of crabgrass in the middle of his new sod lawn. She felt as though a part of her were dying.

"I wish you well, Robbin, and I'm sure you'd like me to be happy, too. So don't think I'm angry; don't think we're parting with ill will between us. You've been a very special part of my life and you've been a godsend to my children. But the time has come for us to say goodbye." At first she thought he was through, but then his voice dropped as he continued more gently, "You hold another solution in your hands, Robbie, but there's nothing more that *I* can do."

Tears spilled over Robbin's red-brimmed eyes. Her lips trembled as she begged him, "Do you want me to lie to you, Ted? Do you want to pretend I feel something for you that I don't?"

"Of course not! I want us to part while I still have some measure of your respect!"

"But Ted, you do! You have more than my respect! I love you more than I love anybody except for my children! So what if it's not romantic love? I had that for

Doug and look where it got me! You're my very best friend. How can you just throw that all away?''

''I don't *want* to throw it away, Robbie, but I don't have any other choice!'' he burst out with feeling. ''I just can't live like a window-shopper. If I spend another minute with my nose pressed up against the pane, I'm afraid I'll break the glass!'' His anguish touched her, shattered her reserve even more than his anger had last night. How could she have hurt him so terribly? How could he have ached for her like this when she hadn't even known? ''Robbin, I've been going crazy for months now, trying to protect you from my needs. I just can't do it anymore, can't you see that? It's not right for you, and—'' he sighed in potent frustration ''—it sure as hell isn't right for me.''

Robbin said nothing as the tears rolled down her face. She wanted to reach out for him, but she didn't dare. Not because they were in public, but because he'd built this terrible wall between them. She couldn't go over it or under it or through it no matter how hard she tried.

''We're just neighbors now, Robbin, and there's a reason for that fence that runs down our joint property line,'' he pointed out objectively. It was his amiable, professional tone, the one that went with the three-piece suit and tie, the one he'd used to address strangers at the meeting. ''It's supposed to guarantee your privacy and mine. As long as we both honor that boundary, we should have no problems.''

Robbin felt bereft, abandoned. She wanted to grab Ted by his stiff white collar and shake him. *I am Robbie, Teddy Bear! Your best friend in the world. The woman who raised your daughter and baby son when Ellen died. The mother of three kids who love you as a second dad! You just can't throw away thirteen precious years!*

But Ted was already turning away from Robbin, his eyes on the far end of the compound where Lila was batting her eyelashes at the security guard, the Erik Estrada look-alike. Ted even took a step or two in her direction before Robbin cried out, "What about the back gate you built to join our two families, Ted? Are you going to nail that shut as well?"

He stopped one last time to meet her weeping gray eyes, but only for an instant. "Robbin—" his tone was kind but final "—I already have."

CHAPTER NINE

TED FELT ROBBIN'S EYES boring into his back all the way across the compound, but he refused to turn around. If he looked at her now he might weaken; he could hardly bear to walk away from her while she was crying. If he hadn't been so furious last night, he never could have ignored Robbin's astonished tears; this morning he had no anger to protect him.

But his determination to make a break with Robbin had not diminished overnight...and neither had his love for her. It tore him up to see her hurting, let alone to realize that he was the cause of her pain. But he simply couldn't go on living in limbo; he'd been treading water long enough.

If Robbie doesn't want me, surely there's somebody else who does, Ted told himself resolutely as he marched across the compound. It was a thought that should have cheered him; in the wee small hours of dawn he'd made a list of half a dozen women who'd recently expressed a vibrant interest in him, fully intending to make sure he had a date with one of them by this evening. But the only call he'd made so far had been to Lila, who wasn't a potential date at all. It galled him to reveal his fiasco with Robbin to the flighty young woman he'd only known for a couple of days, but he'd felt obliged to tell her to cancel the bid on the Crescent Heights house just as soon as possible.

"Howdy, Lila," he greeted his new friend when she finally abandoned the young security guard long enough to trot over in his direction. "Have you found out anything new this morning?"

"I found that Joe likes Chinese food . . . and he's free tonight."

"Joe?" he repeated blankly.

She nodded toward the front gate. "The security guard with the endless lashes and the tight behind."

Ted sighed in disbelief. "Honestly, Lila, I know that you view collecting men as an honest avocation, but we've got more important things to study up here than—"

"Trust me, Ted," she assured him blithely. "You examine the accident your way; I'll do it mine."

She gave him a saucy wink, then sobered as she glanced at Robbin. "Robbin hasn't smiled once this morning. I feel so sorry for her, Ted."

And for you, she might have added. Mercifully, she didn't. Lila's sympathy was more than Ted could have handled at the moment.

"Robbie's in for a rough week, Lila," Ted said softly. He didn't have to reveal all the sorry details of last night's fiasco to ask Robbin's friend to keep an eye on her. "Please be extra gentle with her for a while and . . . keep Frank out of her way."

"I'll do my best," Lila promised.

Embarrassed by the flighty woman's uncharacteristic solemnity, Ted asked briskly, "Did you take care of everything with Mrs. Ruckson?"

"I haven't been able to reach her yet, Ted. I think she's out of town for the weekend. But I did talk to Jane, and we both think you ought to wait until the dust settles before you withdraw your bid."

He shook his head. "Absolutely not. The only way I could look any worse in Robbin's eyes right now was if word were to leak out that I tried to buy that stupid house for her. I've got enough egg on my face, Lila. Promise me you won't ever let her know."

"Ted!" Lila sounded outraged. "I gave you my word!"

He grinned sheepishly, pleased with her spunk. "I know you did. But now that I've seen a sample of Frank's idea of tact, I know I sure can't trust him to keep his mouth closed if he ever stumbles over my bid for that property."

"He won't suspect a thing unless I tell him, Ted. It's not even our listing. And I explained your situation to Jane. Of course she's a friend of Robbin—"

"She is?" The other realtor's name had struck him as familiar, and he realized now that Robbin had surely mentioned Jane Davidson before. "Now that's a stroke of luck I surely don't need."

Lila clucked reassuringly. "Jane has her ethics, too, Ted. She knows how much Robbin loves that house and also how much she thinks of you. She was absolutely delighted to help me play Cupid. Believe me, Jane really is in your corner."

He shook his head. "I don't even know the lady. Besides, a man ought to be able to get a woman to marry him all by himself, don't you think?"

"Depends on the woman, I imagine," was Lila's answer. At the moment her eyes were on a tall, shapely brunette near the front gate who was purposefully moving their way. "This one strikes me as all career and no fun. Take her out for a good time, Ted, but don't try to marry her."

Ted studied the woman in question and decided she was moderately pretty; she had nice legs. Since she was a reporter covering the explosion, any county environmental health inspector would surely be grist for her mill. "I suppose she'll want to talk to me," he concluded, trying to buoy himself with the prospect.

"That's the spirit, Ted," Lila cajoled him. "Other fish in the sea and all that."

Slowly he shook his head. "Unfortunately I'm not partial to seafood." He didn't really want to go out with anybody at the moment, but he'd decided that his first choice was Angela Hartwood, another planner with whom he'd worked for years. She knew him well enough to forgive him for asking her out when he felt depressed, and he didn't think she'd be insulted by an evening's entertainment that ended at the front door.

Lila squeezed Ted's arm, then offered him a cheerful grin. "Is there anything I can do to make you feel better?" she inquired sincerely. "I can cancel this date tonight if you—"

"No, I don't need a hand to hold, Lila. I'll be fine, now that I know...how to make my long-term plans." The reporter was now heading briskly in his direction. Suddenly Ted realized that not only was he loathe to date her, he didn't even want to talk to her about Red Rock today. The county frowned on premature release of information. A week from now he might be able to give the public the news it deserved and wanted, but right now all he had were scraps of paper floating in the wind. "You could...do me a couple of favors, Lila."

"Such as?"

"Keep this gal off my trail today. I don't have anything to tell her yet."

"It would be easier if she were a different gender, but I'll give it my best shot."

Ted shot her a doleful glance. Lila, he'd decided, was a good sport. Not at all his type of woman, but she had a solid soul underneath all that protective fluff. *What is my kind of woman?* he found himself asking, then pushed away the answer that fought its way into his mind. *The Robbin Walker kind.* He was starting to sound like a broken record.

"Thanks, Lila," he answered softly, then forced himself to explore another avenue of thought. "Also, could you drop by my place some time next week? I want you to give me an appraisal of my house. I think chances are very good that . . . I'll decide to sell it."

Lila's eyes grew big. "Oh, Ted, I'm not sure you need to do that. I really think you should wait a few weeks. Robbie really does care for you—she just doesn't know it yet. Sooner or later she'll see the light. I'm sure of it. Just let her get used to the idea."

He shook his head. "I'd rather cut my losses, thank you."

"Have you discussed selling your house with Robbin?"

"Not in so many words. But I made it clear that we were going to have to go our own separate ways."

"You make it sound like you're a couple splitting up, not two people trying to get together."

He glanced at the determined reporter, now just ten or fifteen yards away. She would pigeonhole him any minute if he didn't slip off quickly. "Only one of us is trying to get together, Lila. Don't forget that I'm a man who spent five and a half years in a very happy marriage. I know how it feels to know that the woman I love returns my feelings. Believe me, that is *not* the way I'm feeling right now."

On that grim note he crossed the compound to join Lowell Gregory, hoping that Robbin would stay out of his sight the rest of the morning. He couldn't concentrate on his work when she was around him.

"Uh, Ballard. Thanks for...bailing me out back there," Gregory said by way of greeting, holding out his hand. "I must admit I wasn't expecting reinforcements from your quarter."

Ted took his hand reluctantly, and then felt the urge to wipe his fingers to cleanse himself of Gregory's touch. "The man was about to create a panic situation. It's dangerous enough having civilians loose at this plant when we don't know what's wrong. I couldn't see a stampede helping much." His eyes narrowed in disapproval. "Why did you stage this cart and pony show in the first place?"

Gregory's jaw set in defiance. "Because I'm tired of people making accusations. I've got nothing to hide."

His sudden anger startled Ted, but he didn't comment on Gregory's vehemence. "Has somebody accused you of...hiding something?"

"I'm not stupid, Ballard. You can't pretend that you and Hawthorne haven't considered the possibility that something shifty took place when we installed those new pipes in June."

His openness was not what Ted had expected. "Do you think that bad valve was just a fluke, Gregory? A once in a lifetime occurrence like Hawthorne said?"

He fully expected Gregory to say yes; for, if Ted came to that conclusion at the end of his investigation, Red Rock would be off the hook, and the matter would be put to rest. But to his amazement, Lowell Gregory rubbed fresh beads of sweat off his upper lip and said softly, "To tell you the truth, Ted, I don't know what to think. I haven't had time to ask too many questions up here . . . I spent yesterday down at the hospital with my men." His eyes were bleak. "Bill Rayburn's in an oxygen tent fighting for every breath. He's like a son to me, Ballard. Worked here seventeen years."

Ted didn't answer. He wanted to accuse the man of pulling a fast one, feigning concern to elicit sympathy. But his own feelings were far too raw this morning to risk wounding a man who might be hurting as much as he was. "He's going to make it, isn't he, Lowell?"

Gregory lifted his hands in a helpless gesture. "At first they said he was. But apparently the damage to his lungs was worse than they expected. Now they tell me that . . . they aren't so sure."

Pain shadowed his rotund features, but determination gripped his fleshy mouth. "Look, Ted, I know you don't trust me much. Hell, you've got no use for me at all. But I'm asking you to just set that aside for a minute and look at the facts. This might have been sheer bad luck, but if it wasn't—if we got bum equipment or sloppy installation—then somebody has screwed up my safety record; somebody has messed with my plant. I want to find out who's responsible as much as you do—probably more."

His tone was so intense that Ted could not disagree; he felt only pity for the wrongdoer once Gregory got his hands on his throat.

"Could you bring yourself to pretend that I'm one of the good guys just till this thing is settled?" Gregory's round face looked afraid more than hopeful. "Or at least give me the benefit of the doubt? I'm running an investigation from the inside while you're officially checking me out. If we pooled our information, I think we'd make a lot more headway."

Ted stared at the Red Rock manager's gap-toothed smile and remembered all the superficial banter and downright hostile words he'd endured from him over the years. He had always disliked Lowell Gregory, and he didn't trust him as far as he could throw a bull by the tail. But this time he really wanted to believe that Gregory was on his side.

"Okay," he relented, against his better judgment. "We'll compare notes. But everything you say to me will be on paper and plastered all over my office so there can be no question of collusion somewhere down the line. And if I have any reason to suspect you're trying to pull something over on me, I'll chain you to an ammonia processing valve and jam the controls wide open."

Gregory laughed without humor. "Thanks for the vote of confidence, Ballard."

"Sorry, but that's the best I can do."

Gregory stuffed both hands in his pockets. "Well, it's more than I got from your cohort."

Ted stopped, wary and confused. "How's that, Gregory?"

"Your buddy. Kent Hawthorne. I made him the same offer yesterday, but he got hot under the collar and accused me of offering him a kickback before he refused."

It occurred to Ted, in hindsight, that he should have done the same.

ON SUNDAY NIGHT, Robbin pulled up to the curb in front of Doug's new house in Grass Valley and honked the horn. As the kids came bounding out the front door, Doug waved to her from the living room window. A year ago such a simple gesture would have reduced Robbin to tears. Now she felt nothing as she gazed at the man she'd once loved. Her heart was too full of joy at the sight of her three precious children...and too full of the pain Ted had caused her to think about old wounds inflicted by her ex-husband.

"Hi, Mom!" Ruth greeted her gaily, her dark hair cut in a new, shorter style. "Are we going out for pizza?"

"Will Tina be there?" Allison asked.

"I wanna see Larry!" was Jarrod's contribution.

"We're not going anywhere until I get some hugs," Robbin told her brood, to which she was greeted to a chorus of "Oh, Mom...."

But they all clung to her tightly, joy in the reunion evident in their shining smiles. Jarrod, her baby even though he was now seven, demanded to sit in the front seat beside her. "Mom might need me to give her directions," he explained to his older sisters. "She hasn't been to Dad's in so long."

Allison giggled, and Ruth patted her mother's arm with all the confidence of one who is about to enter the eighth grade. "He missed you, Mom, even though he won't admit it."

"I missed him, too," Robbin was quick to answer, pulling her small son close. "I missed all of you, and I'm not ashamed at all."

"But you're always saying you'd like some peace and quiet," Allison pointed out. "Sometimes you won't even let Captain keep you company."

Robbin jammed the Buick into reverse, biting her tongue on her inexpressible reply. *Not even Captain will have anything to do with me these days. The Ballards have all but disappeared.*

She knew there might be some other reason why she hadn't seen hide nor hair of Tina and Larry all weekend, but Captain's snub was really the straw that broke the camel's back. She'd recently stocked up on his favorite food—canned mackerel—and he knew it. Normally he made a pest of himself on weekends, but ever since the night she'd gone out with Kent Hawthorne, Robbin hadn't had a glimpse of the haughty Siamese cat.

She hadn't gotten much more than a glimpse of Ted's shiny new green van, either. She'd seen him come and go a few times, but he'd seemed determined to spend the weekend anywhere but at home. In the past, when Robbin hadn't had occasion to speak to Ted for several days, she had drawn comfort from the knowledge that he was just next door. Now she was acutely aware of his absence...and of the painful fact that even if he were home, she would not be welcome there.

"Are we going to the Pizza Palace with the Ballards, Mom?" Allison wanted to know when they reached the outskirts of Coltersville an hour and a half later. "Dad got me this new baby doll that—"

"You can show it to Tina tomorrow," Robbin cut her off. Personally, she didn't care where they went to eat; she'd had no appetite whatsoever for two whole days. "The Ballards had . . . other plans this evening."

"Other plans?" Ruth responded instantly, already picking up the hesitation in her mother's voice. "What could possibly be more important than having the whole family together on our first night home?"

What, indeed, Robbin could have answered. Sooner or later she'd have to explain to the children—or at least to Ruth—what had really happened. But it was too complicated to go into at the moment and too cruel a reality with which to tarnish their first night home.

The Pizza Palace was just as noisy as ever. A ball game was blaring out of the sports room, and the video arcade was blasting with the sound of laser guns and would-be starfighters scoring incalculable devastation on some alien fleet. Two human-sized fluffy creatures of unidentifiable origin strolled through the masses of children, shaking hands, squeezing cheeks and patting little people on the head. But with only three children to keep her company, the place was empty as far as Robbin was concerned.

She ordered twice—once giving her standard two-family order, then with adjustments as she remembered that Tina and Larry weren't there to gobble their share of pepperoni, and Ted couldn't help her with the ham. Allison and Jarrod scrambled off to play with the Palace's juvenile delights while Ruth and Robbin waited for the orders.

"So how was your visit with your dad, honey?" Robbin asked.

Ruth shrugged. "It was fine. I like to be with Daddy, but I don't really like to be away from home so long." Her voice dropped as she admitted with a trace of embarrassment, "I really missed you and Uncle Ted."

She said it just as though Robbin and Ted were married; it was hardly the time to point out that they'd just gotten "divorced." Instead, Robbin slipped an unobtrusive arm around her daughter and pulled her close to her side.

"Have you guys finished planning the camping trip? I can't believe we've only got a week left until Labor Day and we go back to school!" Ruth switched topics abruptly, grateful for her mother's quiet display of affection, but embarrassed by her own need of it. "A friend of Daddy's went camping in July and a bear got all their food. Remember that time we saw the bear at Yosemite?"

Robbin remembered vaguely; there were often bears at Yosemite, but normally they kept a safe distance from the campers. At the moment she had a much greater concern regarding their trip: if Ted's mood didn't change by Friday, the only way Ruth would get to Yosemite at all this year was if the Walkers braved the bears alone.

Robbin tugged a napkin out of the steel holder with her free hand and fingered it nervously. She knew she couldn't fend off her daughter's questions about the Ballards for very long. Ted had been pretty blunt about the future relationship he perceived between their two families. It would devastate the children, but sooner or later she would have to tell them the truth. Perhaps now that they were alone she might give Ruth a hint as to which way the wind was blowing on Mulberry Lane.

"Ruthie, Ted has been...well, very busy lately. We had a little trouble at the refinery while you were gone, and he's in charge of looking into it."

"So? He doesn't work on Sundays," Ruth was quick to point out.

"No, but—"

"Ruthie!" a young voice suddenly rang out across the pizza parlor.

Robbin quickly followed her daughter's eyes to the doorway where Tina Ballard was bouncing up and down, tugging on her father's reluctant hand. Larry, not bothering to wait for his father, was already bolting toward the table.

"Hi, Ruth! Where's Jarrod?" he asked, running the words together in one interconnected sentence. Without waiting for an answer, he scrambled off to the video arcade room.

Tina, equally enthusiastic, bounded over to the table to give Ruth a hug. "I thought you guys would never get back! Would you help me go find Allison?"

Ruth nodded cheerfully. "First let me say hi to your dad," she told the younger girl, then sauntered toward Ted with a mixture of girlish spontaneity and adolescent reserve.

Ted still stood at the door, his eyes on the joyful family scene. When Robbin had first seen him, she'd treasured a moment's hope that he'd changed his mind about their forced separation and had decided to drop by the Pizza Palace on the off chance that she'd brought the kids there. But one look at his face—tense and tired—told her the truth. He looked as though he were trying to find a way to escape without hurting Ruth's feelings. It wasn't until she reached his side that he gave up the struggle.

Despite her best efforts to play it cool, the thirteen-year-old threw off her veil of artificial maturity a few steps away from Ted and all but leaped into his arms. And Ted, for all the conflicts raging within him, wrapped his arms around her fiercely and dropped a kiss on the top of her head.

Robbin couldn't hear what they said to each other, but the poignancy of the reunion was hard to ignore. She battled the lump in her throat and tried to think of a way to tell the kids that Ted had nailed shut the gate between their two houses. It was the hardest news she'd ever had to share with her children; mercifully, Doug had been the one to tell them about the divorce.

When the emotional greeting at the door had finally ended, Ruth and Tina disappeared in the crowd, leaving Ted, looking angry and defeated, standing by himself. With the greatest reluctance he met Robbin's eyes. And then, after a long, contemplative moment, he strolled slowly toward her table.

She tried to look at him as a stranger would...after all, the tense expression on his face didn't belong to anybody she knew. To Robbin's surprise, she thought he made a very attractive picture. Despite his loosened tie and rolled-up sleeves, he had a uniquely sexy walk that she'd never really noticed before... sort of a rolling motion that emphasized his long legs. Maybe Ted was right; maybe she'd never really noticed him at all—at least not as an available man. For years he'd been her "brother"—how else could she have viewed him when she'd been married to another man! But things were different now. It occurred to Robbin that if she were meeting this mustachioed family man tonight for the very first time, she might well have hoped he would ask her out. Did that mean that maybe, if she worked at it, she could someday grow to think of Ted as more than just a pal? It was a startling possibility—one that filled her with hope as well as trepidation.

"I take it you haven't told them yet," he said by way of greeting. His voice was tense and cold.

"I just picked them up two hours ago, Ted. They were already crushed that you weren't planning to join us for a welcome-home celebration."

He sighed. "You told me you'd be eating at home," he reminded Robbin as he slipped into the booth across from her. "Otherwise I wouldn't have risked coming here."

The simple truth devastated Robbin, as did the painful realization that nothing had changed from Ted's perspective in the last two days. Nothing had really changed for Robbin, either; her agony had just grown a little more intense as her hope had slipped away.

"Well, now that you're here . . . do you want to order? If I'd known you were coming, I would have—"

"Robbin, don't try to pretend that everything's the way it was. It's not. We've got to tell the children, and we've got to do it soon."

"All right, Ted! But do we have to do right it now when they've been gone all summer? They've missed you—they've missed all of you! Can't you spare them one evening of celebration before you pull the rug out from under them?"

At first Ted didn't answer. His expression was hard to read; the only thing she was sure of was that his eyes held neither friendliness nor welcome. "Look, Robbin, I think it would be better to tell them right away. We're all out of the habit of spending much time together anyway."

He said the words with such cool deliberation that Robbin found herself snapping back, "And whose fault is that, Ted? You started avoiding me long before the kids went to see their dad! Were you already mad at me in March or April? It's been months since—"

"I wasn't mad at you, Robbin."

"Then why were you avoiding me? And you *were* avoiding me, Teddy. Before last week I just thought you were busy. But now that I think about it—"

"Oh, that's rich!" He chuckled without mirth. "You've hardly seen me in six months, and now that it's come to your attention—half a year later—you're wounded and indignant. Do you think I should feel guilty because the shoe is finally on the other foot?"

Tears fought their way into Robbin's eyes as she listened to Ted's stinging words. Before Friday night, he'd never spoken to her like this! She knew he was hurt and bitter, but she couldn't believe that he was indifferent to the fact that she was hurting, too.

"It didn't take me six months to notice, Ted!" The words spilled out in self-defense. "I just had such faith in our friendship that I was sure that if something was wrong, you'd come right out and tell me...and whatever it was, we could make it right."

"Well, we can't make it right, Robbin, so let it rest, okay?" His eyes darkened again as silence gripped the table for a tense moment.

There was nothing left for Robbin to say; if Ted didn't even want to heal the breach between them, what more could she possibly do? Yet, she couldn't believe he could give up their friendship so easily.

Then, abruptly, he whispered, "I'm sorry, Robbie."

Ted's husky words gave Robbin the first glimpse of hope she'd seen in two long days. When she met his eyes bravely, she read the anguish there and knew that his love for her still lingered.

"You know I don't want to hurt you. I just can't bear to talk about this anymore. So give us both a break and let it be."

She didn't get a chance to respond before the kids came bounding back to the table. The same reunion scene Robbin had already witnessed was repeated between Ted and Jarrod, then Ted and Allison. Ruth had collected the pizza, and the younger girls volunteered to order more for the late arrivals. Robbin couldn't even finish one piece tonight, although it was her favorite kind of pizza. Ted was normally a voracious eater, but Robbin noticed that he only got down a few bites himself.

Ted managed to be cheerful with the children, but Robbin was hard pressed to do the same. For the next half hour the conversation bubbled around her. The kids had a lot to get caught up on—like which movies they'd seen, and where they'd gone, and what toys were the latest fad. Ted didn't say much, and he kept his eyes away from Robbin's. The entire meal was a cruel parody of the countless joyful dinners they'd shared in this very booth.

"So have you and Mom figured out what all we need to take on this camping trip?" Ruth asked as she finished off the pizza and the younger children once more set off to play. "I know Dad took a lot of stuff with him when he left, but I'm sure he'd loan it to us if we asked him. It might be better just to buy new stuff, though, since we go camping so often." She turned to Ted as though he, not Robbin, were the head of her family. "What do you think, Uncle Ted?"

Ted stared at her bleakly; his reserve of optimism was wearing thin. "I think…I think it's something your mom and I need to talk over, Ruthie."

"Uh-oh. Grown-up stuff," she intoned melodramatically. "I suppose you want me to get lost?"

A year ago Ruth would not have noticed the subtle implication of Ted's words, but she'd grown extremely sensitive to adult tensions ever since the divorce. It seemed to her mother that she'd grown up even more this summer.

Ted smiled wanly, as though his thoughts reflected Robbin's own. "I'd like you to go check up on the kids, if you would, honey."

Ruth gave him a quick kiss on the cheek, then did as he asked. For a minute he sat perfectly still, reluctant to continue their private conversation; it was Robbin who broke the silence.

"Doug and I already knew our marriage was over before last Labor Day, Ted, but we still went to Yosemite because you and the kids were counting on it. The kind of family dissolution you're planning is going to tear all five of them apart; you know it is. Can't you just put up with me for three or four days?'' She waited while he stared at the big screen over her shoulder. The crowd was cheering; some nameless hero had hit a home run.

''I don't want to go camping with you, Robbin,'' he said bluntly, though his tone was more sad than cruel. Ever so briefly his eyes met hers. ''I don't know how to make myself any more clear.''

Robbin battled the rush of moisture in her eyes, but one determined tear escaped anyway, ignominiously trailing down her flushed cheek. ''Oh, Ted, don't you understand? You're not the only one involved here. It's not just the kids. Ever since Friday night, I've been—''

''I've got other things on my mind besides your problems, Robbin,'' he snapped, clearly irritated by her persistence. ''I've got a refinery that still may be unsafe, a shady character I've been forced to trust, and a hero of yours who might turn out to be a villain. About the last thing I need is to waltz into purgatory for a weekend to give you a false illusion of happiness.''

With those hard words, Robbin gave up the struggle to maintain her composure. Right there in the Pizza Palace, with toddlers whining, ball fans screaming, and the aroma of pizza wafting through the air, she gave in to the tornado inside her. She covered her face with both hands and wept.

''Damn it, Robbie!'' Ted breathed, his voice low and hoarse. ''Don't do that, Robbs,'' he begged her. ''Please don't cry in front of me. I just can't bear it.''

''I'm sorry, Ted! But I've already cried everywhere else.'' She met his eyes through soggy lashes, still sobbing as she spoke. ''Oh, Teddy, I love you so much!

Can't you understand that? What we have is much too precious to throw away just because of... sex!"

He slammed one hand down on the table in wordless frustration. "Robbin, it's more than sex! It's the difference between the way you look at me and the way you look at Kent! You see him as some kind of a god, and you don't see me as any kind of a man at all! I want to be the center of your world, Robbie, not the spare coat you keep in the hall closet in case you can't find your new one when it's raining! I'm tired of being the understudy for...whatever or whoever comes first in your life! Is that so very hard to understand?"

"No, it's not!" she burst out, her hot tears still flowing freely. "But I think you're the one who doesn't understand. If you really mattered to me so little, how could your...abandonment possibly hurt me so much? Maybe I've never thought of you as a lover, Ted, but that doesn't mean you haven't been the center of my world! Nothing's ever torn me up like this except for my divorce. I've hardly been able to eat in two whole days! Doesn't that tell you anything?"

Ted met her eyes but didn't answer.

Robbin reached out to take his hand, but he pulled away as though she'd burned him.

"Don't play games with me, Robbin," he ordered grimly. "Don't pretend that—"

"I'm not pretending, Teddy! But I—I'm not absolutely positive that I'll never feel the way you want me to! All I know is that if I love you this much... if I want to merge my life with yours so desperately...that there must be something special there!"

As she said the words, she truly believed them. What she felt for Ted could never be called girlish, first-love passion, but it was so deep, so profound, that maybe it couldn't be discounted as a seed from which marital love could grow. If he'd just give her a little time to sort things out....

Ted studied her warily. "What are you suggesting, Robbs?"

She took heart from his repeated use of her special nickname; she struggled for words to keep him talking to her. "I'm just saying that maybe in time if I get used to thinking of you in a different light—"

He slumped back in the booth and glared at her. "I'm not a child, Robbin; I won't let you toy with me. We've known each other for thirteen years; the last thing we need is more time to get acquainted!" He gave her no opportunity to defend her position. "There's only one way I could even consider going through with this camping trip, even for the kids, and that's if you promise not to keep me dangling with false hopes about things that will never be."

Robbin didn't know what to tell him. At the moment she would have agreed to almost anything for the slightest ray of hope that Ted would still be her friend. Even for one more week.

"Just tell me what I need to do, Teddy," she whispered tearfully. "I miss you very much. I just can't bear to lose you altogether."

Ted studied her face for a long, tender moment; he didn't try to veil his love. "I'm having a damn hard time of it myself, Robbsie," he confessed in a ragged breath. "I thought it would be impossible to stay close to you under these circumstances, but...pushing you away seems to be hurting me even more."

Again Robbin reached out for Ted's hand by instinct, and this time he didn't pull away. His fingers closed around hers with tender anguish; he closed his eyes, then pulled her palm against his cheek. Gently, Robbin stroked his face, tracing the outline of his mustache with one brave nail. He turned his head to press his lips against the softness of her wrist in a gesture obviously intended to soothe her. But the brush of mustache and the warm, yearning lips aroused a spark within Robbin, a need for... for what?

Before she could begin to think about that question, Jarrod and Larry bounded back to the table. Jarrod scrambled under Ted's free arm, and Larry climbed up on his back.

"So when are we going to Yosemite, Uncle Ted?" Jarrod begged him, his eyes alight with joy. "Since my dad's not going, do you think I could sleep in your tent? Otherwise, I'm going to be stuck with Mom and my sisters."

"And if Tina slept with Allison, it'd just be boys in our tent!" Larry concluded. Clearly, the two had thought out their argument.

Slowly Ted released Robbin's hand. He studied the eager face of one young boy and then the other before he glanced up at Robbin again. Sorrow and fragile hope marred the quiet beauty of her face, which was now tearstained. Never had his love for her—nor his anguish—called out to Robbin more poignantly.

The noisy hoopla of the pizza parlor blurred in the background while Ted debated his decision. He tried not to stare at Robbin, but he couldn't seem to cut himself off from the lifeline of love that radiated from her eyes. For several seconds he drummed the table with five strong brown fingers. Then, abruptly, he clenched them into a fist.

More resigned than joyful, he declared to the boys, "I guess we men have to stick together. Let's go home and pack."

CHAPTER TEN

"HAWTHORNE? Ballard here. We need to get together to compare notes on Red Rock. Are you free this afternoon?"

It had taken Ted several days to come up with the self-control to make the call to his colleague, and the only reason he was doing it now was because he and Robbin were scheduled to leave at noon tomorrow for Yosemite. The last thing he wanted to do at the moment was talk to Kent Hawthorne, but he knew it was imperative for the two of them to work together if they were going to solve the mess at Red Rock. One way or another, Kent was going to help him find out the truth about the explosion.

He still didn't have nearly enough information on the refinery accident—just enough to heighten his basic suspicion of Kent and suspect some possible alliance with Howard Caldwell. Gregory had called Ted three times this week. Once he'd reported that he'd checked his records and discovered that Caldwell had handled the installation of the new equipment while Gregory had been on vacation. Ted had conferred with Caldwell again—an unsavory task at any time—but he hadn't been able to find any holes in his account of that transaction. He couldn't very well convict a man for belligerence.

Gregory's second call was to inform Ted that the contractor from whom he'd bought the valves had suddenly abandoned the trade and disappeared, leaving no record of the crew involved or any other specifics of the transaction. Oil patch gossip had it that he'd been skimming funds and had gone underground. Ted had followed up on that lead, too, and had come up empty. Whether the contractor's fleeing the coop before Gregory's inquiry was sheer coincidence, Ted simply couldn't tell. Just to be on the safe side, he'd asked Angela Hartwood to listen in on his conversations with Gregory so he'd have a witness to all statements and accusations. He still didn't trust the man as far as he could throw him.

Gregory's third call, just an hour ago, was by far the most alarming. The man had just returned from the hospital in Morgantown where Bill Rayburn was holding on by a thread. If he died, not only would Red Rock be left open for a suit, but anybody convicted of shady dealings with the urea unit equipment would be culpable in a charge of second degree murder. The guilty party could even do hard time.

That possibility hadn't bothered Ted very much when the finger of suspicion had pointed at Gregory. Nor would he shed any tears, Ted thought to himself, if justice were to sling its noose around Howard Caldwell. But he still wasn't sure where Kent fit into the picture, and that troubled him a lot. If Caldwell had sold off the new valves and pipes and pocketed a tidy sum, Kent had approved unsafe equipment—there was no way around that simple fact. The only question was, had he done it out of ignorance, or simple greed? Ted couldn't be sure of the answer.

Why am I making excuses for the man? Ted asked himself. *If he's guilty, he needs to be found out.*

In his heart, he knew why he was being so cautious. Last Friday night, nothing would have pleased him more than stumbling over evidence that would have sent Kent to the gallows. But for Ted Ballard, anger was a rare and fleeting thing; honor and friendship were always abiding. Despite his recent rocky encounters with Kent Hawthorne, he had once considered the man a friend. Knowing how unhappy Kent had been in recent months, it was hard for Ted to hold his own irrational behavior against the man. Moreover, he didn't want to hound Kent out of a sense of revenge over what had happened with Robbin. Such behavior would only cause Ted to lose face in Robbin's eyes. If Kent was really what she wanted, he reasoned, so be it. But he was haunted by the possibility that Robbin was falling in love with a shady character who might actually come to be convicted of a crime. No matter how strained matters grew between Ted and Robbin, he would always protect her if he could.

If Kent was surprised at Ted's straightforward tone on the phone after their last rocky encounter, he concealed it well. "I've got a few leads myself, Ted," he answered suavely, "but I'm afraid this afternoon is out. Any chance we could meet for lunch tomorrow?"

This time it was Ted who demurred. "Sorry. I'm leaving town as soon as I tie up a few loose ends here in the morning. I won't be back till Tuesday."

"Where are you going this weekend?" Kent asked in a conversational tone. "Didn't you tell me once that you always went camping over Labor Day?"

"Nope, I didn't. Robbin must have." Somehow he managed to keep his voice low and even. "We always go to Yosemite."

This time Kent did hesitate for just a moment. "Robbin's going with you?"

Ted couldn't suppress a brief sense of triumph; clearly Kent hadn't been in touch with her this week or he'd already have known. Maybe Robbin didn't really want to see him; maybe he'd just been playing with her after all and hadn't bothered to call. Either way, it didn't change the way Robbin felt about Ted... or the fact that going on this trip with her was an act of sentimental folly that he was most certainly going to regret.

"Yep," Ted told the other man as nonchalantly as he could. "It's a family thing we've done together for thirteen years."

"Even though the... family has changed a bit, I gather."

"Some things don't really change, Hawthorne."

Ted's words lingered in the air for several moments before Kent said quietly, "I'm sorry about Friday night, Ted. I knew you had your eye on Robbin, but she didn't mention breaking a date with you; I honestly thought she was free for the evening. I was already upset before you came barging in because things weren't going quite the way I'd planned. Once I cooled down a bit, I realized that I had no call to chew you up like that."

And no call to paw over my woman like that, either, Ted wanted to snap back. But he rose to the occasion—he knew how hard the apology came to Kent—and forced himself to say, "Let's just forget the whole thing, okay? Robbie's a big girl. She's got the right to pick her own friends."

"No hard feelings?" Kent asked cautiously.

"If I said yes, I'd be lying, Kent. Robbin's damned important to me and you knew that before you asked her out. But she doesn't belong to me, obviously—" he kept a tight rein on his feelings as he forced out the words "—and if she wants to date you, that's her business." Ted's voice dropped a bit as he tacked on, "But if you keep seeing her, Hawthorne, you better be damn sure that you treat her right. Robbie's not one of your love 'em and leave 'em types. Do you understand?"

"I know a first-class lady when I see one, Ballard," Kent replied a bit tersely.

"Glad to hear it. If we're clear on that, I've got to go. I won't be in until about ten on Tuesday—I've got personal business in the morning—but I'll call you as soon as I can."

"Sounds good. Have a good trip, Ted, and don't worry about anything here. I'll keep an eye on Gregory while you're gone."

Ted wanted to laugh. Gregory was practically accusing Kent of taking a bribe, and Kent was still trying to convince him that Gregory was the guilty party. Nothing could be proven yet—including the fact that anybody had committed a crime—but he felt queasy about leaving Kent in charge of the Red Rock investigation in his absence. It was rather like leaving a fox to guard the hen house.

Oh, well, it could be worse, Ted consoled himself as he hung up the phone. *I'd rather leave him alone with Gregory than alone with Robbie.*

For the next few days, at least, Robbin would be safely beyond the reach of Kent or any trouble that might be brewing at the refinery. It was almost enough to make Ted glad he had agreed to go on the trip.

ROBBIN HANDED TED ANOTHER SLEEPING BAG and waited while he stuffed it into the van. He'd hardly spoken to her in the thirty minutes he'd been packing. Nervous, she'd made enough conversation for both of them. "Is there going to be enough room, Ted, or do we need two cars?"

Ted's tone was terse. "I didn't buy a Japanese import, Robbin."

He could have said more, but mercifully he refrained. Obviously he'd bought the van with just this sort of venture in mind. Robbin wondered how much camping he'd do with Larry and Tina alone. An unwelcome notion shook her: maybe he'd find another outdoor woman with children. Maybe now he'd marry someone else.

It certainly wouldn't be Lila; of that Robbin was certain. Despite the occasional twinge of jealousy she still felt whenever she thought of the two of them together, Robbin hadn't really believed that Ted's interest in Lila was romantic even before Lila had spelled it out for her on Saturday morning. Nonetheless, she hadn't been able to stifle a sense of discomfort when Ted had called the real estate office yesterday to speak to Lila. Robbin had answered the phone, but Ted had greeted her with only the briefest of hellos and had sidestepped her courteous questions about the progress of his investigation. He didn't have time to share his problems with Robbin, his number one confidante, but he'd managed to talk to Lila for almost fifteen minutes. And when Robbin had quizzed Lila on the content of that conversation, the other woman had been friendly but evasive.

Jane had called a little later in the day and had also passed over Robbin for a chat with Lila. Kent Hawthorne hadn't called all week. Although Robbin still wasn't sure whether or not she wanted to go out with him again, she would have preferred the option of telling him yes or no.

Robbin picked up Captain, who was lounging on the roof of the van, and stroked his ears as she watched Ted load up the vehicle. He'd thwarted every effort she'd made to help him today; nonetheless, she felt the need to try one more time. "I've just got one more box of kitchen supplies, Teddy. Should I go get them now?"

"You mean this box?" He gestured toward a cardboard box on the ground. "Ruthie brought it out fifteen minutes ago." He couldn't hide the note of censure in his voice; he seemed to be saving all of his sunny smiles for the children.

"Are you going to be like this for the whole weekend, Ted?" Robbin decided to ask him bluntly. She knew what was wrong; he still didn't want to go camping and he hated being near her. Even though she knew it was because he loved her too much to pretend they could just be friends, it was hard to enjoy his company when he was so blue.

"Like what?" he said grumpily, poking a pillow behind the Coleman lantern.

"Grouchy and rude to me. I'm not used to it, Ted, and it's not really much fun. You've said more nasty things to me in the last seven days than you have in the last thirteen years."

Ted turned to stare at Robbin. His hair was still combed from his morning at work, but the ratty T-shirt and paint-splattered jeans he wore for camping were as familiar to Robbin as the old Ted—the one who had wrestled with her during the commercials and plopped the popcorn bowl on his stomach when he stretched out on her blue carpet to read. His expression was still foreign—strained, hurt, and angry.

"You're the one who insisted on this trip," he reminded her. "I told you I didn't want to go; I still think it's a lousy idea. Now if you—"

"Aunt Robbin! Telephone for you!" Tina trotted eagerly across the Walkers's front lawn as she called out her news. She wore cutoff shorts and a bright red T-shirt, and her braces framed a brilliant smile. Like all four of the other kids, she was thrilled that they were going camping.

"Ruthie says it's Mr. Hawthorne. I told her to ask him if it was really Daddy he wanted to talk to," she informed Robbin. "But she double-checked and said you're the one he wants."

Her inadvertent choice of words didn't help the awkward situation. Ted, already irritated, now turned back to the van. "We're just about packed up here, Robbin. I'd like to get moving before everybody and his brother hits the road."

Robbin should have gone directly to the phone, but now she stopped and reached out to touch Ted's left shoulder. She couldn't bear to start out the trip like this. If being near her was really this hard on him, maybe it really would be better if they cancelled the trip.

At first Ted didn't respond to Robbin's touch, but she waited anyway. With her usual timing, Mrs. Griswald took this moment to stroll down the street with Peppy, hoping, no doubt, to get the latest scoop on Ted's and Robbin's trip.

"So where are you kids off to?" the old woman asked amiably, her old T-shirt almost as ratty as Ted's. "Lots of room here in the new van."

Ted flashed her a dutiful smile; he'd always felt sorry for Mrs. Griswald. "Going to Yosemite, Mrs. Griswald," he reported. "And we're late as it is or we'd stay to talk to you and Peppy. We'd sure be grateful if you'd keep an eye on the houses while we're gone. Sarah's going to be feeding Captain, but if you see him outside I'm sure he'd like a little company."

Mrs. Griswald positively glowed at the realization that Ted was giving her an assignment, but Robbin had to stifle her impatience as she bid her neighbor goodbye and waited while Ted did the same—albeit more gently. She knew that Kent was still waiting on the phone, and she knew that Ted didn't want to be alone with her. But still she stood in back of the van, one uneasy hand on his shoulder, while Mrs. Griswald wandered off with her dachshund and the boys chased each other around the lawn.

Robbin stood close to Ted, immobile, until he finally turned to meet her eyes. Ever so gently he lifted his right hand to pat her fingers. "I'm sorry, Robbie," he whispered in a strained tone too low for his daughter to hear. "We'll make it a good trip. A good last memory for all of us." For the briefest of moments he met her sad gray eyes and added, "I promise you, Robbsie. I won't spoil the fun."

Robbin wanted to hug him and whisper, "Thank you, Teddy Bear!" But she knew that that was more than he could handle at the moment. It was enough that he'd broken down the barriers with his gentle words and a healing touch; enough that he'd called her "Robbsie."

Resisting the urge to kiss him on the cheek, Robbin just smiled her gratitude, then marched quickly into the house to talk to Kent before fate—or Mrs. Griswald—had a chance to rob her of the peaceful moment.

"Hello?" she said into the mouthpiece.

"Robbin, this is Kent Hawthorne." His tone was subdued, almost humble. "I understand you're leaving town for the weekend, but I hoped . . . I'd like to get together when you get back."

Robbin wasn't sure what to say. Granted, it hadn't been *that* long since their date; she really didn't have a right to be angry that he hadn't called her sooner. But something in his timing struck her as deliberate, as though reminding Ted of his interest in Robbin just before they left on their trip was more important to him than spending time with her. Besides, their last encounter still rankled. The more Robbin thought about the events of last Friday evening, the more certain she was that Kent had tried to initiate lovemaking without the slightest concern for her own feelings in the matter.

"Well, Kent, the van is packed and we're ready to go. I'm sorry I can't really talk right now. Why don't you call me back next week some time and I'll . . . look at my appointment book."

There was a lengthy pause before he answered, "Okay, Robbin. I'll do that. You have . . . have a good trip."

"Thanks, Kent. You have a good weekend, too."

She was about to hang up when he stopped her with a wistful tone. "Robbin?"

"Yes?"

"I didn't . . . I didn't just call to ask you out again. In case you . . . in case we don't get to spend much time together in the future, I just wanted to apologize."

"Apologize?" *I didn't think that word was in your vocabulary.* His tone confused Robbin; despite his display of cockiness on their date, he now sounded disappointed that she probably didn't want to see him again.

"Robbin, I was a total boor with you on Friday night. I put on an act that I . . . use quite successfully with a certain sort of woman. You're so many cuts above that kind that . . . well, I guess I was afraid to take the risk of just being myself. Ladies are always quick to fall for my face. I'm never quite sure how they'll take to the rest of me once they get past that."

Robbin was dumbfounded. No wonder he'd treated her as he had—she'd given every sign of being the kind of woman who wanted to go out with Robert Redford!

What did she know about the real Kent Hawthorne? She remembered traces of openness and laughter in him, moments when she'd found him likable and fun. But had she really encouraged him to relax with her? She'd started off the evening drooling over his good looks and his orchid...and she'd exuded more joy over a trip to The Old Mansion than the possibility of seeing him again.

Truthfully she told him, "Kent, I don't know you very well, but I have the feeling that your real personality would appeal to me a lot more than the role you played on Friday night."

For a moment he was quiet, then he asked, "Is that a compliment or an insult?"

Robbin smiled, wishing he could see her perplexed expression. "I don't know, Kent. When it comes to you, I—I really don't know."

He sighed audibly. "Well, that's pretty honest, I guess."

"Honest is the only way I really know how to be with people, Kent. If you...if you want to play it that way, why don't you call me for lunch next week, and maybe we can give it another try."

"Fair enough, Robbin. I'll call you for lunch on Tuesday."

"Sounds good, Kent, but make it Wednesday or Thursday. Tuesday's out for me; it's the first day of school. By the time I get five kids settled into new classes, I won't be able to take more than a minute for a drive-through lunch."

"Five kids?" he repeated. "I thought you only had three."

Robbin wasn't sure how to answer, so she told him the truth. "I only gave birth to three, Kent, and only three live in my house. But I've raised Larry Ballard since he was a baby, and I don't think Tina's orthodontist even remembers that I'm not her mom. The school even calls me when Ted's kids get sick!"

"I see." His tone was thoughtful. "Do your children also think of Ted as a . . . second father?"

Robbin didn't try to deny it. "We've always been an extended family, Kent. You know how it is."

The long silence at the other end told Robbin that Kent didn't know how it was; it reminded her of the painful emptiness of his own paternal life. Sometime, she vowed, she'd talk to Kent some more about his own daughter; she'd get to know the real man behind the mask. But right now she didn't have time. Another man—a far more important man—was waiting for her.

"I'll talk to you next week, Kent," she finished the call. "Teddy's got the van packed, and he's waited long enough."

The alternative meaning to her words struck her as she hung up and returned to the van. And as she looked at Ted—so strong, so loving as he wrestled with Jarrod and Larry on the grass—she couldn't stifle the sudden strange, illogical hope that maybe Ted could manage to wait for her just a little longer.

A few days alone in the mountains might be just long enough.

THE LENGTHY DRIVE TO YOSEMITE was very hard on Ted. He managed to keep his promise to Robbin; he was cheerful and friendly every step of the way. But it was an inordinate strain on him, and he was already counting the hours until he could go home. It didn't help any that in every place they stopped—every gas station and every restaurant—somebody made a comment on Ted's large family, assuming that Robbin was his wife. One elderly waitress even asked how long they'd been married—she didn't think Robbin showed enough wear and tear to have given birth to five children.

"I don't remember how long we've been together," Ted responded with a valiant effort at humor. "Sometimes it seems as though we've been married forever, and other times I might just as well still be down on one knee waiting for her to say yes."

The waitress thought that was hilarious, and Robbin had feigned a smile. Nobody had commented on the incident as the van pulled into one campsite after another and seven people voiced their opinions.

"It's too windy here," was Ruth's inevitable comment. A nippy night breeze was sweeping through the mountains.

"It's too far from the river," was the younger girls' lament, while Jarrod and Larry complained, "All the trees are too big to climb, or else they're seedlings and are still too small."

Ted, only one of three grown-ups on most of their previous trips, had never before interfered with their time-honored tradition of democratic campsite seeking. But for some reason he found the group's indecisiveness enormously aggravating this evening. It was already dark, of course, which didn't help matters any.

"Well?" he asked Robbin as he pulled into Possible Campsite Number Eight. "What's wrong with this one?"

Robbin laughed. She'd been a good sport on the trip, and now seemed to be in genuinely good humor. "Have I complained about any of these choices, Ted?"

"No, but that's only because everybody else is doing it for you. You always want trees for a hammock and a tent flap, and water and rest rooms close enough to be handy but far enough away to forget."

She grinned with pleasure. "You've got my number, Teddy. I'm content to leave the decision in your hands."

Why don't you leave some other decision in my hands? he wanted to ask her. *And why don't you stop calling me 'Teddy'?* After he'd growled at her about her reference to him as a "teddy bear," she'd been careful not to use her private nickname for him again. But even "Teddy" seemed entirely too intimate a sobriquet for a woman he planned to see no more than absolutely necessary after this weekend of perdition was over.

Pondering her last words, Ted realized with a jolt that he'd never really made a solid decision about anything to do with Robbin before he'd asked her to marry him. With his own children, he did whatever disciplining needed to be done, and at work he was known for his efficiency. But with Robbin he'd always tried so hard to be amiable that he now feared he might have come across as wishy-washy. Suddenly, he decided that it was time to be firm.

"I like the third one we looked at, tucked back in that cluster of trees," he declared with calm authority. "That's where we're going to pitch the tents."

"But Uncle Ted, it didn't have—"

"Tough," he cut off little Jarrod. "This caravan can only have one commander, and since I'm the one who's going to be driving in the tent stakes, it's going to be me."

Robbin said nothing, but he glimpsed a whisper of a smile on her face in the moonlight. He couldn't tell whether she was pleased or just amused.

They unloaded the van by the light of the Coleman lantern. Although it had been hot on the drive up, it was chilly now, so Ted started a fire while Robbin set up the kitchen supplies and the girls hauled in several buckets of water. He ordered the boys to collect firewood so they could roast some frankfurters for a quick supper, then asked Ruth to help him set up the tents.

"Seems kind of silly to have two tents now that we've only got seven people," Ruth pointed out after they'd hoisted the Ballards's old army-surplus model. "If we got one giant tent, couldn't we all sleep together next time? We all fit in the van and we've always driven two cars before."

Ted unzipped the front of the tent and slipped inside to check for any critters that might have moved in since the tent had been stored in the garage. He knew Ruth very well, and he suspected that her comment was not coincidental. "Ruthie, if you're leading up to something, I think you—"

"Well, it does make sense, Uncle Ted," she pressed on hurriedly. "If you and Mom got married, then we'd—"

Ted turned to face her so swiftly that he banged his head against the tent pole and strangled an oath he'd never use in front of the children. "Ruth, I'm only going to tell you this once. Put that notion right out of your head. It's not a joke, and it's not a possibility, either. Is that clear?"

Ruth's adolescent ego deflated quickly as she hunched against the tent flap. It was so rare that Ted spoke harshly to any of the kids that his words were like a cat-o'-nine-tails' lash. "I'm sorry, Uncle Ted. I was just . . . thinking of a way we could always be together. I missed you so much this summer."

Her quiet confession nearly undid him. For the little ones to confess to missing him would have been no surprise. But Ruth tended to be more reserved. A spontaneous hello kiss was one thing, but a carefully rehearsed plea like this was something else altogether. She'd been the hardest hit by her parents' divorce, and Ted had always done his best to comfort her. He hated the knowledge that his break with Robbin would intensify Ruthie's pain.

Slowly he crossed the dark interior of the tent, using his flashlight to brighten the darkness. He laid one gentle hand on top of her head and pulled her against his chest.

"I'm sorry, Ruthie. Just because I can't marry your mother doesn't mean that I don't love all you kids like I love my own."

Ruth went into his arms and hugged him mightily. Ted was deeply moved by her spontaneous embrace. Until the kids had come back from Doug's, he'd tried to pretend that Robbin was the only Walker he'd have trouble leaving. But the moment he'd stumbled into the pizza parlor on Sunday, he'd realized that he would have to tear himself away from three other people he dearly loved. This last trip together was only going to make the separation harder.

"Why can't you marry Mommy, Uncle Ted?" Ruthie's words were muffled against his chest. "It would be so perfect for all of us!"

Ted gave her a tender hug, then released a heartfelt sigh. "It would be perfect for you, Ruthie, and maybe for Tina and Allison and the boys." He considered explaining the whole soggy tale to Ruth—she was old enough to hear it—but he decided that it was Robbin's place to share her version of the truth with her own children. Awkwardly he concluded, "What's right for your mom, honey... well, that's something only she can decide."

Before Ruth could answer, Jarrod called out from somewhere in the darkness, "Uncle Ted! Come quick! There's a bear!"

Ruth ducked out of the tent first, and Ted followed right behind her. All the kids were in plain sight, huddled near the fire. Most of the food was still in boxes stacked by the table and the cupboard, though some of it was strewn helter-skelter on the ground. In the midst of the pile of Tupperware and cutlery prowled a great shaggy beast, relishing the remnants of their weekend food supply.

Ted took in the scene in an instant. Bears were common at Yosemite, and nothing to fear if you stayed out of their way and let them eat their fill. Nevertheless, he'd heard some frightening tales in recent years about aggressive bears in the park. Besides, it was one thing to take risks with his own safety; another altogether to take risks with five kids in his care.

Not to mention Robbin, he added in his head. He didn't see her at first, but he knew she must be nearby. Still, her absence with a shuffling bear in their camp caused a wild pounding in his heart, a sudden flash of terror that he was powerless to deny. "Jarrod," Ted asked her son in low, calm tones, hoping not to alarm the bear, "where is your mom?"

"I don't know!" the little boy cried out, the excitement of the bear's arrival now giving way to fear. "She was right here just a—"

"She's in the van, Uncle Ted," Allison whispered breathlessly. "He trapped her in there when she went back in to get the wienies. She—"

Allison never finished her sentence. The bear, as if it had overheard her words and understood them, sauntered a few feet farther from the table and lazily plopped both of its huge front feet on the open tail end of the green van. And then, while Ted watched in sudden, irrational panic, it clambered up between the open doors and hauled itself inside.

CHAPTER ELEVEN

ROBBIN SCREAMED. She didn't plan to; it was foolish, and only served to aggravate the bear. But the sight of the enormous bruin charging at her—or at the very least, grabbing for the package in her hands—was more than she could handle. The sound of her panic echoed through the van as the bear lunged at Robbin, batting the hot dogs out of her hands with one swipe of his massive paw. She could actually feel his savage claws scrape her fingers as he seized his prize.

An instant later, Ted slipped into the van through the door behind her, brandishing a piece of firewood that still glowed with flame. Robbin couldn't see his face, but tension and strength radiated through every line of his long body as he scrambled over the back seat and jammed himself between Robbin and the bear. Robbin was too stunned to think, but from the instant she realized that Ted had come to her rescue, a curious sort of safety net seemed to close around her. Even in her fear she was suddenly certain that Ted would protect her. Nothing could ever harm her as long as Ted was near.

The bear snarled at Ted's intrusion, and Ted promptly bashed it in the snout with the burning log. "Get out of here! Get out!" he hollered, jabbing his weapon into the thrashing animal's chest. It howled in surprise and fury, and batted at the flames, but Ted lunged at it again. "Get away from her! Get out of my camp!" To Robbin's amazement, he sounded furious with the animal, but not in the least bit afraid.

This time the bear had had enough; it stood upright, banging its massive head on the top of the van, then backed out, snarling, as Ted continued to clobber it with his log. Even when the bear fell over the bumper and hit the ground, Ted didn't ease off. He chased the shaggy creature through the brush for nearly fifty yards.

Robbin kept trembling long after both Ted and the bear were out of sight. It had all happened so quickly that she'd barely had time to think, but Ted had reacted in the blink of an eye with a courage and power that amazed Robbin. She remained perfectly still in the van, until Ted bolted back into camp and handed the burning log to Ruth with sharp orders to stow it safely in the fire. Robbin was breathing hard and wanted to cry, but she couldn't seem to move until Ted hustled back into the van beside her.

"Robbsie?" he whispered, quickly taking hold of her hands as he pressed his cheek against her beloved, frightened face. "Are you all right?"

Ted's love for Robbin was so profoundly healing that all her lingering terror fled. Her pulse now throbbed with relief instead of fear. At least, she thought it was relief; whatever it was, it proudly wore Ted's name. Instinctively, Robbin reached out to pull him closer, and he did not demur.

She felt his arms tighten around her, and she felt as though she'd reached a safe harbor in a storm. She felt curiously light-headed and terribly happy for a woman who'd just endured a minor trauma. At the moment she couldn't imagine anywhere else she'd rather be, and certainly no one else she'd rather be with. "Oh, Teddy, I'm so glad you're here," she whispered truthfully. "I just don't know what I'd do without you."

Ted dropped to his knees in the short-ceilinged van and pulled Robbin right down with him. "I'm always here if you need me, Robbs," he promised, his breath sweet and warm against her hair. "No matter what happens down the road, I'll always be there for you. Don't you ever forget it."

Robbin trembled as she pulled back to meet his eyes. "Teddy, I..." As she met his deep brown eyes, words just wouldn't come. She'd hugged Ted a thousand times for one reason or another, and she had a very good reason to hug him now. But right now she wanted more than Ted's offer of platonic relief and healing, more than his fraternal embrace. She didn't understand it, wasn't quite ready to believe it was true. But she was afraid to lose the precious moment, afraid it was a miracle that might never come again.

Ever so gently Robbin touched Ted's face, wondering what was taking place inside her. They were so close she could have kissed his warm, inviting mouth, and so in tune with each other that for the first time in her life, Robbin wanted to do exactly that. She let her fingers tug softly on his mustache, and she tried to remember why she'd never touched him quite like this before. She tried to find an answer for her troubled questions in Ted's ever-watchful eyes.

"Teddy," she whispered again. "I—"

"Mom!" It was Jarrod's frightened squeal.

"Aunt Robbin! Are you all right?" another voice chimed in.

"Dad, that was super! I never knew you were so brave!"

"Mommy, please tell me you're all right!"

"Did he cut you, Mom?"

The voices chattered on endlessly. Robbin dropped her eyes from Ted's dark gaze in confusion and turned to her worried children as one after another scrambled into the van.

"I'm okay. He didn't hurt me. Your father—Uncle Ted—scared him away."

"You were super, Uncle Ted!" Jarrod called out with rapt admiration. "Wait'll I tell Bobby Roland at school! He's always bragging about how tough his daddy is!"

"All right already," Ted finally intervened, deflecting the host of compliments. "I just did what anybody would do. I'm sure if I'd been trapped in the van, Aunt Robbin would have done the same for me."

It was the first time on the whole trip that he'd referred to her as "Aunt Robbin" with his children, and the old honorary title filled Robbin with a fresh surge of hope. Now she followed Ted out the back of the van and surveyed the mess on the ground.

"Oh, boy! And here I had everything so carefully arranged!"

Quickly Ted put his arm around her. His touch was comforting...and more than comforting, somehow. She felt a twinge of disappointment when he released her and started to clean up their supplies.

"Never mind, Robbie," he said. "Bears are just part of the fun of a camping trip. The kids will help you clean up while Ruth and I get your tent assembled. Everything will look brighter after supper."

Ted was only half right. Robbin did feel better tucked snugly in her tent for the night, especially since Ted had slipped a rock from the fire that he'd wrapped in newspaper, into her sleeping bag to keep her warm; it was a tradition that had started years ago when he'd first learned that Robbin was troubled by poor circulation in her feet. He also loaned her the Coleman lantern so she could read before giving in to sleep. Considering the rocky ground beneath her and the uncertainties in her mind, she really didn't have too bad a night.

But in the morning Robbin discovered that she should have let Ted check over the new stove she'd bought to replace the one Doug had taken. It hadn't been oiled correctly and couldn't be used at all. Robbin had also forgotten to pack the bread, the can opener, and the only pot big enough to cook enough beans for the Ballard-Walker army. As if that weren't enough, Jarrod had outgrown his hiking boots over the summer and ended up with such a terrible blister that Ted had ultimately carried him for the last mile of the family hike. Tina got a bee sting and complained about it all the way back to camp.

But Ted remained bright and cheerful throughout the day, directing the children to collect tiny pinecones as they hiked along the trail. All five of them grew secretive after dinner, snickering in delight about a surprise they were cooking up for Robbin. Ted sent her off on a fool's errand—collecting several pails of unnecessary water—while he collaborated with the animated brood on some furtive project. She had no idea what he had in mind, but it was wonderful to see Ted in a playful mood again.

"Okay, Robbs. We're ready now," he called out after an hour of private negotiation with the kids.

"Come on, Mommy!" Jarrod cajoled her.

As soon as Robbin joined the giggling group by the fire, all six of them burst into a spirited, if slightly off-key, rendition of "Happy Birthday." The table was covered with a paper tablecloth and a plastic vase full of freshly picked wildflowers. Ted, the mastermind of the whole affair, bequeathed Robbin with a "corsage" he'd put together with tiny pinecones and broken bits of evergreens gathered earlier on the trail. While it wasn't at all like the one that had been delivered by the clean-cut boy in the white truck, Ted's corsage was uniquely beautiful in a rustic sort of way. Robbin would have loved it even if Ted hadn't made it for her.

Using a giant silver safety pin, he attached the pinecone corsage to Robbin's baggy gray sweatshirt and gave her a genuine smile. "Happy birthday, Robbsie. I hope this year you get everything you've always wanted."

Confused and touched by the gesture, Robbin fought a compelling mist of tears. "Thank you, Teddy." She caressed the tiny cones lovingly. "But it's not my birthday for a month yet."

This time his smile was sober. "I know, Robbs. But I might be too busy to celebrate it then." He swallowed hard as he met her eyes. "And I did promise you that thirty-five would be a good year for you."

His gentle words reminded Robbin of the reality of the way things stood between them, but she brushed away the threatening tears. She didn't have much time left to convince herself she could fall in love with Ted. She knew that something very strange had happened between them last night in the van; or at least, something had happened to Robbin. Maybe her surge of sensual need for Ted had been nothing more than the relief of being saved from the bear. But whatever it was, Robbin was hopeful it might be repeated. If there was any way in the world she could convince herself she could marry Ted Ballard, she would do it.

"You really are just too good to me, Ted," she told him sincerely.

Ted kissed her on the nose, the way he often kissed Tina, then laughed as he moved quickly away. "I know it. But you know what I always say. Life isn't fair, but—"

"—it's fun!" all the children finished in unison. Then, overcome by their own brilliance, they laughed hilariously while Ted served the cupcakes he'd secretly packed for dessert.

"Wait till you see what we've got planned for the evening's entertainment," Ruth told her. "It would even put The Old Mansion's orchestra to shame."

"Well, I don't know about that," Robbin replied without thinking. "That orchestra is really incredible. I've never heard—"

"*You've* heard The Old Mansion's orchestra?" Ruth's eyes bulged with glee as she turned to Ted and asked, "You guys went to The Old Mansion without us?"

When he didn't speak, she glanced at her mother, then at Ted again. "I, uh, well, like I said, we're going to do a great show tonight," Ruth mumbled uncertainly, confusion and distress evident on her young face. "Aren't we, Uncle Ted?"

"Right." Ted's answer was swift and artificially cheerful, as though Robbin's thoughtless blunder had cost him no pain. "Ruthie wrote the script, more or less, and everybody's got an outstanding part. Right, gang?"

The other kids shouted out in agreement, but Ruth was silent. *She knows,* Robbin realized sadly. *She doesn't have all the pieces of the puzzle yet, but she knows that something's terribly wrong between her mother and her beloved Uncle Ted.*

Suddenly Robbin wished she'd never heard of The Old Mansion, never seen Kent Hawthorne's face. She knew it was irrational; she and Ted would have reached this impasse sooner or later, anyway. But the transition could have been more gentle, and they both might have made the adjustment with less pain.

But do we have to make a change? she asked herself as Ted playfully led the children through the rest of the evening's festivities. *If I can find a new way to reach out for Ted, is it possible that I won't have to give him up after all?*

She'd promised him, of course, to play no games or make false promises. But surely searching her own heart for new answers didn't fall into that category, especially if that heart was giving her reason to believe that what she felt for him might be what he longed for after all. But Robbin knew that it was vital not to give Ted any clues about her confusion until she was sure what direction she was heading in. The last thing Ted needed to hear was, "Teddy, I want you as a lover... maybe." Until she was absolutely certain, she didn't dare give him any hints at all.

As Robbin touched her pinecone corsage and gazed softly at Ted's fresh growth of beard, she had the strangest feeling that by the time they left Yosemite, she wouldn't have to worry about *pretending* to fall in love with Ted. If the strange blur of tangled feelings that threatened to overwhelm her tonight were to become habitual, it was not at all beyond the realm of possibility that their future would take care of itself.

TED HEAVED A GREAT SIGH OF RELIEF when the last silly scene of "This is Your Life, Robbin Walker" was finally over. He'd cavorted like a clown and made the children laugh; Robbin was still giggling as she readied the children for bed. He had kept his promise this weekend. This last trip would be a happy memory for all of them.

Except for me, he could have added. *But my feelings don't seem to count where Robbin is concerned.*

Ted had volunteered to do the dishes in honor of Robbin's birthday, despite the fact that he was allergic to household chores in general and cleaning up after meals in particular. His motivation tonight was twofold: he wanted to make her happy, and he wanted to get her out of his hair. If he had to spend another half an hour smiling and laughing and pretending that this trip was a lark, he would either go stark raving berserk, or blow up at her again. Ted was sure that his performance these past twenty-four hours was worthy of an Academy Award.

"Oh, Ted, you don't have to do the dishes!" Robbin chastised him, returning from his tent where she'd just tucked in the two boys. "It isn't really my birthday. Besides, you and the kids got dinner."

"Don't bite the hand that feeds you," he retorted lightly, certain that he'd used up his last corny joke. "I said I'd do them and I will. You go on to bed; it's been a long day."

Robbin perched on a big rock near the fire and leaned closer to the flames. "If you won't let me help, the least I can do is keep you company while you work. It's been a long time since we've been able to chat in peace around a campfire."

He couldn't suppress a stab of pain as he realized that after this weekend, he would no longer have quiet evenings with Robbin to sustain him. Sometimes they talked for hours; sometimes they just watched TV or read separate books on opposite ends of the couch without exchanging a single word. They'd been married in so many ways for so long that he couldn't believe that Robbin didn't feel the strength of their bonding the way he did. Whatever she felt for him—no matter how intense—fell far short of his own potent need to have her be at the core of his existence. He enjoyed her as a neighbor and he loved her as a friend, but those roles could no longer satisfy him.

School would start the morning after they got home from Yosemite, and so would their lives as two separate families. Ted planned to explain the sorry situation to his children as soon as they got home, and he expected Robbin would do the same. He'd even considered telling all of the kids together, but that would only have prolonged the myth that they were one extended family. *If we were really that close, I wouldn't have to make a break with Robbie. The only problem we'd have to solve was whether or not to move to Crescent Heights.*

He certainly hoped Lila had taken care of his bid on that exorbitant house; every time he called to firm up his plans for selling his home she gave him an evasive answer about reaching Mrs. Ruckson and tried to talk him out of moving away from Mulberry Lane. He knew he ought to discuss his plans with Robbin, but somehow he couldn't bear to do it on this trip. What was the point of making her happy just so he could break her heart?

"I always think about Ellen when we're camping," Robbin murmured from the fire. "The first time we came here she was sure she would hate it; she only agreed to give it a try because I promised to keep her company while you and Doug were off hiking."

Ted couldn't help but share a smile with Robbin; it was one of many joyful memories that they shared. "And then she wore all of us out on the trail."

Robbin laughed. "Well, you and Doug were both carrying babies on your backs; no wonder you were tired!"

Ted stuck a sponge in another dish and gazed out at the pristine night. How many years had they shared this glorious wilderness! He and Robbin had been little more than acquaintances the first time they'd camped at Yosemite; she and Ellen had been close, he and Doug closer yet. The special bonding between Ted and Robbin had been slow in coming, but now it was as solid as the granite boulder on which Robbin sat.

"I still miss her sometimes," Ted admitted. In a way he wished that Robbin hadn't brought the subject up, yet he was grateful that there was one person alive besides his mother who could so fully understand his mingled recollections of joy and grief. "Sometimes I'll meet a woman her age—the age she was when she died—and think 'Ellen looked like that.' And then there are times when I'll meet women who are twenty-eight, fifty, even sixty-five, and I'll think, 'Oh, Ellie, how beautiful you would have been.'"

For a moment Robbin was silent, battling with recollections of her own. Then she replied, "At least all of your memories are good ones, Ted. When Doug left, he took all those happy years with him."

And he left me sitting on a powder keg, Ted couldn't help but think. He never would have allowed himself to fall in love with Robbin while she was married to Doug. The rules were different then; it had all been very easy, very clear.

He finished drying the last pan by the dim light of the Coleman lantern and joined Robbin by the fire. There was only one rock big enough for a man to sit on, and she was already ensconced there. It was natural to settle down beside her as she slid to one side to give him room.

"Are you over Doug, Robbin? Have you really let him go?"

Her pause was brief but thoughtful. "Yes, I think I finally have. When I picked up the children last week, he waved from the window and I thought, 'Oh, there's the kids' father. I hope they all had a good time together.'" She smiled, pleased that she'd left the dark times behind. "Of course, at the time I had...well, another man on my mind."

Ted seethed at the slightly coquettish tone in her voice; he stiffened and angled himself farther away from her. "I'd just as soon not talk about Hawthorne on this trip, if you don't mind. You don't see me parading my dates before you in a verbal display of conquest."

"Teddy!" Robbin was incensed; she pulled him around to face her. "I was talking about *you*! I've hardly been able to think about anything else all week!"

Ted only shook his head and studied the fire. "Robbie, I thought we had an understanding. My job on this trip is to pretend I'm having a good time; your end of the deal is *not* to pretend you've changed your mind."

Beside him, he felt her body go slack. *Damn, I hate it when I hurt her!* he swore with inner vehemence. But Robbin made it so hard for him... harder than it had to be. Last night after he'd chased off the bear she'd practically thrown herself in his arms...and not just because she was in need of comfort. She'd nearly kissed him on the mouth... and would have if the kids hadn't interfered. At the time he'd been too surprised to protest, but now, in retrospect, the memory made him angry. Although her pretense of wanting him was an indication of the depth of fear she felt at losing him, it was still no compliment to his manhood. And it was clear from the wistful look on her face that she was thinking about kissing him again.

I know you too well, Robbsie, he protested in his heart. *If you truly ached for me, I'd have you in bed before you could say, 'Please, Teddy Bear.' But you're just trying to talk yourself into wanting me, and I won't have it.*

"Ted, we've all had a really wonderful time on this trip," Robbin declared unhappily. "Are you telling me that . . . it's all been a pretense on your part?"

Her face was lovely in the firelight; she'd never looked more kissable. Worse yet, he could tell that she knew it. *What I'd give for the privilege!* his heart cried out. Her eyes were big and soulful; her lips soft and parted, all but inviting him to claim them for his own. If the woman beside him had been anybody but Robbin, he would have sworn she was coming on to him.

He rose quickly and sought refuge in rearranging the fire, throwing on enough logs to last all night. It wasn't really a waste; he knew he had no chance of sleep anyway. He'd be better off enjoying the stars than rubbing his nose against the icy zipper of his bag, pretending that he could find a way to thrust Robbin from his mind long enough to doze off for the night.

"Robbin, I know you'd like to think that my entire life is tied up in you and your kids," he answered rather stiffly. "But quite frankly, I've got some other concerns right now that make it hard to have fun."

To some extent it was true; the mess at Red Rock was worrying him a lot. The more he discovered, the less sense the whole thing made. There was always the off chance that the blown valve had really been a freak occurrence, but his instincts as an investigator belied that notion. Worse yet, he thought Kent Hawthorne was just too clever to be taken in by a man like Caldwell. It was growing harder and harder to believe in his innocence.

"Are you still having trouble figuring out what happened at the refinery, Ted?" Concern rather than hurt laced her tone.

"Yes."

"You promised to explain it all to me when we had a chance."

He met her eyes tiredly. That promise had been made a lifetime ago, minutes after Robbin had met Kent Hawthorne. Now that he suspected Kent of taking kickbacks, he wasn't even sure it was safe to confide in Robbin; her loyalties might already be confused. It was easy to put Lila off when she asked for information—she knew they weren't close enough for him to divulge his secrets to her. But he'd always told Robbin everything, and she was clearly wounded by his failure to trust her with his private thoughts.

"This isn't really a good time, Robbin."

"When would be better? It's been a long time since we've had a chance to be alone, Ted. And from the way you talk, it might be a long time before we're alone again."

Truer words were never spoken, he vowed to himself. He had to put an end to this charade; he couldn't spend every night at Yosemite sitting alone with Robbin by the fire. Abruptly Ted stood up and walked back to the table; he picked up the Coleman lantern and planted it firmly by Robbin's side.

"Robbin, I'm going for a walk now—by myself. I'd like you to go to bed and read now. I don't want to share this campfire when I come back."

He said the words without anger, but Robbin looked as though he'd slapped her in the face. For an instant she didn't even try to answer; her gray eyes looked huge and haunted in the uneven light, full of moisture that had nothing to do with the smoke from the fire.

Ted squatted beside her, his gaze honest and direct, his voice ragged and low. "Robbie," he confessed as honestly as he could, "whether you mean to or not, you're putting me through hell. If you give a hoot for my feelings, please go to bed and give me a little time alone to get myself together. It's bad enough having to keep smiling when the kids are around; I can't keep up the act when I'm alone with you, too." Ever so gently, he reached out to touch her face. He knew it was a mistake, but he just couldn't keep his hands away from her anymore. He pushed a strand of dark hair out of her eyes, then let his fingers trail along the delicate bone of her jaw. "Robbsie," he breathed hoarsely, "you just can't afford to play with me tonight. I'm hanging by a thread."

Ted didn't wait for her to answer; he didn't want to take the risk of getting lost in those glistening gray eyes that stared at him with such hurt and dismay. Abruptly he stood up, grabbed a flashlight from the van and stalked quickly out of the camp.

Ted wandered alone in the moonlight for more than an hour, grappling with the wars in his heart. He tried not to think about the helpless grief in Robbin's eyes when he'd left her sitting alone on the rock; he tried not to think about how empty his world would be when they returned home on Monday and he started his Robbinless life. *I love her so damn much!* he told the stars over and over again. *The instant I get back, I'm going to call Lila and insist that she list the house. If she tries to stall me again, I'll call somebody else,* he decided once and for all. *Robbie and I won't last another month with only a fence between us.*

With the painful decision made, a hollow sense of relief buoyed Ted ever so slightly and lasted the last half mile back to camp. But the instant he laid eyes on the family campsite, that faint feeling of relief was kicked aside by fresh panic.

Robbin's tent was on fire.

CHAPTER TWELVE

ROBBIN WASN'T SURE what woke her up first: Ted's shouts, the heat of the flames, or the water pouring onto her face through a burned hole in the tent. Although she was too confused to think clearly, she knew she had to get the kids out of the tent.

"Ruthie!" she screamed. "Get the girls! Jarrod! Larry! Where are you?"

She felt dizzy with panic, too hot and too cold. Little girls, crying with fear, seemed to be springing up all over the place, but she couldn't find the boys. It was not until she'd searched every sleeping bag in the tent, hysteria mounting, that she heard Ted call out, "Robbie, get out of there! Are you hurt? Can you move?" Each question was punctuated by another bucketful of water pouring in through the canvas wall. "Answer me!"

"I can't find my boys!" she shrieked. "I can't find—"

For the second time in twenty-four hours, Ted saved Robbin from her own fear. He bolted in through the now smoldering hole and pulled Robbin into his arms. "For God's sake, Robbie! They're both in my tent. You could have been killed looking for them in here!"

The boys are sleeping with Ted! she realized in panicky hindsight. *I tucked them into bed!* She felt stupid; she felt relieved. More than that, she felt absolutely confident that as long as Ted was holding her in his arms, everything would be all right. She clung to him, weeping, while Ruth continued to douse the charred remains of canvas.

"Oh, Teddy, I feel so dumb! I wasn't sleepy, but I knew you didn't want me out there when you got back! I brought the lantern in to read by and I fell asleep. I must have knocked it over somehow and—" She broke off, her sobs forestalling talk.

Ted pulled her closer, and cradled her wet head with his big, quiet hands; he kissed her forehead as though she were a child. "Shh, Robbsie, it's okay. None of the kids are hurt. I'm here. It's okay."

I'm here. It's okay. What beautiful words, what simple words. What more was there to say?

Robbin pressed herself against him, drawing more than comfort from his touch. She was shivering now—soaking wet in the cold—and too confused by the recent chain of events to know what she wanted at the moment. The only thing she was sure of was that she didn't want Ted out of her sight until she got a grip on herself.

"Come on, Robbs. We've got to get you dry." Gently he tugged her out of the tent—through the zippered flap this time—and pushed her gently down on the rock by the campfire.

"Ruth, are there any dry clothes in there?" Ted asked her. "Check the sleeping bags, too." He glanced quickly at both of the smaller girls. Reading the lingering terror on both their faces, he abandoned Robbin for just a moment to take them in his arms.

"Daddy, I was so scared!" Tina whispered, weeping now as a delayed reaction set in. "I didn't know what was happening!"

"I know, baby. I know." He drew his daughter more tightly to him, then crouched on the ground to let Allison crawl into his arms. Too frightened to cry, Robbin's little girl hadn't yet turned to her terrified mother. Robbin suddenly realized that in a crisis, one parent was just about as good as another, and so Allison turned to Ted as easily as she would have turned to her own father.

"My clothes are dry, Uncle Ted," Ruth informed him; she'd been sleeping near the wall farthest from the fire. "And I found a bag of Tina's clothes in your tent that ought to have enough clothes for Allison, too. The trouble is Mom. She's a mess and all of her stuff was right near her head. Some of it's burnt and all of it's soaking wet."

Robbin's teeth began to chatter, from both the cold, and delayed shock. There was a brisk wind sweeping through the trees, which didn't help her icy-wet skin. Ted glanced back at her, then at the girls, obviously trying to decide who needed his help first. Quickly he made a decision. "Larry go get that old quilt I threw in the back of the van. Ruth, get your mother out of those wet clothes and wrap her up in the quilt until I can find something else for her to wear. I'm going to take care of the girls."

On his way to his tent, Ted turned back to Robbin, stopping to lay one soothing palm on her face. Robbin found herself gripping it with both hands. His fingers were warm compared to hers; his skin rough, but his touch infinitely gentle as he promised her, "I'll be back just as soon as I can."

While Robbin studied Ted's beloved face in the smoky campfire light, she felt a wash of love for him as she realized how desperately she craved that reassurance. She knew she was scared, and nothing about tonight was normal, but she also realized, albeit vaguely, that this wasn't the first time in her life that she'd turned to Ted in a crisis. The difference was that this time, even when the crisis was over, she didn't think she'd want to turn away.

"Just give me a few minutes, Robbsie, and then I'll warm up your cold feet."

Robbin nodded hopefully, then turned to the girls before they followed Ted to his tent. She took Allison's hand, then Tina's, as she promised, "I'll come tuck you in later, okay?"

Tina was still blinking back tears. "Even if we're already asleep, Aunt Robbin?"

"Of course, honey. I imagine I'll be sleeping in your tent, too." She turned uneasy eyes to Ted. "Won't I?"

"Of course," he assured her. "If we line you up like sardines, we can fit six in there." He didn't say where he expected to sleep, but Robbin knew that Ted's own needs would come pretty far down on his list of concerns tonight.

He and the little girls disappeared into his tent. While Larry and Ruth marched over to the van, Jarrod, eyes big, came to sit beside his mother. "Uncle Ted said my job was to keep you company till Ruthie gets back," he informed her. "Are you really okay, Mommy?"

Robbin took his hand—she was too wet to dare hug him—and squeezed it hard. "Yes, honey. I just kind of went crazy there for a minute because I couldn't find you and Larry. I was too scared and sleepy to remember where you were...only that I loved you."

For once Jarrod didn't bother with "Oh, Mom"; instead, he leaned up to kiss her cheek. "I wasn't too scared, Mom. By the time I woke up, Uncle Ted was already throwing water on the fire, and I knew that as long as Uncle Ted was taking care of you, everything would be okay."

Robbin swallowed hard, eyes full of love for her youngest child. "So did I, Jarrod. So did I."

HALF AN HOUR LATER, all five children were bedded down in Ted's tent, doubling up in dry sleeping bags. Ted had put a hot rock in his bag since Robbin would be sleeping in it. He'd assured her that he wasn't likely to sleep at all tonight, but if he did, he'd just stretch out in the van. He'd dug up several ratty sweatshirts and a pair of his underwear for Robbin—a skimpy blue model that was a far cry from the baggy white things she used to sort when she'd been in charge of his laundry—but his jeans were just too small. So Robbin kept the quilt wrapped around her legs as she stretched them toward the fire. Ted had also loaned her a pair of socks—with Ballard-sized holes in both heels and one toe—and now was busy rubbing her freezing feet in an effort to get her blood circulating again.

"Are you sure the girls are okay now, Teddy?" she asked, feeling guilty that she'd been so little help in the calamity.

"Yes. I wouldn't have left them otherwise. Ruthie's just been a tower of strength this weekend. Can you believe how much she's grown up this summer?"

Robbin didn't answer, partly because it was, to some extent, a rhetorical question. But more than that, she was finding it hard to concentrate on mundane conversation at the moment. Not because of the cold; not because of the fire. But because the foot rub Ted was giving her was demanding her full attention.

His fingers were square and warm and very, very thorough; there was not a single nook and cranny of toe and ball and heel that they failed to stimulate. The ratty socks—with those holes that had provided Robbin with countless opportunities for ribbing Ted—now served as an instrument of totally unexpected delight as Ted's skin slid over hers. In and out, over and around, promising, delivering....

The sensual awareness came slowly, and at first Robbin tried to pretend it did not exist. In the aftermath of her panic, her major concerns were her children, her own safety, and her demolished tent. The last thing on her mind right now was talking herself into feeling sexual hunger for Ted. Yet as his warm hands caressed her feet—ever so intimately—her increasingly intense arousal was becoming an undeniable fact.

More than a year had passed since the last time Robbin had made love with Doug, and it hadn't been particularly rewarding. But she was a mature woman with plenty enough years of a loving marriage behind her to remember the prelude to passion, and she realized now, with a curious mixture of fear and wonder, that Ted had just taken her through the first few measures of sensual delight.

The irony of the moment was that Ted didn't look the least bit aroused himself. He was concentrating on her feet as an act of healing, worry for her and the children still evident in the taut lines of his face. She knew that he was thinking about all the details he would now have to attend to: scrounging up more clothes, salvaging the sleeping bags for another night...and possibly saving her tent.

As the crickets called from the distant creek and a lone coyote howled at the moon, Robbin lost interest in troubling thoughts. She was wrapped in a blanket of lazy, incipient hunger, and she wanted nothing more than to open her quilt and beckon for her beloved Teddy Bear to come inside.

Abruptly, Ted stopped. "Is that better?" he asked.

"What?"

"Are your feet warmer now? I'm sorry I don't have any socks without holes, but—" he shrugged apologetically "—you know what my clothes are like."

Robbin grinned, still deliciously warmed by his touch. "I thought I did," she replied with the lilt of invitation in her voice. "But you seem to have changed your style in underpinnings since I last did your laundry."

Instantly Ted's face was consumed with that embarrassed grin she knew so well. He even seemed tongue-tied; he had no reply for her.

Following her feminine instincts, Robbin leaned toward him and let the quilt fall open below her knees. "I think you'd look good in blue," she suggested wickedly, delighting in the sudden flush of his cheeks. Making only a vague effort to keep the quilt wrapped around her waist and her borrowed blue underwear, Robbin reached out to touch Ted's face, splaying her fingers over his sooty, unshaven face.

The stubble was coarse and virile, but his skin was soft and warm. Robbin let her fingertips trail over his bushy mustache—how she loved the feel of it!—then float lower over his slightly parted lips.

She didn't dare meet his eyes; it was a risk she couldn't take. If his expression said anything but "Yes, Robbsie, yes!" she wouldn't have the courage to kiss him. And yet Robbin was suddenly certain—as certain of anything as she'd ever been in her life—that she wanted to kiss Ted Ballard; she wanted to be held in his arms.

It had nothing to do with comfort, nothing to do with fear. Oh, her love for him was too bound up in their years together to say it had nothing to do with friendship, but Robbin knew that this newborn desire was not the result of her vow to find a way of keeping Ted near her. It was a simple evolution from one kind of love to another, a striving for the highest peak of the mountaintop after a long, satisfying hike up the slope.

Slipping her palm around his jaw to gently tug him nearer, Robbin leaned forward to find his warm, full lips. She ached to feel his mouth on hers; she longed to tingle from the feel of his mustache. She wanted his hands to keep rubbing her feet, then her legs, then—

"Goddammit, Robbin!" Ted burst out in sudden fury, all but leaping to his feet. "You promised me you wouldn't do this! I've kept my end of this lousy bargain one hundred percent, and here you are playing sophomoric games that—"

"Teddy, that's not fair! I was only trying—"

"I *know* what you were trying to do, Robbin! You're not the only woman I spend time with, you know." His anger lashed at her, shredding her brief moment of feminine confidence. "I won't be patronized by you, Robbin, and I won't be used. You're going to have to find yourself another teddy bear to hold onto when you're scared of the dark!"

"Ted, if you would just listen to me—"

"Damn it, Robbin, I am tired of listening! I am tired of turning down whatever crumbs of artificial passion you deign to throw my way. And I'm *damn* tired of pretending to be such a swell guy . . . a patsy who'll put up with just about anything from you!"

Robbin slumped on the rock. It was hard to say "I want to be your lover as well as your friend" to a man who was yelling at you, especially when your conviction of that fact had been so sudden and so surprising. Besides, Robbin wasn't used to taking the lead in such things. And she didn't really trust her instincts at the moment; the fire had left her badly shaken, and she wasn't at all sure that her arousal had been more than a knee-jerk reaction to the incident, which might fade away by morning. *With five kids a stone's throw away, the timing couldn't be much worse, anyway,* she thought dejectedly.

For the first time, Robbin understood why Ted hadn't wooed her in the traditional fashion, why he'd asked her to marry him without any prior hint of sensual overtures. Making love with someone for the first time was always a delicate process, but the transition from dear fraternal friend to erotic lover was a leap of incredible proportions. Robbin had the eerie feeling that it would have been easier for her to seduce a total stranger than this man she loved so dearly. With Ted, so much more was involved than sexual hunger. The emotional risk was staggering.

Suddenly Ted crouched down before Robbin, his eyes full of anger and fresh pain. "You know, Robbie, last week when you turned me down, I took comfort from the fact that you still had enough respect for me—for what we've meant to each other—to tell me the truth, even if it hurt. Well, let me tell you, lady, no honest statement from your lips will ever hurt me more than these phony 'come hither' looks you've been throwing my way ever since we started out on this trip. I won't have it; do you understand? I deserve better, Robbie. You know I do."

Robbin didn't know how to answer that. Her feelings were in such turmoil now that it was impossible to say for sure what she wanted. But Ted, at least, was sure. He wanted to get on with his life . . . apparently without her. A week ago, she could have chanced an honest revelation of her urgent but conflicting feelings. But under the circumstances, such a convoluted confession would only drive him further away, and that was a chance that Robbin just couldn't bear to take. She was beginning to realize that this weekend had already done her relationship with Ted a great deal of harm.

"Here's the way we're going to play it, Robbin," he ordered grimly. "You are going to get up and keep that damn quilt wrapped around you until you're in that tent. Then you are going to crawl into my sleeping bag and stay there until morning even if the whole damned high Sierra burns down! You are not going to say or do one single thing that a sane man could misinterpret, and you are not even going to say good-night." His glare was all but venomous. "Is that clear?"

It was a new side of Ted that Robbin had never seen before this week—a depth of rage that only her insensitivity seemed to trigger. It should have made her angry, but she knew she deserved his wrath. He was a strong man, and she'd treated him like a child. A week ago, she hadn't thought him mature enough to be a match for herself. Yet now, in the dim firelight, she had the definite feeling that her teddy bear had somehow outgrown her. He'd even outgrown the nickname.

Robbin got up slowly, wrapping the quilt tightly around her body. She could feel tiny rocks through the holes in Ted's socks, but she didn't ask for shoes to walk the few short yards to the tent. When she got there, she didn't turn around—she couldn't bear to look at his eyes again—but she did say softly, "Thank you for putting out the fire, Ted. Thanks for everything."

There was a long silence. At last, in spite of his orders, Robbin turned around to face him. *I love you, Teddy,* she longed to confess. But his dark eyes held such pain that she couldn't speak. At the moment she was still powerfully aroused, but she wasn't at all sure that she would be in the morning. So she just stared at him helplessly until he whispered, "Good night, Robbin. Try to get a good night's sleep." And then, on a jagged note of defeat, he added, "I'm going to start packing up the van. We're pulling out at dawn."

THE RIDE HOME SEEMED TWICE AS LONG as the happy trip down had. Both breakfast and lunch were eaten at drive-in stops, and Ted insisted on driving himself every mile of the way. By late afternoon everybody was tired, and Jarrod and the girls fell asleep. Larry, sitting right behind Robbin, nibbled on crackers and told his father silly jokes.

"Would you like me to drive for a while, Ted?" Robbin finally asked. "You don't look like you got much sleep last night."

Actually, he looked terrible. The scraggly growth of new beard had made him look quite sexy the night before; now it gave him a bleak, haunted look. His eyes held no more anger or even pain. They were utterly blank and devoid of feeling. On the rare occasions when he looked at Robbin, it was as though he didn't know that she was there.

Robbin, on the other hand, was keenly aware of Ted's presence. For hours in the night she had stared into the dark, listening to the gentle breathing of her five children in the silence as she rubbed her feet against the newspaper-wrapped rock until it was icy cold. Ted's sleeping bag had smelled of wood smoke and Ted. Robbin had tried to imagine what it would have been like to share the bag with Ted, but it was a fantasy that had come true only in her fleeting dreams, which had only heightened the intensity of her arousal.

In the morning, Robbin's surge of sexual hunger had disappeared, but the intense ache for peace with Ted had not. Now—after miles and miles of stony silence and tepid courtesy—Robbin was no longer sure what she wanted from Ted. She missed Teddy Bear Ballard; she longed to laugh and wrestle with her friend. But how she felt about this chilly stranger who sat beside her was anybody's guess. Robbin knew she had to get away from him for a few days and let the dust settle before she could honestly sort out her confusing emotions.

"You're the one who had a rough night, Robbin," Ted observed shrewdly. "Just relax. Take a nap if you like. I don't need any help."

Taking the hint that he wanted to be left alone, Robbin tried to engage Larry in conversation. "Jarrod says you've got Mrs. Paulson this year, honey."

"Yeah. I'm going to be in room 17."

Robbin twisted in her seat to see him better. "Allison had her in second grade. She's a strict teacher, but very good."

Larry wrinkled his nose. "What does 'strict' mean?"

She laughed. "It means you can't sneak frogs into your desk or tickle the girl sitting next to you."

"Ugh! I wouldn't *touch* a girl!" he vowed, clearly appalled at the notion. Then, more brightly, he asked, "Will she let us play kickball?"

"I suspect so. Why don't you ask her when I take you in Tuesday morning?"

The surprise on Larry's face was the only warning Robbin had that her very last tie with Ted's family was about to be cut. "You're taking us in on the first day of school? I thought Daddy was going to do it this year."

"Oh, your daddy's too busy, Larry," Robbin answered without thinking. "I always—"

"Not any more." Ted's voice was quiet, tired, but firm.

Slowly Robbin turned to face him; his eyes were still on the road. "You're taking time off work when you know I'm going to be at the school anyway? You've never done that before."

"I've made different arrangements this year, Robbin," he informed her factually. "Sarah's taking all of her classes in the morning so she can be at my house every day by the time Larry and Tina come home from school," he replied tersely. "I'll take the kids to my mother's if I get stuck with an evening appointment."

For several seconds Robbin stared at him speechlessly. *You can't mean this, Teddy. You can't mean you don't want me to help you out at all!*

Into the silence Larry babbled cheerfully, "Daddy says it'll really be great for all of us this way, Aunt Robbin. We can still go play with Allison and Jarrod when we want to, but you won't have to worry about us anymore now that you're working full-time." He grinned cheerfully. "Gee, Aunt Robbin, with Sarah coming every day and Grandma helping out at night, we won't need you at all."

CHAPTER THIRTEEN

"WELL?" Ted asked as jovially as he could. "What did you find out while I was gone, Hawthorne?"

Kent shrugged uncomfortably as he perched on a swivel chair in the office he called home. "Not much. But Gregory is mighty determined to keep me happy. He even offered to share notes with me. I have a feeling that if I'd accepted, he would have paid me well."

Ted wasn't sure how to respond to that. There was a good chance that Kent just didn't trust Gregory any more than he did, but there was also a chance that he was still trying to wave his virtue in Ted's face as a smoke screen.

"Gregory's pretty upset about his men," Ted pointed out. "I hear one of them is still in pretty bad shape." Unfortunately, Gregory had been called out of town on some family emergency over the weekend, so Ted hadn't gotten a chance to touch base with him again before this meeting with Kent. He was not prepared for Kent's reply.

"If you're talking about Bill Rayburn, he no longer needs your sympathy, Ted. He died last night."

Ted didn't know the man, but he was still shocked by the news. He couldn't shake the feeling that this was in one way or another his fault; somehow, he should have prevented the explosion.

Kent tugged on his tie as though it had suddenly tightened up on him. Ted saw his own guilt reflected on Kent's face.

"We've got to find out what happened, Kent," Ted declared with renewed determination. "Even if it was just an accident—"

"What makes you think it wasn't an accident?" Kent asked a bit shrilly.

Ted's eyes met Kent's, but Kent quickly looked away.

"I don't like coincidences, Hawthorne," Ted said bluntly. "I don't like the fact that the equipment was installed while Gregory was gone, and I don't like the fact that the contractor who did the work has flown the coop without giving us a list of men who could tell us what really happened out there."

"What do you think happened out there?" Ken asked uneasily.

Ted was very direct. "I think Caldwell and the contractor sold off the equipment and pocketed the profits. The contractor's crew was either told to refurbish the valves and weren't informed that a con was going on, or else they were paid a token sum to keep quiet. Either way, if we could interrogate some of them, we'd be bound to turn up something."

Kent licked his lips and tugged on one ear. "I don't think you have any proof that that's what went down, Ted. It's more likely that somebody fouled up putting in a valve—or else the materials weren't up to code in the first place." The words made sense, but Kent's deep voice quaked unconvincingly.

"You checked the new valves, Kent. You did hydrochloric acid tests and cleared that whole unit in July. How could you miss faulty equipment or lousy installation?"

When Kent began to sweat, Ted felt ill with suspicion.

"I know how to do my job, Ballard! I know when equipment is inadequate!" Despite the proud words, it was obvious that Kent's confidence was deteriorating.

"Damn it, Kent, I know you do!" Ted swore, hating the implications of his investigation. "So how could Caldwell pull a fast one on you? Can you answer me that?"

Kent didn't meet his eyes; he tugged on his tie again as though he were strangling. "You have no proof that Caldwell did anything wrong," he finally rasped out. He began to cough as he insisted, "What happened at Red Rock was pure bad luck. It was just an accident."

"Tell that to Bill Rayburn," Ted replied grimly, the memory of the Red Rock worker's death dissolving any pity he might have felt for whoever was responsible. All of his instincts told him that Kent was somehow involved in the mess, but he still couldn't prove it. "You know, Hawthorne," he added as a sober thought hit him, "now that Bill Rayburn is dead, if Caldwell or anybody else messed with those valves, he could be tried for second-degree murder." Kent's face grew pale as Ted concluded, "He could even do hard time in prison. Not a pretty thought."

"MOM, when are you going to tell me about your fight with Uncle Ted?"

Ruthie, already in her nightie, lay stretched out in the armchair in the corner of her mother's bedroom with her head on one armrest and her feet dangling over the other. Captain lay curled up on her chest as though he lived on Robbin's side of the fence that separated her property from Ted's. Apparently nobody had told the Siamese cat that Ted had nailed the gate shut.

Ruth had already told her mother everything about her first day in the eighth grade—the highlight of which had come when a boy she liked had let her cover third base while he was pitching—and she'd listened patiently while her sister and brother had shared the details of their new classes as well. But Robbin had sensed that her eldest girl was merely biding her time until the little ones were in bed. She had cornered Robbin the minute Jarrod's door was closed. Now she prodded, "It must be pretty bad for him to miss work to take Tina and Larry to school."

Ted had pulled his new van into the school parking lot just as Robbin had been trying to leave that morning. Though her battery had struggled repeatedly to come to life, he hadn't offered to help her. By sheer luck she'd finally gotten the Buick started, but that didn't change the way she felt about the startling difference in Ted's attitude. It wasn't something she felt like explaining to Ruth.

But Ruthie had been frighteningly quiet since the camping trip, her eyes sadly trailing her mother around the Ballardless house since Sunday. Ted and his two kids had loaded up the van and taken off again just hours after they'd all returned from Yosemite, and Robbin hadn't spoken to him since. Three days had now passed since she'd thanked him for the trip—three days of turmoil and confusion that had left her weak and anxious but no closer to an answer.

What troubled Robbin the most was that both times she'd felt a rush of desire for Ted, she'd been terribly afraid, relieved, and grateful. She *wanted* to fall in love with him, but she was afraid that circumstances had made her feel things that had nothing to do with the sort of passion that Ted might engender within her on a day-to-day basis. In order to see how she would react to his touch under other conditions, Robbin wanted to see him again—alone—when her life was calm. Considering how hard he was working at avoiding her right now, that wasn't going to be easy. She couldn't very well leave a note on his refrigerator that said, "Ted, drop by and try to make love to me some time; I want to see if you really do turn me on." For the first time in her life, Robbin couldn't afford to be totally honest with Ted. That in itself was troubling.

Robbin still hadn't found the courage to tell her children the way things were going to be on Mulberry Lane from now on. It wasn't just cowardice on her part; she still had hope that her tangled feelings for Ted would sort themselves out in the near future.

"We didn't exactly have a fight, Ruthie," she managed to tell her daughter. Avoiding Ruth's eyes, Robbin tugged a nightgown out of her closet and started to get dressed for bed. "You know Ted never gets mad." It wasn't strictly true, but he rarely got mad in front of the children, and he certainly wasn't mad at Ruth.

"Come on, Mom! I'm not a little kid anymore," Ruth protested. "You've acted funny every time we mentioned the Ballards since you picked us up at Dad's. Uncle Ted was so edgy all weekend that I thought he was going to jump out of his skin. And the other kids may buy his story that you guys decided to go home because of the fire, but I heard him swearing at you that night before you came to bed, and I've *never* heard Uncle Ted swear before. You guys were so loud it woke me up."

Robbin was alarmed by her daughter's revelation. She couldn't remember exactly what she and Ted had said to each other by the fire on that last night in camp, but she was certain that most of it should not have been said in front of Ruth. But Robbin had dodged Ruthie as long as she could, and some kind of explanation was now in order.

Defeated, Robbin sat on the bed and faced her eldest girl. This wasn't going to be easy, and she didn't know how to begin. "Ruthie, Ted and I aren't really mad at each other, but we do have . . . well, a problem."

"A problem?"

Robbin sighed. How did she explain to a thirteen-year-old what she didn't really understand herself? "Do you remember when you were in fifth grade and Laura Wilson wanted to be your best friend?"

Ruth nodded.

"You liked her a lot and you didn't want to hurt her feelings, but she wanted to spend all her time with you. And you had . . . well, other friends who were more important to you."

Ruth looked confused. She sat up more intently and tugged on a lock of dark hair. "Well, Kim Pritchard has always been my best friend, just like Larry is Jarrod's and Tina is Allison's and yours is Uncle Ted."

Robbin sighed deeply. "Honey, maybe that was a poor example. What I'm trying to say is Ted and I aren't . . . well, we aren't going to be best friends anymore. We're going to spend a lot more time with other people."

A dark, frightened look stole over Ruth's face. "Why? Who could you possibly want to be with more than Uncle Ted?"

"Nobody. I want to be with Uncle Ted more than anybody else."

Ruthie blanched. "You mean Uncle Ted doesn't want to be with us? Oh, Mom, what did you do to him? Or is it my fault? Should I have called him over the summer like I called you? I—"

"No, honey, it's not your fault," Robbin was quick to reassure her. Ruth had suffered from far too much imagined guilt when her father had moved out; it was grossly unfair for her to feel such pain again. "I'm not even sure that it's my fault. The simple truth—" it was anything but simple, yet Ruth knew she had to start somewhere "—is that Ted thinks he wants to marry me."

"Oh, Mommy!" Ruth leapt out of the chair and threw herself in her mother's arms. "That's terrific! How soon can we—"

Robbin shook her head and disentangled herself from her eldest girl. She felt tearful and more than a little sick inside. "Honey, I told him no."

Ruth plopped down onto the bed and stared at her, openmouthed. "I don't believe it! Why would you do a dumb thing like that?"

At the moment, Robbin didn't have a very good answer for that question. "Ruthie, marriage is . . . well, it's a different thing for grown-ups than it is for kids. Ted is like an uncle to you; it's an easy relationship to have. You can have lots of uncles—"

"Well, I *do* have lots of uncles, and they're all just swell, Mom. But Uncle Ted is... well, he's special. At first I always went to him when Daddy wasn't home, and now I... well, as long as I find Uncle Ted I don't even need to find Daddy. He's my family, Mommy, as much as Tina and Larry are. We've always lived together! I think it's the most natural thing in the world for you and Uncle Ted to get married."

Robbin struggled for words. "Oh, Ruthie, in some ways it is. But in other ways—" she broke off, frustrated. Ruth had grown up a lot this summer, but she was still a child. There were some things Robbin couldn't share with her for another five or ten years, and even then . . . "It's hard to explain, honey."

"Don't you *dare* tell me I'll understand when I'm older, Mom. I hate that."

Robbin bit her lip and gave her daughter a quick hug. "Okay, honey, I won't say it. To tell you the truth, I'm not even sure it's true. As old as I am, I don't understand what I'm feeling at all. All I know is that I miss your Uncle Ted something awful."

"Oh, Mommy!" Ruth's exasperation almost overwhelmed her hurt. "I don't know what's wrong with you, but one thing I'm sure of: if you don't marry Uncle Ted, you're just plain crazy! I'm going to tell him that myself."

Robbin shook her head. "No, you're not. The last thing Ted and I need right now is a bunch of children messing in our affairs. He's asked for the four of us to go our way, and he wants to go his. Until I can figure out if the way I feel about him has anything to do with marriage, that's the way it's got to be."

A terrible darkness had settled on Ruthie's face. When they'd begun the conversation, she'd been prodding for information without any realization of the depth of the trouble between her mother and her Uncle Ted. But now, for the first time in her life, her mother was telling her to keep a distance from the family next door.

"What do you mean, 'he wants to go his own way'?" Ruthie whispered, unable to still the note of panic in her voice. "We practically live together! That's why he built that gate in the fence!"

Robbin stood up briskly and pulled down the covers of the bed. She couldn't bear to face her precious child as she revealed, "Ruthie, honey . . . Ted has nailed the gate shut. From now on, there's just one endless fence."

"GOT A SPARE SANDWICH for a passing stranger?" Ted asked his mother as he tapped on the door once, then poked his head into the house. It was Wednesday afternoon, the first time he'd talked to her since the aborted trip to Yosemite. "I've got a whole hour for lunch today."

"Well, that's the best news I've heard in a month of Sundays!" Martha Ballard greeted her only boy with a hearty hug. "Though I do wish you'd drop by more often—and I wish you'd bring good news."

"Good news? What makes you think I don't have some?"

Martha shook her head. "Because you look like death warmed over, Teddy, in spite of that fancy new suit. Any fool could see it, and I'm not just any old fool; I'm your mother." She clucked sympathetically, then hoisted her generous form toward the kitchen to start fixing his lunch. "I didn't think you could look much worse than you did the day after Robbin turned you down, son, but I do declare, the crows are going to start pulling straw out of your head if you don't get some meat on your bones and some sunshine back in your face."

Ted pulled out a chair at the kitchen table and turned it around, straddling it so he could lean forward onto the back of it and rest his head on his hands. He knew he looked mournful, but that was how he felt. After so many days of determined cheer and levity with his kids, he sorely needed to let his hair down.

"I'll skip the meat, thank you kindly, but I wouldn't mind some sun. In fact, I might even be willing to take some advice from you next time around."

Ted hadn't told his mother much about the terrible night when Operation Cinderella had blown up in his face. He'd just picked up the children, feeling black as the ace of spades, and told her tersely that she'd been right all along. His continually bleak mood ever since had made it clear that Robbin had dealt him a blow from which he was still staggering.

"You didn't ask my advice about the camping trip," Martha reminded him. "I suppose it was as bad as I could have warned you it would be."

Ted sighed. "Nope. Worse. You were probably just worried about my *feelings*. You forgot to worry about the bear, the fire, and the length Robbin was willing to go to in order to keep me around." Mercifully, his mother didn't press him for an explanation; he'd already said too much. But it galled him unspeakably that Robbin would pretend to issue a sexual invitation to him after she'd made it so clear that her feelings for him, though strong, were anything but romantic. How hard he'd tried during all these awkward months never to cross the lines of their platonic friendship...never to let Robbin know he ached for her until he'd asked her to marry him outright. She'd turned him down honestly; he'd never begrudged her that. But now she was playing all sorts of games, trying to string him along with false hope, convinced that he'd get over his "infatuation" in time and everything could return to normal. She still wanted to have her cake and eat it, too. She thought she could keep him on a short leash if she tossed him enough doggie bones. She couldn't have been further from the truth.

"Mom," he declared without preamble, "I've decided to sell the house."

Martha didn't respond at once. She finished cutting a ham and cheese sandwich in half, then set it on his plate with a carrot curl. It was just the sort of touch Robbin would have added; he could have cared less about the gourmet flourish but he appreciated the evidence of love in the extra attention.

"Thanks, Mom," he told her with a quick kiss on her cheek. "Just what the doctor ordered." He ate the carrot first just to prove that he'd noticed it.

Martha smiled as he started chewing, then poured him some cola and sat down. "You're sure there's no way you can stay? The children love it there."

"I've never heard of children who didn't try to keep their folks together during a divorce, and that's what this is, for all intents and purposes. Robbin and I have irreconcilable differences. I want her to be my wife, and she wants to be my friend."

"I wouldn't think those terms were mutually exclusive."

"Neither would I, but if we keep up the way we're going we won't even be civil to each other anymore. I'm like a raging bull around Robbin; I've yelled at her more in the past week than I have in the whole thirteen years we've been neighbors. I feel awful about it, but every time I apologize, things get . . . sticky. It was bad enough when I was afraid she'd lost her respect for me, but the way things are going, pretty soon I'm going to lose my respect for *her*. And that scares me, Mom. That really does. I'd rather lose Robbin altogether than watch her lose herself because of me."

He knew he wasn't explaining it very well, but his fear was real and justified. Robbin was halfway to convincing herself that if she could just find a way to sleep with Ted—to "endure" his body close to hers—that she could somehow hold on to what they had. Part of him was flattered that she loved him that much, but another part was far too proud to accept her under those circumstances. Every time she gave him an opening, he pulled back a little further. He wasn't being chauvinistic; he would have jumped at her invitation if he'd believed she was sincere. But Ted had never been a bed-hopper at any time in his life. He'd been utterly loyal to Ellen and virtually celibate since her death. There were times when he thought he would explode if he couldn't make love to Robbin Walker; but just as he knew that no other woman could begin to slake that thirst, neither could a half-hearted bedding of Robbin meet his potent needs, either. If she wanted him any less than he wanted her, it would tarnish not only their future, but eat away at his precious memories of the past. He refused to let that happen. His memories of Ellen had sustained him through many dark years because they were unblemished. From this point on he'd have nothing left of Robbin but the same kind of nostalgic dreams; he would never give them up to satisfy the needs of his body.

"Have you thought about where you'll move?"

"Probably to Morgantown, Mom. Closer to work, closer to you—"

"—and farther away from Robbin," Martha finished for him. "I'm glad to be included in your list of reasons, but I know where I rate." She smiled to ease any imagined sting of her words.

Ted knew he'd put his mother in a bad position by coming to see her today; there wasn't really anything she could say to cheer him up. He loved her dearly, but there were only so many holes in one's life a mother could fill. His need for Robbin was as hard to ignore as a front door torn off its hinges in a rainstorm.

"The worst thing is the children. I think hers are taking it worse than mine."

"Why's that? Because they've already gone through this before?"

"Partly. But I've got a better set of answers to give Larry and Tina. I told them the truth: I love Robbin, I asked her to marry me, she said no, and it just hurts too damn much to live next door anymore. I promised them that they could still see the Walkers, just like Jarrod and the girls still see their dad. They know that Robbie will always be glad to have them visit."

He took a bite of his sandwich, then washed it down with the cola. "But Robbin's stuck with a whole lot of wishy-washy answers. She loves me, but not that way; yes, you'll see the Ballard kids, but only when Ted wants them to play with you. They know I've put their mother on ice, and they're not sure whether or not they can still count on me. While I was jogging this morning I passed Ruthie on the way to school and tried to say hello." His voice dropped a notch or two. "She burst into tears and ran away. Can't say it made my whole day."

Martha rustled up an old cookie tin and slipped two homemade chocolate chip rounds on his plate. Gently she turned the conversation to more productive channels. "What have you found out about the refinery?"

"Whew. Now that's a hard question."

"I've got all day."

"Well, I don't. I've got two meetings back-to-back this afternoon and another one this evening, plus a report to write before noon tomorrow."

Martha sighed; she always thought he worked too hard. "Okay, tell me in a nutshell."

He gave her a brief report, starting and ending with his suspicion of Kent and the difficulty of proving that the valves had only been refurbished. As long as they tested out safely, there wasn't a great deal he could do. He needed hard evidence. If he could find any of the men who had worked on the project, one of them might be willing to tell him the truth.

When Ted finished his story, Martha touched his hand lightly, then pointed to the untouched cookies. "Is that really your biggest problem, Ted? Do you really lack the facts you need to clear this up, or just the concentration?"

He chomped on a cookie and studied her uncertainly. "What's your point?"

"My point," she said gently, "is that you like feeling in control of your life. You're making some pretty big decisions about Robbin—maybe unnecessary decisions that are going to hurt a lot of people—just to protect yourself from what might be some short-term pain. At the same time you're so upset about Robbin that you're having trouble concentrating on your work. My advice—which I'm sure you'll eventually get around to asking for—is to put selling the house on hold for a while and concentrate on clearing up the mess at Red Rock. You won't feel right about leaving Robbin on Mulberry Lane if there's some chance she's in danger, and I know you'll feel a lot stronger once you tie everything up at work. As much as you and Robbin mean to each other, it seems to me that if you'd give this some more time, the two of you might be able to work out some new parameters to your relationship that you can both live with. That's a lot less likely to happen if you move to Morgantown. It might not be as good as it was before, but it surely would hurt less than losing each other altogether."

Ted smiled, but it was an effort. "Thank you, Dr. Ballard. This has been a most productive hour on your couch."

Martha patted his cheek—a doting maternal need she only indulged when they were alone—then squeezed his hand. "The time will come for you, Ted. At least you're finally over our dear Ellen. I know you had your heart set on Robbie, but maybe there's some other fine girl out there who'd be proud to be your wife."

Ted held her hand for a minute, then stood up to take his leave. "Actually, I think there are several. I believe I'll set up a date with one for Friday night. I had a pretty good time with Angela the last time we went out, all things considered." He didn't mention that he'd realized halfway through the evening that she'd caught his eye mainly because she had long black hair like Robbin's.

"That's a great idea, Ted. One I might even have suggested myself."

He rolled his eyes in patient exasperation, then thanked her again for the food and the company. He was halfway out the door when the phone rang.

"If that's for me, tell them I'm on my way. Fool that I am, I told my office where I was going for lunch."

Ted kissed his mother on the cheek, tightened his tie and moved briskly down the walk. He'd just climbed into the van when his mother came barreling out of the house, tears mottling her round, frightened face.

"Teddy, it's Red Rock School! There's been an accident and they need you at the hospital!"

"My God!" he breathed in panic. *I'm too late. All five of our children attend that school!* "The refinery blew up? How bad is it?"

Martha shook her head, crying so hard that her words were slurred. "It's not the refinery, Ted! It's Ruthie! She's been—" the words spilled out in one great sob "—she's been hit by a car!"

CHAPTER FOURTEEN

ROBBIN SMILED AT KENT over the butcher-block mini-table and licked up the catsup dripping off of her hamburger. He grinned at her, then pulled loose his sober black tie.

"I thought this might be a good change of pace," he told her easily. "Sort of a chance to start over."

"Well, it's no match for The Old Mansion, that's for sure, but I feel a little more at home here."

He laughed. "When I was young, eating out at a place like this was a big thing. We never had two nickels to rub together."

Thinking of the extravagant tip he'd dropped so nonchalantly two weeks before, Robbin said, "Well, it looks as though you've come a long way." It occurred to her somewhat distantly that Kent must make a lot more money than Ted did. Funny that two men who did such similar work would be in such different income brackets. A Dodge van, even a new one, couldn't compare with the cost of a Mercedes. And although Ted wore clothes that matched these days, they were still department store specials; Kent's looked custom-made.

"Where did you grow up, Kent?"

"Indiana. Little farm town near the Illinois state line. My dad owned a gas station."

Robbin wasn't sure that she wanted to keep him talking. In the past few minutes she'd discovered that his deep voice, once so intriguing, could be grating on the nerves. She didn't recall his voice vibrating quite so heavily when they'd gone out to dinner. Today something about his tone injected Robbin with uneasiness instead of inspiration. Still, she asked dutifully, "How did you get interested in fire protection?"

Kent shrugged. "I think I just liked the uniforms. Originally I wanted to be a cop, but I never liked the idea that I might have to kill somebody in the line of duty. I didn't think I could live with that." His tone grew softer, despite its manly depth. "So I became a fireman instead."

"Well, now you're saving people's lives. That must be very rewarding."

Kent didn't look as though he felt it were rewarding. A hint of despair colored his handsome face. "To tell you the truth, Robbin, nothing's been too rewarding since my divorce. I'd like to be noble and tell you it was my fault and I've reformed, but I honestly don't know whose fault it was, and I don't really think I've changed—except that I'm lonelier than I used to be," he admitted with a cautious smile.

Robbin understood his feelings only too well. Although it was a depressing subject of conversation, she was glad Kent had revealed a little bit of himself. She felt a need to get to know the real Kent Hawthorne, not just for his own sake—he still wanted to make up for his boorish performance on their first date—but also because she was still unhappy with her own early attitude toward him. In some strange way, her reactions to this man were still tangled up with the way she felt about Ted. Maybe if she could tie up the loose ends with Kent, her future with Ted would become more clear to her.

Lila, of course, could hardly believe that Robbin had come back from her trip even more estranged from Ted than she was when she'd left and had freely voiced her disapproval. Frank, surprised by Lila's vehemence when he overheard her in the hall, had popped his head in to ask what the ruckus was about, then shuffled off to his own office when no one bothered to give him an explanation.

Ted had already called Lila once since the aborted camping trip—apparently to bring her up-to-date on the refinery investigation. Although Robbin knew without a shadow of a doubt that Lila's interest in Ted was quite different from her own, it had taken all her willpower not to cut in on the line and say, "Teddy, *I'm* here. If you want to share your problems with a friend, *I'm* the one you should call!"

She had refrained, of course, but the memory still rankled. Now that her kids were back in school, and life seemed to be settling down, Robbin knew she had to find some way to get Ted by himself for a while. Whatever she felt for him wasn't growing any weaker. She missed him all the time, and every now and then a whisper of desire would sneak up on her and add to the confusion in her mind. Even while she was trying to listen to Kent's troubles, her thoughts kept straying back to Ted. It was the foot rub, more than anything, that she couldn't quite forget.

"How often do you see your daughter, Kent?" Robbin asked, determined not to dwell on the memory of her inexplicable arousal.

"I used to see Connie every other weekend like clockwork; for a long time after the divorce we were still close. But she's in high school now, which is a hard enough time to keep up with a daughter. There were lots of times when she was bored at my apartment; she wanted to see her friends and go to parties. Then my ex moved to Colorado last fall. I couldn't afford plane tickets very often, so I was just crazy to see Connie by the time summer started. It took me a while to realize that Connie didn't really care whether she came to visit me or not." His eyes darkened, and his tone grew unspeakably sad. "She came for her court-appointed six weeks in the middle of June and was ready to go home in three days. I did everything I could to make her change her mind—threatened, cajoled, bribed—but I couldn't make Connie *want* to spend the time with me. Finally I called her mother and put her on a plane." His sigh was sorrowful. "I haven't heard from either of them since."

Instinctively Robbin reached out for his hand; she knew what the admission had cost him. "I'm really sorry, Kent. I can imagine how hard that must be."

He shook his head, but he didn't withdraw his hand. He seemed eager to tell her more. "You don't know the half of it. I just went crazy for a while. I was terrible to everybody and did things that...well, that I'm still trying to undo." His glance shifted nervously, but did not meet her eyes. "I don't think Ted's forgiven me yet for the awful things I said to him the last time we played tennis. And now it's even worse since...well, you know, the other night."

Robbin didn't want to talk about "the other night"; she didn't even want to think about it. Maybe if she and Ted had been alone...maybe if they had gone out to dinner instead of having a fight...maybe if he'd rubbed her feet then...

"Has Ted told you what he's found out about the refinery?"

"No, Kent. We haven't talked about it much." The question made Robbin uneasy, but then again any mention of Ted would probably have upset her today. She'd hoped that a lunch date with Kent would help clarify her feelings for Ted, but so far it had done little to push him out of her heart.

Why do I have to push him out of my heart? she asked herself. *Couldn't I just call him or pop next door and say, 'Teddy, I want to marry you,' and he'd come bounding back?*

The answer was simple in some ways, but very complicated in others. If she meant it with all her heart and soul, surely Ted would tear open the nailed gate between their yards with his own bare hands, like Superman rescuing Lois Lane. But he knew her too well—knew every nuance of her soul—and if she made an offer like that while she still harbored the slightest doubt about what she wanted from him or was prepared to give him, he would turn his back on her for good and walk away. He'd come perilously close to that already.

"Robbin, I really would like to spend some time with you this weekend," Kent suggested as their meal came to a close. "There are some things that . . . well, I'd like to say to you. I mean, some things I'd like to get off my chest."

It was an odd request, but a sincere one. Reflecting on their conversation of the last half hour, Robbin realized that Kent had been working up to a confession of some kind, and she hoped it didn't have to do with his feelings for her. She was having enough trouble right now just coping with Ted's.

When Robbin didn't answer right away, Kent started gathering up their napkins and hamburger wrappers with nervous, jerky gestures. "Robbin, I can't say I'm a great cook, but I can barbecue a decent steak. Any chance I could lure you up to my apartment this weekend with the promise of a home-cooked meal?'' His smile was tentative, almost vulnerable, as he waited for her response. ''I'm really in need of some advice right now, Robbin. Some advice from a friend.''

Robbin found herself smiling back. This was a need she could respond to. ''I'd like to come over for dinner some time, Kent,'' she assured the man with the fragile ego who sat before her. ''Why don't you call me later in the week.''

''Thank you, Robbin. I will.''

He sounded so relieved that it was hard for Robbin to remember that just ten days before she'd been absolutely thrilled at the possibility of his asking for her number. Of course, ten days ago she'd also been certain that nothing could ever shake her relationship with Ted.

When Robbin left the drive-in and started up her Buick, the battery struggled to life with an effort. She knew it needed to be replaced, but Ted had always taken care of her car trouble, and coping with this small problem by herself was admitting, in some way, that she could no longer depend on Ted. First she had to make things right with Ted—then she could buy a new battery. Robbin knew it was illogical, but nothing about her feelings these days seemed to make much sense.

Her thoughts were a haze of camping trip memories when she pulled into Three Star Realty a few minutes later. The last sight she expected to greet her was Lila bolting out the door, crying out Robbin's name, tears staining her ever-perfect makeup as she waved a pink message note in her hand.

"Oh, Robbie!" she cried out, her panic numbing the joy Robbin felt at the sun's bright light. "Your daughter's been hit by a car."

WHEN ROBBIN GOT TO THE HOSPITAL in Morgantown, Ted was waiting for her in the lobby. The only reason he hadn't gone back to her Coltersville office to break the news to her himself was that he wasn't sure how long Ruthie's surgery would take, and he was determined to be the first face she saw when she came to.

"Robbie!" He called out when he saw her rush into the lobby with Lila. "Robbie, she's okay!"

Robbin burst into tears the minute she saw Ted, and ran to him with the speed of a gale force wind. She didn't look the slightest bit surprised to find him waiting for her.

"Where's my baby? What happened? What happened to Ruthie, Ted?"

Ted pulled her close and muffled Robbin's sobs against his chest. He only had bits and pieces of the story; Ruth had been prepped for surgery and had been pretty groggy by the time he'd arrived. "She was playing softball at school during lunch. One of the kids hit a grounder into the street. She ran out after it. A car was coming...it couldn't stop...." He felt Robbin's body shudder against him in agony and he pulled her tighter yet. "She's pretty scraped up, Robbs, but the doctor doesn't think there's any internal damage. He'll know for sure when she gets out of surgery. The car wasn't going that fast. Her right arm is broken in a couple of places—it's going to take a lot of work to fix. The doctor said he can't tell us much more until he looks her over."

Robbin sobbed convulsively. "How long will that be?"

"I don't know. At least another hour or two, I imagine. I've been here quite awhile already. I got to see her before she went under."

"You did?" Palpable relief flooded Robbin's face. "Did she talk to you? I mean, could she talk?"

He nodded quickly. "Yes, but she didn't say much."

"What did she say?"

Ted swept a loose lock of black hair out of Robbin's face and repeated her daughter's last conscious words. "She said, 'Don't leave me, Uncle Ted. Don't leave me all alone.'"

He closed his eyes, still angry with himself for having hurt Ruth so badly in the wake of his recent separation from Robbin. "I told her I wouldn't leave the hospital until she woke up. I told her that you and I would be waiting here together."

Lila slumped in relief, then laid one hand on Robbin's shoulder. "She's going to be okay, Robbie. Ted says she's going to be okay." She was struggling for composure, but her blotchy red face put the lie to her image as a shallow swinger.

Against Ted's shirt, Robbin nodded. She was still too hysterical to think clearly, so Ted did her thinking for her. Quickly he gave Lila directions to cancel all appointments for Robbin and himself for the next two days, to call Sarah and the school to make baby-sitting arrangements for Allison and Jarrod, and to keep trying to reach Doug Walker with the news. Lila promised to take care of everything, then gave Robbin a quick hug before she flitted off down the corridor.

As soon as they were alone, Ted bent over to whisper in Robbin's ear, "The doctor's going to take care of Ruthie, and I'm going to take care of you. All the other details are in Lila's capable hands. Now trust me,

Robbsie—" he kissed her temple almost reverently "—it really is going to be all right."

Still weeping, but more quietly now, Robbin pulled back to meet his eyes. "You're sure, Teddy Bear?"

"I'm sure." For some reason her old endearment touched him deeply. It was the first time she'd called him that since the night she'd forgotten their date. At the time that nickname had incensed him, but now it felt loving and right, and so did holding Robbin in his arms. "She'll probably have her arm in a cast for a while, but I really don't think she was hurt that badly. She was more scared than hurt, Robbsie, and one of the nurses told me that after I talked to Ruthie she was a lot more calm."

Robbin swallowed hard and hugged him again, then allowed Ted to steer her down the hall to a small alcove in a sunny corner of the corridor where they nested together on a vinyl couch. Ted kept his arm tightly around Robbin's shoulders while she clung to his free hand.

They sat that way for hours, exchanging no more than a comforting word. Every now and then Ted would drop a kiss on Robbin's hair, and sometimes she'd start to cry again, then subside when he pressed her face against his chest.

Ted hadn't lied to Robbin; from what he could tell, Ruthie really was going to be all right. But the enormity of the danger she'd been in terrified him, and the fact that he'd hurt her so much the past few days only intensified his inescapable sense of parental guilt. *If only I had been there; there must have been something I could have done....* There was nothing original about his feelings; he knew that any parent waiting for a child in surgery would feel the same way. But he also remembered—albeit vaguely—that Ruthie wasn't his own child, and the sobbing woman in his arms was not, and never would be, his wife.

It doesn't matter, he realized hopelessly. *I could run from here to Siberia and I'd never escape my love for this family. I can move to Morgantown or Timbuktu and it will make no difference. I belong to Robbin Walker and her three precious kids, and I will for the rest of my life.*

A THOUSAND FEARS CRIPPLED ROBBIN while she waited for the doctor to bring them the news. Never in her life had she experienced quite this level of panic. Without Ted's steadying presence, she didn't know what she would have done. At the moment, Robbin couldn't remember why she and Ted had been so at odds lately, only that it was somehow her fault. All that mattered now was that Ted was here—here for Robbin and here for Ruth—just as he had always been. And, if she had anything to say about it, he always would be.

"Mr. Ballard?"

"Yes, sir!" Ted stood up quickly, then gestured to Robbin. "And this is Ruth's mother."

Robbin rose and shook the red-headed doctor's hand. He looked like a bouncy child himself with his mass of freckles, but the lines on his face proved that he was at least ten years older than Robbin.

"Your daughter is going to be fine," he assured her at once. After a moment to let the relief set in, he went on more slowly, "Her arm has multiple fractures, but we were able to deal with them without undue complications. There may be a great deal of swelling, and we'll have to watch it closely for the next few days. It's possible we'll have to change the cast. One leg is pretty badly cut on the outside, but there doesn't appear to be any structural damage. We'll want to keep her under close observation for a while yet, but I see no internal injuries at this time."

Vaguely Robbin realized that Ted was thanking the doctor, shaking his hand. She knew she should have done the same, but her relief was so intense that speech was beyond her. When the doctor had left them, Ted turned and held out his arms to Robbin with a look of paternal joy on his face that was positively majestic.

"Oh, Teddy!" Robbin burst out, ready to explode with the intensity of her relief.

Ted must have felt the same, because he crushed Robbin to him fiercely, then picked her up and swung her around him in tiny circles.

"She's okay, Robbs!" His relief sounded every bit as intense as her own. "Our little girl is going to be okay!"

He kissed her cheek, her chin and her forehead in rapturous relief; in the same spirit Robbin pressed her lips against his beloved face. She never knew just how it happened, but suddenly his mouth found hers—or was it the other way around?—and the world tripped, then tumbled off its axis.

Never in this lifetime would Robbin have guessed that Ted Ballard's touch could affect her so. The first kiss was leftover joy and relief—and perhaps the second one was, too. But suddenly the kisses weren't fast and light anymore. When Ted kissed Robbin, *really* kissed her for the very first time, it was as if a tidal wave had rocked the California coast. She trembled with desire and joy; she clung to him with a wholly different kind of need.

Suddenly Robbin could feel every one of Ted's fingertips pressed against her ribs; her hands tugged on his thick brown hair. He drew her closer, too, as he kissed her yet again, his lips warm, demanding, as his hands slipped up to cup her face.

"Robbsie..." he groaned from a place deep within him.

She silenced him with a kiss of her own, too eager and needy to waste time on old apologies or explanations. The world had narrowed to the two of them, and the two of them had just condensed to one. Robbin pressed herself against his chest, wanting nothing more than to merge with this marvelous man for all purposes and for all time, to make their bonding complete in every possible way.

His hands slid over her ears, arousing the sensitive lobes; his mustache erotically stroked her face, calling, inviting, and answering her own desperate call.

"Oh, Teddy, I love you," she whispered fiercely. "You are everyth—"

"Mr. Ballard?" The voice was as white and starched as the nurse's uniform. "Excuse me for interrupting, but you asked me to let you know when your daughter was back in her room. You can go wait with her now if you'd like."

Robbin was amazed at how calmly Ted released her and found words to respond to the nurse. Only his fingers—still trembling as they abandoned her face ever so slowly—revealed the depth of his aborted desire.

"Thank you, ma'am." He didn't correct her reference to Ruth as his daughter. "What room is Ruthie in?"

"Three-oh-three. If you'll just take the elevator at the end of the hall you shouldn't have any trouble finding it."

"Thank you," Ted repeated. Then, without meeting Robbin's eyes, he put a light hand around her shoulder and steered her down the corridor. "I imagine it'll take awhile for the anesthesia to wear off, but I promised Ruthie I'd be waiting in her room when she woke up."

Mutely, Robbin followed his lead. She was unspeakably embarrassed by the nurse's untimely interruption; more embarrassed yet that her desire for Ted had eclipsed her concern for her daughter, even for a moment, and even if it was just a by-product of her relief after so many tense hours of fear.

But if that's all it was, then nothing has really changed, she realized dimly. Why did she only reach out to Ted in a crisis? Just once couldn't she ache for him in the clear light of day, when her world was calm? But this was hardly the time to try to sort out the blurry roles Ted had recently assumed in her life. He seemed to be willing to treat the whole episode as a mistake, and until Ruth was back on her feet—or at least conscious—it seemed to Robbin that it would be wise for her to do likewise.

Silently they walked to Ruth's room together and just as silently waited for her to awaken. This time Ted didn't sit beside Robbin, but paced back and forth around the empty second bed, his eyes on the sleeping little girl, the window, and the door, but never once on the woman whom he'd asked to be his wife.

When at last Ruth came to, she was groggy, aware of little except that her Uncle Ted was holding her hand. "I told you I'd be here, sweetheart," he told the child.

"I knew you would," she answered weakly, struggling for a smile. But when she spotted her anxious mother on the other side of the bed, Ruthie began to cry.

Gingerly, Robbin reached out to hug her. "The doctor says you're going to be fine, honey," she whispered. Though Robbin had sobbed freely with Ted and fully expected to do so again, now she gulped back her own tears, knowing they would be of no help to her young daughter. "Everybody will want to write on your cast. You'll be a celebrity."

Ruth clung to her mother with one hand and Ted with the other. Groggily she battled her tears. "I think I need to sleep some more," she whispered after a few minutes. "As long as you two are friends again, I know everything's going to be okay."

Robbin stroked her forehead, and Ted kissed Ruthie's cheek.

"You are friends again, aren't you?" she repeated. "You'll take the nails out of our gate?"

Robbin had never seen Ted cry—not even when Ellen died—but she could have sworn that his eyes looked a tad bleary now.

"You bet," he promised the pleading child. "That gate will be wide open by the time you get home."

Ruth smiled at him, then hugged her mother once more before she drifted off to sleep.

For several moments, Ted said nothing, but Robbin knew he was trying to find a way to deal with the promise he'd made to Ruth. Under the circumstances, Robbin suspected he would have promised the child anything, and he certainly would open the gate. What steps he would take beyond that she didn't know, but surely the accident would buy her a little time to influence his plans.

After Ruth had been snoring peacefully for several minutes, Ted murmured, "Well, now that I've got something to report, I think I'd better go call Lila."

The mention of the other woman's name jarred Robbin; it was as though the outside world had just invaded their own private cocoon. She wanted to beg Ted not to leave her; she wanted to tell him that she was very, very close to being sure that she truly wanted to be his wife. But she felt so dizzy—so weary and confused—that she couldn't bring herself to say the words . . . words that she might have to retract in a day or two.

Ted's eyes met hers as he reached down to touch Ruth's hair once more before he left the room. His tone was bleak as he added softly, "I'll call Doug for you, too, Robbin. He needs to know everything that's happened today. That is—" his voice grew hoarse "—everything that's happened with Ruth."

CHAPTER FIFTEEN

IT WAS LATE THE NEXT DAY when Ted arrived at the hospital with the stuffed teddy bear. It was huge and ludicrously expensive, but cute as could be in its little black tuxedo. After a restless night with a fair amount of pain, Ruth was getting well enough to be bored at the hospital, and Ted wanted to take her mind off her troubles.

"Hi, Uncle Ted!" she greeted him enthusiastically, as though days, not hours, had passed since he'd left her room. Either Ted, Doug or Robbin had been with her almost continually during the daytime since her accident the afternoon before, and it both worried and warmed him that Ruth seemed to regard his parental support on an equal par with that of the other two. It had forced him to reevaluate his position with all three of Robbin's children, and he'd finally decided what he was going to do. He'd open the gate as he'd promised Ruth, and then he'd sit down with all of them and tell them the truth. *I love you guys, and I'm going to ask your mother for visitation rights when I move. I can't handle living next door to your mom, but you three monkeys will see me just as often as you see your dad.*

It wasn't the perfect solution, but it was the best he could do. It was better than losing them altogether. He was sure Robbin would approve.

"Howdy, Ruthie," he greeted the child warmly. "I brought you something to make sure you didn't forget me."

Ruth giggled as she reached out for the bear. "Oh, he's beautiful!"

Another voice, right behind him, echoed, "He certainly is. And he looks just like you, Ted."

Ted met Robbin's eyes for just a minute, surprised that she was still at the hospital. The plans they'd agreed on called for her to leave at two-thirty; it was already three.

"Hello, Robbin." He gave her a supportive smile, one of dozens he'd managed during the past twenty-four hours. Not once since that sizzling kiss had either of them alluded to that unexpected burst of passion; by now he was certain that it had been a mirage—a merging of Robbin's relief and his own long-suppressed desire. It wasn't something he dared pursue even now that Ruth was feeling better. Robbin knew that he wanted to marry her, and she had flatly turned him down. If anything had happened to change her mind, she could easily let him know it. So far, she'd given no sign.

He'd always been sure that he knew Robbin so well that any change in her feelings would be instantly clear to him. On the camping trip, he'd remained convinced that she was putting on a show of romantic interest. But yesterday, she'd been in no condition to feign anything when she'd all but swooned from the impact of their kiss. And for a moment there—a long, dizzying moment there—he'd actually been certain that she'd ached for the follow-up of that spontaneous beginning as much as he had. But if that were true, he wouldn't be relieved that Lila had already found a young couple who wanted to look at his house, and he wouldn't have set the wheels in motion to find a new place in Morgantown. Ted had always been a practical man, not a dreamer, and he wasn't about to start lying to himself now. Despite that moment of understandable aberration in the hospital alcove, nothing had really changed.

Quietly he asked Robbin now, "What are you still doing here? I thought I got the late afternoon shift today."

She smiled warmly—with gratitude, not passion. "Ruth was feeling a little lonely. I just thought I'd stay until you arrived."

I'm lonely, too, he could have told her. *When was the last time you held my hand and brightened up my day?*

"Well, I'm here, Robbie. There's no rush to get the kids from Sarah, but you might want to get some rest before you come back again tonight."

Robbin laid one hand on his arm. "You're so good to us, Teddy. I just don't know what we'd do without you."

Deliberately he avoided her eyes as her touch jarred fresh hunger within him. For twenty-four hours he'd been just as loving as he'd been able to be; he'd taken her through this last calamity without a moment's thoughtless word. But now that the crisis was over—now that he knew for sure that he had to escape his love for her—being close to Robbin was more than he could bear. It was time to lick his wounds in private.

"Always glad to help a friend, Robb," he answered casually, then pulled up a chair next to Ruthie by the bed. "I'll go into the office first thing in the morning and plan to get back here by two or three. Doug's going to have dinner with Ruthie, so maybe you can get a little rest tomorrow afternoon after you check in."

He felt Robbin's luscious black hair spill over his shoulder—tantalizing in its quiet warmth and clean

Robbinish scent—as she leaned over to kiss Ruth good-bye.

"I'll see you tonight, honey."

"Okay, Mommy. Don't worry about me. I'm just fine with Uncle Ted."

"I know." Robbin's voice echoed Ruth's utter confidence in the man who sat beside her; the tender kiss she dropped on his cheek gave mute testimony to that fact. "I wish I had a teddy bear like that."

She could have been talking about the bear on the bed, but Ted had the uneasy feeling she was talking about him. He'd never forget the look on her face the night he'd told her he was no longer her "teddy bear"—no longer hers to count on, to believe in, to trust in when all else failed. Surely he'd proven that those words were only spears of self-defense hurled in fear and anger. Struggling for a safe but loving answer, he said simply, "Maybe Ruthie will share hers with you, Robbin."

Robbin met his eyes, and the expression on her face confused him more than any of the strange moments between them in recent weeks. There was a longing there that almost matched his own. But a longing for what? For the good old days when everything between them had been so simple? Or a need for something new and different, a need that had been born in the hospital alcove last night and was still struggling for a breath of life?

He waited tensely for her to speak, to reveal some hint of the avenue her thoughts were taking. Clearly she was troubled, struggling with some decision that she eventually chose not share. When Robbin finally stood up straight and slung her purse over her shoulder, all she said was, "Any messages for Sarah, Ted?"

He shook his head, once again defeated. "She knows what to do."

Robbin patted his head—like a dog, he decided—and disappeared from the room. *You're such a damn fool, Ballard,* he berated himself. *They say that hope dies hard, but you've lied to yourself long enough.*

He turned back to Ruth and listened while she filled him in on her day's experience with pills and tests and needles, smiling at her juvenile jokes and patting her good hand whenever she lamented her hurts. It occurred to him that he'd need to find the courage to tell Robbin he was moving before Lila inadvertently revealed the listing of his house. They had discussed splitting Lila's commission with Robbin and sparing her from the sight of a For Sale sign stuck in the middle of his yard. But the Johnsons had asked to come over tomorrow, and he still hadn't told Robbin his plans.

As Ted watched the vibrant young face before him, he knew he couldn't possibly break the news to any of the Walkers until Ruthie was home safe and sound. He hated to put off the inevitable, but he'd have to reschedule the Johnsons for some time next week. He couldn't bear to tell Robbin he was moving when her daughter was still in the hospital, and he didn't want her to find out from any other source. For some reason, breaking the news himself was important to Ted, though he didn't really know what difference it would make in the long run. No matter how gently he told Robbin, it would still break her heart when the Ballards moved away from Mulberry Lane.

ROBBIN CHECKED INTO THREE STAR REALTY at four o'clock on Friday afternoon just to see if anything pressing was waiting for her. It was the first time she'd given much thought to work in over forty-eight hours, and even now it was hard to concentrate.

Ruth, of course, still weighed heavily on her mind, even though she was starting to enjoy her celebrity status and no longer felt much pain. The doctor said everything was fine and she could come home in the morning.

Allison and Jarrod were going to spend the weekend with their father. It was officially his time with them anyway, and he felt so badly that he couldn't take care of Ruth when she left the hospital that Robbin hadn't begrudged his desire to help out with the other two. Besides, she could give Ruth more attention without Allison and Jarrod making demands on her time.

By the time Ruth came home, the family network that included the Ballards would once more be on the ropes, she knew. For the past two days, Ted had been the perfect second father, the perfect loyal friend. Robbin could not fault his warmth, his steadying influence, his willingness to do everything he could possibly do to help. For a while there—for a long while there as they'd cuddled and traded fears in the alcove—she'd felt the rebonding that she'd ached for. But ever since he'd kissed her—or she had kissed him—there had been a wariness in Ted once more, a subtle sense of separation, a quiet recognition that this reunion was only temporary. As soon as Ruth was safe and sound, she knew that Ted would pull away again.

I can't lose him, Robbin vowed as she studied the mass of notes on her desk. *I've got to make a decision; I've got to be honest with Ted and honest with myself.*

She was almost certain that she was ready to marry Ted. She didn't really know what accounted for the crippling sense of hesitation; all she was sure of was that it wouldn't go away. Maybe it was the result of so many upheavals in the past two weeks; Robbin didn't think a decision as vital as marriage should be made at a time when her emotions were so fragile. Possibly it was just because she'd only learned in the past few months how it felt to be a free woman, how it felt to seek and enjoy the admiration of men like Kent Hawthorne.

And how much do I seek his admiration? Robbin asked herself yet again. *Not much,* came the answer. *When push comes to shove, a man like Kent doesn't hold a candle to a man like Ted.* When Robbin heard that Ruth was injured, informing Kent hadn't even crossed her mind, though she'd left him at lunch less than ten minutes before Lila had broken the news. It was Ted she'd wanted near her, Ted to whom she'd flown just like a homing pigeon. Ted whom she'd wept over and kissed until—

The phone rang shrilly, reminding Robbin that she was the only one at the office. She wasn't really in the mood to handle business calls—especially inquiries from potential clients. Still, there was always the chance that somebody from the hospital was trying to reach her, so she picked up the phone and said hello.

"Robbin? This is Kent. I've been trying to reach you for two days. I hear your little girl got hurt."

His concern was genuine; with a burst of warmth for the man, Robbin remembered his love for his own daughter. "She was in a small accident, Kent. At the time it seemed like the end of the world, but actually she only has a broken arm. Multiple fractures and a lot of pain at first, but everything's going to be fine."

"That's a relief. I left a half a dozen messages at your office, but that ogre who owns the place wasn't about to give me any information."

Robbin chuckled. "It's a wonder Frank does so well in a business that requires dealing with the public. Of course, he's been awfully upset lately about the trouble at Red Rock," she tacked on loyally. After all, Frank *had* been even more irascible than usual since the accident. For that matter, so had Robbin, but her troubles with Red Rock were somewhat different than Frank's. Without pausing to consider the effect of her remark on Kent, she suggested, "You should have called Teddy, Kent. He always knows how to reach me."

Kent didn't answer at once, and then he replied briskly, "I tried that, Robbin, but he was hard to reach, too. They told me he had a family emergency. I figured that he was with you."

Of course he was with me. We are a family—where else would he be in a time of crisis?

Before she could voice any of her thoughts, Kent continued, "When does Ruth come home from the hospital, Robbin?"

"Tomorrow morning."

"Great. Does that mean you're at loose ends tonight?"

Robbin didn't have to think about that. She'd eaten lunch alone at the Pizza Palace; without Ted and the kids it had been the loneliest place in the world. Tonight Doug was going to eat with Ruth, then take Allison and Jarrod home with him, so Robbin had no family obligations. Normally she might have welcomed having some time to herself, but after all she'd gone through in the past few days, she was feeling lonely and adrift. She needed to spend the evening with a friend, and from what Kent had said on Wednesday, he needed a friendly ear, too.

"Robbin? What do you say?"

After a moment's hesitation, Robbin concluded, "I'm free for dinner, Kent."

"Super. Okay if I cook for you? I imagine you're a bit worn to feel like going out."

He gave Robbin the directions to his apartment before he hung up. She barely had time to tuck the note in her purse before the phone rang again.

"Robbin, this is Jane Davidson. I hear you've had a family problem this week."

Robbin told her friend the whole story, omitting her struggle with her feelings for Ted, before she asked, "Is that the only reason you called?"

"No. I've got some business to discuss with Lila."

"She's not in. May I help?"

Jane hesitated uncomfortably, then hedged, "Tell her I've got another buyer for the Crescent Heights house, and before I do anything final, I wanted to make sure that...the buyer we discussed before is definitely not interested."

"What buyer?" Robbin asked. "The last client who came through this agency was Paul Hawley, and he never made a bid."

Again Jane hesitated, then she said awkwardly, "Robbin, we've been friends a long time, and I hate to be party to a deception, however noble. But there is a matter of confidentiality involved here."

Robbin was miffed. She remembered Jane's last call for Lila, when her friend had so quickly shunted Robbin aside; it still rankled. "What are you talking about? What deception? What client? Why are you telling me if you don't want me to know?"

"Oh, Robbin!" Jane burst out, her frustration blatantly clear. "I *do* want you to know. I'm just not free to tell you! But somebody ought to. I can't believe—"

"Jane, what on earth are you babbling about? If there's something I should know, just tell me!"

"Let me ask you a question instead. How are things between you and Ted right now?"

"Ted? What does Ted have to do with the Crescent Heights house?"

The minute the words were out of her mouth, Robbin knew the answer. All those secret calls and giggles from Lila, who cared for Robbin enough to cry for Ruthie! Ted had remodeled his own house to Robbin's specifications; he knew how she longed for the house on Crescent Heights. Was it possible that he'd considered buying it for her? He didn't even like the massive place! Could it be that he really cared for her that much?

"Jane, are you trying not to tell me that Ted is trying to buy that house for me?"

There was a long pause. Jane's silence told Robbin what she needed to know.

"Oh, Jane!" Robbin was unspeakably moved. "I can't believe he would do that for me. He never hinted...never said a word—"

"He didn't want you to know. He wanted it to be a gift with no strings attached, not a bribe. Once he was sure you wouldn't marry him, he asked Lila to withdraw his bid. But Mrs. Ruckson thought the whole idea was so romantic that she's reluctant to sell it to anybody else as long as there's a chance for you and Ted. She's thrilled by how much you love the house, and she's touched by how much Ted loves you. And Lila and I both think you're stark raving mad," she added for good measure.

Robbin felt ill. *I am positively looney-tunes,* she decided. *If I live to be a hundred, no man will ever love me the way Ted Ballard does. And I will never love anybody the way I love Ted.*

"I adore Ted, Jane, but I've never felt any fireworks with him," she whispered uncertainly, trying to justify her incongruous behavior. *At least, not until recently.* "Shouldn't I feel lightning and thunder with the man I marry? Shouldn't I feel dizzy like a kid?"

"Who wants to feel dizzy?" Jane demanded. "Who likes to get stuck in a storm? Your love for Ted Ballard is like a slow-burning fire. It may never scald you, but it'll always keep you warm and dry. You're not looking for a date for the prom, Robbie! You need a best friend to hold your hand, walk beside you for the rest of your life!" Jane breathed a great sigh of frustration, then asked, "What ails you, girl?"

"Nothing, Jane," Robbin replied with firm conviction. Suddenly she couldn't think of a single reason why she hadn't said yes the first time Ted had ever mentioned marriage. "My temporary insanity has just been cured. That old house is going to be loved by a family again."

Jane whooped in glee. "Do you mean it, Robbin? Are you ready to tell that to Mrs. Ruckson?"

"You tell Mrs. Ruckson; I've got to call Ted." At the moment, even a ten minute delay seemed overwhelming to Robbin. "I've put him through such hell, Jane—"

"Well, go release the man from his torment, Robbin. You can talk to me any time!"

The instant Jane hung up, Robbin dialed Ted at work, then at home. Nobody knew where he was or when he'd be back, but both Sarah and Angela promised to give him a message to call Robbin at once when he checked in.

In a way, she was relieved she hadn't found him; she hadn't had time to decide what to say. She also hated to pour out her potent new feelings on the phone. As difficult as things had been between them lately, Ted might take some convincing that her change of heart was real.

The front door to the agency opened just as Robbin hung up the phone. She was dying to talk to Lila, but it was Frank who barreled in. "Well, look who's here!" he greeted Robbin almost jovially. "Decided to come see us since you had nothing else to do, huh?"

Robbin knew that gruffness was his way, but this afternoon she had no patience with his rough humor. She wanted to go home to wait for Ted's call. "My daughter's doing much better now," she greeted him with a tinge of sarcasm. "Thank you for asking."

Frank stared at her a minute, then said almost gently, "Yeah, I know. I called the hospital Wednesday night, and ever since then Lila's been keeping me up-to-date."

Robbin could hardly believe that Frank had cared enough about Robbin—let alone Ruth—to call the hospital himself, but she couldn't put her feelings into words that wouldn't have embarrassed him.

"I've been kind of nervous about hospitals ever since my brother-in-law died at Red Rock," he confessed in a somber tone. "I spent five days in that big lounge, waiting for word on one friend after another as they just curled up and died...."

His voice faded away, then brightened somewhat as he said, "Lila tells me she's got some information that may help crack open Ballard's investigation of Red Rock. He just called here a little while ago to—"

"He did?" Suddenly Robbin didn't care about the refinery, didn't care what Ted had confided in her friend. She simply had to speak to him *at once*. "Where is Lila supposed to call him back?"

Frank shrugged. "I don't remember. But I just left the message on her desk. Let me check."

He wandered down the hall, rifled some phone messages in Lila's office, then came out with a pink piece of paper. "Yep. Here it is." As he studied the note, his expression grew sour. "He didn't say anything about Red Rock. He's going to call her back at home tonight to reschedule an appointment to look at the house."

"The house?" Robbin repeated, wondering why Ted would be going to see it now instead of two weeks ago when he'd first asked her to marry him. "You mean the house on Crescent Heights?"

"Does Ballard own property up there, too?" Frank asked in surprise. "I thought he was your neighbor."

"Well, of course he's my neighbor. But I thought he submitted a bid for the Ruckson property."

Frank shook his head. "If he did, I don't know anything about it. But I guess he put his Mulberry Lane house on the market earlier this week. Lila already found him an interested buyer."

Confused and decidedly uneasy, Robbin studied her boss. "He wants to sell right away? Even though he asked Lila to withdraw his bid on the other house?" *And even though we've never discussed selling my house along with his?*

Frank shook his head. "I don't think he's had time to make a bid on any of the property he's looked at in Morgantown. I don't even think he's found a suitable house."

Robbin struggled for words as the realization hit her, but she was lost in a tailspin of pain. *If he's looking at land in Morgantown, he's not planning to buy me the house on Crescent Heights Lane! He's leaving Coltersville, and he's not planning to take me with him at all!* The blow hit her full in the solar plexus, and she reeled in shock. *Teddy wants to move away. He's going to abandon me!* Never in her darkest nightmares had she ever considered this possibility. Nor could Robbin have imagined that Ted's abandonment could hurt this much.

"Humph. I wonder why he didn't ask you to handle the sale, Robbin," Frank mused, oblivious to her anguish. "You don't do half bad in this business, you know."

Under any other circumstances, Robbin would have rejoiced at Frank's offhand praise. But the panic within her had rendered her mute, and her heart had dissipated into a cold, frozen wasteland of grief. She knew with full certainty that a part of her had died.

CHAPTER SIXTEEN

"LILA? Boy, you've been hard to reach today," Ted declared when Lila answered the phone at six o'clock. "Did Frank give you my message?"

"Yes... and he also gave it to Robbin."

Ted felt a rush of nausea. He'd received a message from Angela that Robbin had called, but there had been no answer at her house when he'd tried to reach her. "He told Robbie I'm moving?"

"The man's got the tact of a buffalo in rutting season, Ted. Fool that he is, he told her you were real eager to move to Morgantown, and he left her thinking you were giving me the whole commission, too."

"Damn!" Ted couldn't have imagined a worse way to let Robbin know his plans. The only reason he'd left that message in the first place was to give Robbin a few more days with Ruth safely home before he broke the news! He hadn't expected her to check into her office until Monday or he probably wouldn't have risked talking to Frank at all.

"Have you talked to Robbie yet?" he asked Lila.

"No, she was gone when I got here. But all I can do is explain to her that she and I are going to split the commission. There's no way to ease the sting of having you walk out on her bag and baggage."

"Damn it, Lila, I'm *not* walking out on her. If I thought there was a chance at all—"

"I'm sure there's a chance, Ted, if you'd just give her a little more time! I *know* she loves you! You can't imagine how miserable she was when she came back from Yosemite. She hardly spoke to anybody for days."

"Well, she managed to speak to Kent Hawthorne. It didn't take her very long to pick up where they left off."

Lila sighed. "Look, Ted, can we get on to the good news?"

"Yes. Anything would help brighten this day."

"I had dinner with Joe last night, and—"

"Who the hell is Joe?" Ted snapped, his temper too frayed to be plagued with Lila's endless collection of beaux.

"Joe Chacon is a security guard at Red Rock. You know, the one who looks like Erik Estrada?"

"Who's Erik Estrada?"

"Oh, never mind! The point is, Joe's worked there for three years, and he told me some things about the goings-on this summer that I think you should know."

"This summer? You mean when the new valves were put in?"

"When the new valves were *allegedly* put in. Joe isn't at all sure that any such installation took place."

Ted took a great breath. A breakthrough at last! "Does he have any proof?"

"No, but he's got some good reasons for his suspicions, and he promised me he'd ask around before he came over for dinner tonight. He ought to be able to turn over some stones that an outsider couldn't manage."

"I wish him luck. Every one of my leads has run dry, Lila." Ted was awed by the implications of Lila's discovery and amazed that she'd stumbled on such vital information that he himself had failed to obtain. "How on earth did you get him to agree to do that? And how did you get him to talk to you about it in the first place?''

Lila snorted. ''Ted, do you want to rephrase that question?''

''Never mind. No wonder I couldn't find anything out. All the folks who have anything to do with Red Rock are men.''

''And all *man*, if I do say so myself. Believe me, I've made no sacrifices for the good of the cause. My time with Joe has been so glori—''

''Lila, for Pete's sake—''

''Not that you couldn't hold your own with any of them, Ted, if you—''

''Never mind. When can I talk to this character?''

''Tonight at my house. He works the graveyard shift tonight, so he'll be coming over for dinner early.''

''You cook, too?''

''Mistress of the domestic arts, Ted. I learned at my mother's knee that the way to a man's heart is through his stomach.''

''Can't argue with you there. When do you want me to drop by? I wouldn't want to . . . interrupt anything.''

Lila laughed out loud, delighted with Ted's attempt at tact. Robbin, he knew, would have made a comment about the embarrassed grin he always wore at such times, but fortunately Lila didn't know him all that well.

''Why don't you join us for dinner in an hour, Ted? That might loosen him up enough to talk.''

''If you can't loosen him up, I don't know what makes you think that I can.''

Again she chuckled. ''Just come over as soon as you can.''

''I'm on my way.'' Ted hung up feeling better than he had in two weeks. He still didn't expect to sleep well for a long time to come—not with a fantasy image of long black hair on the pillow beside him—but if he could wrap things up at Red Rock before he sold the house, at least he'd be able to leave Robbin without worrying about her safety.

ROBBIN GOT TO KENT'S around six-thirty. Whatever enthusiasm she had summoned for this evening had totally evaporated with Frank's killing news, and the only reason she'd kept the date at all was that she couldn't bear the idea of spending the evening alone. Her plan was to eat dinner, listen attentively to Kent's troubles—a welcome distraction from her own—then cut out early. Considering her stressful week and Ruthie's imminent homecoming early in the morning, Robbin didn't think she'd have too much trouble slipping away by nine without offending her host. By then Ted should be home, Sarah would be gone and the kids would be in bed. Groveling for his love would be hard enough to do without an audience, and by now Robbin knew that she would do whatever it took to bring him back to her side. The only doubt in her mind was whether or not she was already too late.

Since she'd put on an attractive pair of black slacks and a bright pink blouse in the morning, Robbin decided not to change her clothes or do anything fancy to her hair before she drove to Kent's. She couldn't imagine that he'd be planning a formal meal on such short notice, especially since they were eating at his apartment. Under the circumstances, she was amazed when he greeted her at the door in a three-piece suit with a white carnation in the top buttonhole.

"Well...hello," she stammered awkwardly. "I thought this was just going to be a casual barbecue."

Kent smiled. It was the same golden smile he'd given her on the very first day they met, but now she realized that it was only part of the wrapping paper—it didn't have much to do with the man inside. "It is. But I felt the need to buy you a corsage, and I couldn't very well do that in blue jeans."

Robbin couldn't imagine why he'd buy her a corsage for a date like this, nor could she summon much pleasure as she glanced at the box in his hand, considering the memories it engendered.

The corsage was an orchid just like the one he'd sent before. How thrilled she'd been the night it had arrived! And yet that memory had already withered, just as the corsage itself—her lifetime dream—had wilted in just a matter of days. Instantly Robbin recalled the corsage that Ted had made for her at Yosemite, a rough blend of tiny pinecones and evergreen needles lovingly collected and assembled in the woods. Ruth had salvaged it for her after the fire, and she still had it in a drawer in her kitchen. It had been an honest gift, like the love of a man whose devotion to her would never dry or fade. *He won't leave me if I beg him to marry me,* Robbin assured herself desperately. *All I have to do is tell him the truth.*

"You asked me to be honest," Kent said simply. His eyes shifted uneasily; to Robbin's surprise, beads of sweat were forming on his upper lip. "I have a lot to tell you tonight, Robbin, starting with this corsage."

Robbin didn't know what to say. Holding his hand while he unloaded his troubles was one thing, but tonight she was in no mood for a convoluted confession of love from Kent Hawthorne. As Kent took the beautiful orchid out of the box, Robbin was suddenly loathe to even wear the glitzy thing. She was heading in another direction now; the orchid was an unhappy throwback to the past.

"Robbin, the night we went to The Old Mansion, you were already wearing the corsage when I got there. You were so pleased—and you looked so lovely—that I just didn't have the guts to tell you that...I had nothing to do with it."

Robbin gawked at him; one hand rose instinctively to block the pin from touching her blouse as he tried to fasten the corsage. "What do you mean you had nothing to do with it?"

Kent sighed uneasily. "I mean, I didn't order that corsage. I didn't know if the florist had made a mistake, or lost a card, or what had happened. All I was sure of was that somebody else's bad luck had just put me right in the driver's seat. I should have told you the truth that day. So many things have happened since then that I, well, I feel the need to come clean about a lot of things, Robbin, starting with—"

"Ted!" The word leaped out of Robbin's mouth of its own accord as the realization grew crystal clear. "Ted sent it! He wanted to give me every silly bit of my romantic dream! White tux, Crescent Heights house...the boy even said there was some confusion with another Mulberry Lane address! Mrs. Griswald is the one who told him where I lived!" Remorse all but overwhelmed her. How Ted had stared at that corsage. How nobly he'd refrained from robbing her of the joy of "Kent's" gift! Dismally Robbin murmured, "It was Ted all along."

Kent shrugged unhappily and once more tried to pin on the orchid. "But this corsage—" he flashed her his best ladykiller grin "—is all mine. And once I put it on you..."

. . . you'll be all mine, too. Robbin heard the words as clearly as if he'd hollered them right out loud. Suddenly she hated orchids, hated the corsage, hated Kent Hawthorne, too. *I've got to get out of here! I've got to go home and wait for Ted!* she realized with a rush of panic. She didn't know why the corsage discovery affected her so, but she couldn't shake the feeling that she'd sold Ted Ballard for thirty pieces of silver the night she'd gone to The Old Mansion. Ignorance had been her only defense. Now that she was sure of her feelings—and pretty darn sure of Kent's—it was obvious that this well-intentioned evening was likely to turn out even more disastrously than the last.

"I think . . . I'd better pass on the corsage," she declared gently, regretting her bluntness but knowing that her loyalty to Ted had to come before tact. "I'm sorry, Kent but—"

"Come on, Robbin!" he cajoled her, trying unsuccessfully to stab the pin through her blouse as she took a step back. "I got it just for you. I want you to feel just as romantic as—"

"Kent, I *don't* feel romantic." Her tone was firm but still kind. "You asked me to come over as a friend. You said you had some things to tell me—"

"And I do—but in my own way." He grabbed one shoulder almost roughly as he bent to kiss her mouth. "Just relax, Robbs. I—"

"Don't call me 'Robbs'!" she burst out, her patience finally evaporating in the wake of his bold touch. "Only Ted can call me that, and only Ted can kiss me!" Suddenly Robbin realized that the mere thought of Kent's lips against hers was untenable. Now that Ted had branded her with his own kind of passion, kissing any other man would feel like a flagrant act of adultery.

In a whirlwind of determination, Robbin could have shouted her passion for Teddy to the whole wide world. Still, she would never have levelled Kent if he hadn't handled her so roughly. When he made another crude grab at her shoulders and pulled her close enough for a kiss, she slammed both hands into his chest, stopping him before he could sully her lips.

"I mean it, Kent—don't touch me," she rasped out, her words even more adamant than her physical rejection. "I never should have gone out with you in the first place, and I certainly shouldn't have come here tonight!"

Kent stepped back as though she'd slapped him in the face. He looked utterly stunned...and keenly disappointed as he dropped his hands and stared at her in disbelief.

For a minute Robbin wondered if she'd overreacted; surely Kent would not have forced himself on her though his raw insistence on both the corsage and the kiss had been clearly out of line. Yet there was now a vacant desperation in his eyes that had nothing to do with sex or pride or even, perhaps, with Robbin.

"In that case, I guess you'd like to go now," he gravelled out bitterly, tossing the corsage at her feet.

Robbin felt awful, but she couldn't deny his words. She wanted to soothe him, somehow, to apologize. He wasn't a hero, but he wasn't a total jerk, either. Part of his misunderstanding had been her fault, anyway; she shouldn't have come here at all. But before Robbin found words to express her mixed feelings, the doorbell rang. When Kent didn't answer it at once, a heavy fist started banging on the door.

"Hawthorne! Are you in there?"

As Robbin watched, Kent visibly cowered as the angry shout snaked through the room. It was obvious that he knew his visitor well, and the threatening voice filled him with fear.

"GLAD TO MEET YOU, Joe," Ted greeted the other man, taking the limp fingers in his firm right hand.

Joe was much younger than Ted—maybe younger than Lila for that matter—and appeared visibly shaken by what lay ahead of him. Determined to put him at ease, Ted continued, "Lila assures me that she's a terrific cook, so we've both got something to look forward to this evening."

Joe gazed at the deep V of Lila's gold lamé jumpsuit as though he hoped she had more to offer him than her cooking, and Lila smiled back in a way that promised that his wishes would come true.

"Do you two think you could keep each other company for just a minute while I finish up?" she asked, eyes aglow as she batted her lashes at Joe.

Joe grinned back, obviously putty in her hands.

Ted felt as though he were watching a scene from a soap opera, but he restrained his laughter. Whatever hold Lila had on this young guard was clearly going to work to Ted's advantage. "I imagine we can find something to talk about, Lila," he assured her.

She giggled—by now Ted knew it was not a spontaneous sound—and gave Joe a lingering goodbye kiss on the mouth as though she were leaving for a month. "I'll be right back," she promised. The only thing she didn't add was that she might slip into something more comfortable.

"Lila tells me you work at Red Rock, Joe," Ted started off conversationally as both men sat down in Lila's pink and mauve living room. "A security guard, I believe she said."

Joe nodded uneasily, then flicked his eyes toward the kitchen when the phone rang. Lila, purring like a kitten, picked up the receiver and deflected the caller with some silken retort and voluptuous laughter.

"Yes, I'm a guard, though I don't know how long I want to be doing this kind of work at a place like that." He sighed unhappily. "Do you really think the refinery is that dangerous...if those valves weren't really replaced, I mean?"

Ted nodded; he had to impress the younger man with the seriousness of the situation right from the start. "You bet I do. Those regs aren't written up just for fun, you know. If anything, they're too laissez-faire to begin with. The fact that one valve has already blown tells you how weak the equipment can grow with time—or faulty re-welding. That explosion is just a drop in the bucket compared to what it could have been." He paused again, pinning the young guard with an intent "I'm counting on you, Joe" stare. "Will you help me find out what really went on out there?"

Slowly, Joe nodded. "I really don't know a whole lot, Mr. Ballard. But the day the materials contractor showed up—to install new equipment, as far as I knew—I recognized one of the crew. A guy I went to school with. We weren't real tight, you know, but we'd had a few classes together, that sort of thing."

Every nerve in Ted's body told him that he'd stumbled onto the last piece of the puzzle. He'd worked his tail feathers off trying to sort out this mess, and he was a trained professional. How ironic that Lila, playing the oldest and least original of investigative games, had uncovered the missing link to this complex chain of events.

"Go on."

"Well, after I got to know Lila—" Joe's face reddened slightly, revealing exactly how well acquainted they'd become "—she asked me to go talk to this fellow and see just what he'd actually done out there. So I called him, you know, to set up a meeting, but at first he was real squirrelly about the whole thing."

"Squirrelly?"

"Well, he was afraid, or angry, or something. And he asked me to make sure that nobody at Red Rock knew I was talking to him."

"Did he mention anybody in particular?"

Joe shook his head. "He didn't have to. If anybody at the plant did anything illegal, Mr. Ballard, I know who it is."

"You do?"

He nodded. "I'm the one who sees who comes and goes at the refinery. I don't have anything else to do but listen to what people say and watch what they do." He looked uneasy. "Ever since Lila first talked to me about this, I've been trying to remember what I saw in June—what sort of equipment went through the main gate."

"And what do you remember?"

"Not much. I mean, not enough to hurt or help anybody. But right after all those realtors came up to visit, and Lila came over to introduce herself to me—" again his face grew red "—Howard Caldwell started grilling me on who she was and what she wanted. He thought she was the lady reporter who somebody told him had been sniffing around, and he wanted to know what I'd told her."

"And what did you say?"

"Well, I was embarrassed to tell him the truth about Lila. I mean—" he dropped his tone and cast a conspiratorial glance toward the kitchen "—just between you and me, Mr. Ballard, I usually do the asking myself, you know?"

Ted suppressed a grin as he nodded. Lila was still on the phone, so he was sure she hadn't overheard.

"It was none of his business anyway. So I said, 'I just answered the lady's questions, Caldwell. Is that all right with you?'"

"And?"

"And he said, 'No, it's not all right. I'm in charge here and you clear everything you say with me.'"

Ted studied the young man carefully. "You say this was during the realtors' tour?"

"Yes."

"Well, I was there that morning, Joe. Gregory was, too. *He* arranged the tour and answered everybody's questions. I don't understand why Caldwell would claim he was in charge when Gregory was on the premises. At ten or eleven in the morning, I don't know why he was still there at all."

Joe leaned forward intently. "That's just my point, Mr. Ballard. He never comes in so much as ten minutes early, and he always leaves the minute the whistle blows. He never decides anything if he can put it off until Gregory gets there in the morning, and he's never shown any interest one way or another in any other emergency we've had out there. But he must have asked me a dozen times what the hospital said about Bill Rayburn while he was still alive, and every time you've come through that gate since the accident he's grilled me about it later."

Ted assimilated this news carefully. "Does Gregory ask you about me, too?"

Joe shook his head. "The only time Gregory's ever mentioned you was the day of the accident. He told the whole crew that we were supposed to tell you and Mr. Hawthorne anything that might help clear up what had happened. He was so shook up about the men who got hurt that he almost cried in front of us, Mr. Ballard."

It was obvious that the memory had made an impression on Joe. "I know everybody thinks he's a real hardnose, but Gregory's not really so bad. Every now and then he loans somebody money or gives it to them outright when they're in a jam. He makes jokes all the time, but he listens to you if you've got a problem." Joe paused to glance once more at Lila—still in the kitchen and still on the phone—before he continued. "I bet if you asked half of the other guys, you'd find out that Gregory really isn't half bad to work for. Everybody heaves a sigh of relief when he shows up in the morning. We're always a little uneasy when Caldwell's in charge, and we always breathe a little easier when Gregory's there."

Ted was ready to breathe a little easier himself. He was ninety-nine percent sure now that Caldwell was the criminal who'd endangered Red Rock. Despite his reservations about Gregory, Ted's instincts had been right; Gregory, baby-kisser though he might be, had been playing straight with him.

Ted knew he had to get Joe to finish his story about his friend on the contractor's crew, but first he had a question that just wouldn't keep. "Joe, when Caldwell told you to keep an eye on me—to report whatever I asked and whoever I talked to—did he ask you to keep an eye on anybody else?"

"Like who?"

"Like . . . another inspector, for instance."

Joe thought a minute, then shook his head. "Nope. In fact, the next day when I told him that Mr. Hawthorne had come through the gate, he told me not to worry about him; you were the one to watch." He tried to smile. "Only he didn't put it quite that nicely, Mr. Ballard."

Ted could imagine how he put it. What Caldwell thought of him caused him no pain, but Joe's implication of Kent's collusion was a source of growing discomfort for Ted. "Do you recall exactly what he said about Kent?"

"Not much, Mr. Ballard. It was something like, 'Don't worry about Hawthorne. I've taken care of him.'"

Ted's shoulders sagged. Kent was a fool, but he wasn't a criminal. He'd probably started out innocently enough, maybe even been duped by Caldwell at first, but now that Rayburn was dead, he was in trouble up to his eyebrows. Ted didn't relish explaining it to Robbin.

"Okay, Joe," he prodded the young guard to continue. "So you called your friend. And he said—"

"Ted?" Lila's voice, soft but uneasy, beckoned him from the kitchen. "May I see you just a moment, please?"

Damn! Just when we were getting somewhere. He stifled his irritation with Lila—he'd really thought she had too much savvy to interrupt him at a moment like this—and excused himself as casually as he could.

Lila drew him just out of Joe's visual range and dropped her voice. "I'm really sorry, Ted, but it's Robbin. I told her you were terribly busy, but she won't be put off. She's not angry, but she sounds . . . well, pretty shaky and upset. Maybe even scared. I tried to get her to tell me what's wrong, but she insists on talking to you."

Ted was surprised. "That's what I get for calling Sarah to tell her where I'd be. I couldn't reach Robbin this afternoon; I'm sure she's still upset about the house."

"I'm sure she is, Ted, but I don't think that's why she called. I've got the feeling that it's something more urgent."

Reluctantly—but uneasy now—Ted took the receiver. With one hand over the mouthpiece he whispered, "Could anything be wrong with Ruthie?"

Lila shook her head. "No. I asked her that first thing."

Thus assured that her problem couldn't be anything cataclysmic, Ted steeled himself to whatever petty domestic concern Robbin had this time. In the past he would cheerfully have dropped whatever he was doing to be of service to her, but the time had come for her to learn to stand on her own. Besides, he desperately needed to hear the rest of what Joe had to say. By now Ted had a pretty clear picture of what had happened at Red Rock this summer, but not one shred of proof. Robbin's safety—and the safety of everybody in Coltersville—depended on the leads Joe could produce.

"Hello, Robbin." His tone was carefully casual. "What's up? I don't have much time to talk."

For a moment his words were greeted with dead silence. "Robbin, are you there?" he prodded.

"I'm here," she answered in a small voice. "I'm sorry I had to interrupt you, Teddy. I know you're busy. But . . . I need you."

So what else is new? he wanted to ask. *If it's the sink, call the plumber. If it's the car, call a cab.* But something in her tone deterred him. It wasn't like Robbin to sound so rattled. "Robbin, I don't mean to be abrupt, but I don't have time to chat. If it's brief, spit it out. If it's long, can it wait until tomorrow? I'm in the middle of something very important right now."

Again there was a long, empty silence. He didn't know whether it was the current strain in their relationship or something about Robbin's problem that made it so hard for her to talk to him right now. He'd vowed to let Robbin take care of her own troubles from now on, but the minute he'd heard her say "I need you," his determination had begun to dissolve.

"Teddy, I'm in Morgantown at a gas station. Corner of Third and Parker," she finally explained, sounding more embarrassed than afraid. "My car died a couple of blocks from here. It's already dark and—"

"And you're almost at Hawthorne's back door," he pointed out, irritated with Robbin for continuing to lean on him for practical help as though nothing had changed between them. Ruth's accident had called for its own set of rules—it was a family problem. But any friend could bail out Robbin when she had car trouble. "I'm sure your new boyfriend would be delighted to come collect you."

As soon as he uttered the bitter words, Ted wondered if it was time to tell Robbin the truth about Kent. But he still didn't have any proof, and he wasn't likely to get any if he went tearing off to Morgantown right now.

"Considering what I said to him when I marched out of his place half an hour ago, I rather doubt it, Ted," Robbin answered in a subdued and humble tone. "Besides, he's not alone. This awful apelike person—"

"You had a date with Kent and you walked out on him?" Ted asked incredulously. "What did he do to you?" When he'd first mentioned Kent it was jealousy that had spurred his guts; but now, as he considered Robbin's words, his throat felt raw with anger.

"Oh, Teddy, it's a long story. I'll explain it all when you get here."

"Robbin," he snapped, "I'm not at all sure I want to hear it. Besides, I told you, I can't come right now. I'm in the middle of something very important here!" Ted was appalled that Robbin expected him to bail her out of a problem caused by Kent Hawthorne. Was there no end to the amount of salt she was willing to rub in his wounds? Of course, she surely had to swallow a lot of pride to call him under the circumstances. Between them, pride had always taken back seat to loyalty and love.

Ted tried to tell Robbin to call some other friend, but he just couldn't force himself to be so cruel. Despite all his resolutions, he just couldn't turn his back on the woman he adored. Instead, he suggested, "Look, Robbie, why don't you call my mother? She doesn't live too far away from that end of town. When I finish up here I'll meet you at her house and—"

"Oh my God!" Robbin's cry was so shrill that Ted knew at once she was responding to something even more painful than his tepid offer of assistance. "It's him! That terrible man!"

"Hawthorne? Hawthorne's at the gas station?" Embarrassing, perhaps, after he and Robbin had had a spat, but why would the mere sight of Kent trigger such a note of panic in Robbin's voice?

"No! The one who works at the refinery! I don't know his name, but he walks like a gorilla!"

"Caldwell?" For the first time, Ted felt the snap of alarm in the pit of his stomach. "Caldwell's there with you, Robbs?"

Robbin didn't seem to hear his question. Frantically she babbled on, "He was so mean to me at Kent's door, Ted, and I could hear him yelling at Kent when I was clear out in the street! He just pulled in here driving this snazzy red car and—"

"Robbie, slow down! I can't understand you!"

It was the beating of his own heart he couldn't understand. A wild sense of urgency was gripping him, a sense of panic that eclipsed his need to talk to Joe, to solve the mess at the refinery, to do anything in this world but protect his woman from harm. Hawthorne wasn't strong enough to protect her from a man like Caldwell, and from what she'd just said, might not even care to. He couldn't believe he'd ever let her get tangled up with Kent; couldn't believe he'd dawdled an instant when she'd turned to him for help. "Robbsie—"

"Ted, he's coming this way! Teddy, please—"

"Stay where you are, Robbs!" he ordered, instantly abandoning his plans and his common sense. "I'm on my way."

CHAPTER SEVENTEEN

ROBBIN COWERED IN THE PHONE BOOTH while the simian creature—Caldwell, Ted had called him—filled up the booth beside her and made a call. She couldn't hear a word he said, but his gravelly voice echoed eerily around her for several minutes before he slammed open the door and plodded heavily toward his red Z28. It seemed like a lot of car for an oil field worker, and a pretty poor choice if he were trying to follow Robbin inconspicuously. Her relief as he drove off was followed by a sense of humiliation as she realized that his arrival at the gas station had been purely coincidental. This was primarily a residential neighborhood, after all—there wasn't another gas station for several blocks! Because of her fear, Ted was galloping up here to rescue her from this nasty but surely innocuous man who had long since disappeared. And Ted who had made it agonizingly clear that he did *not* want to help Robbin solve her problems tonight.

Stalwartly she prepared to meet him. Thank God she'd managed to escape without that orchid corsage Kent had tried to pin to her blouse; that would have been very hard to explain to Ted. And Robbin had enough difficult things to explain to him tonight. If only he'd relinquish his defenses long enough to listen to her...if only he still loved her enough to give her a chance to be his wife.

While she waited, Robbin touched up her makeup and combed her long tresses back into some semblance of order. She wanted to look beautiful for Ted, but in a way she was glad she wasn't dressed up for the evening. Things between them always felt more natural when they were wearing the homey clothes that spoke of the family intimacy that had bonded them together for years.

The new green van screeched into the station in twenty minutes flat. Ted bolted out of the front seat and hit the ground running; he had Robbin in his arms before the van door slammed shut.

"Robbsie? Are you all right?" Panic radiated from his beautiful brown eyes.

Robbin took a deep breath; dark crimson stained her cheeks. "I'm fine, Teddy. I—I'm sorry I made you hurry so much. Caldwell wasn't after me. He just wanted to use the phone."

Ted's hands were still gripping her shoulders, but the panic in his eyes quickly changed to rage and disbelief. "You got me up here on a wild-goose chase? I'm surprised at you, Robbie. I really am."

"I didn't trick you! I was really scared!"

Ted studied her face for a moment as if to verify her words. A few minutes ago, her wide-eyed, disheveled look might have been more convincing. Now he said wryly, "About the last impression your appearance gives right now is *fear*, Robbin. You must have been taking cat lessons from Lila."

From some other man, such an observation might be flattering, but from Ted, it was no compliment. Defeated, Robbin glanced at the ground, wishing she could slide away with the stream of oily water eddying by her feet. "I'm sorry if my call was . . . inconvenient for you, Ted," she managed to stammer. "But when I phoned you, I really was . . . upset. The main reason I'm so much calmer now is because . . . you said you'd come."

It was true, and she knew that Ted believed her. But it was only the beginning of what she had to tell him tonight; unfortunately, she suspected it was the sum total of what he'd probably be willing to hear.

Ted dropped his hands from her shoulders. "Well, for better or worse, I'm here. Get in the van. I'll drop you off at home on my way back to Lila's."

Robbin followed his directions in silence. She had only a half an hour to convince him that she belonged to him now; half an hour to convince him he didn't need to sell the house, didn't need to shield his heart from her...and he surely didn't need to go back to Lila's tonight! No matter how poor the timing might be for a confession of lifetime love, Robbin knew that she wouldn't last another day without making things right with Ted.

Robbin used the first few minutes of the drive back to Coltersville to marshal her thoughts. She found herself missing Ted's pathetic old car; the new van, impressive though it was, only increased her discomfort. The dear Teddy she loved belonged in a battered Volkswagen bug.

Ted's hands gripped the wheel tensely, but he said nothing as the miles slipped away. His expression was dark but unreadable; it certainly didn't encourage conversation.

Finally, Robbin started cautiously, "Do you want to know what happened?"

He didn't take his eyes from the road. "I'd like to know if you heard anything that Caldwell said to Kent. There's no reason why the two of them should be seeing each other socially."

"Well, it wasn't exactly a social call, Ted," she answered quickly, glad that he was at least speaking to her. "I was just leaving after Kent and I had—"

"I don't want to know about you and Kent," he cut her off grimly. "I'm only interested in Kent and Caldwell."

Robbin decided to get Caldwell out of the way before she tugged Ted back to the more crucial subject at hand. "When I was . . . getting ready to leave, Caldwell showed up. He rang the doorbell and started shouting. When Kent opened the door, Caldwell looked me up and down and said something nasty."

"Nasty?"

"Well, something that implied that . . . well, he could find some good use for me if Kent couldn't. I don't remember exactly—"

"I get the idea." His tone was dark. "What was Hawthorne's brilliant reply?"

"He said something like 'Leave her out of this.'"

"How original."

"Well, all he meant was—"

"I *know* what he meant! What I don't know is why Caldwell was visiting Kent in the first place! Did you find that out?"

"No," Robbin admitted in a small voice. "I was already eager to leave, and I didn't want to hang around for another ugly scene. So I just kept going, and Caldwell went inside. A minute later I could hear him yelling at Kent again, even though I was clear out in the street."

"Did you hear what he said?"

Robbin thought for a minute. "Something about a day burn. I guess it's some oil term—"

"Rayburn," Ted corrected her, his tone dark and hard. "It's a man's name."

She waited for Ted to tell her more, but after a moment's silence, he prompted, "What happened then?"

Robbin shrugged, feeling ridiculous. She didn't want to talk about Kent and Caldwell; she surely didn't want to talk about some other man she'd never even heard of. Somehow she had to lead the conversation toward the topic of marriage. At the moment that seemed as easy as swimming the English Channel.

Quietly she said, "Well, I drove a block or two to get away from there, then pulled over and shut off the motor while I tried to get myself together. I was really too upset to drive." Even now she trembled at the memory; she still wasn't sure whether it was Kent, Caldwell, or the news that Ted was moving that had upset her most today. She wanted to hide in the shelter of Ted's arms . . . or at least wrap herself in the security of his corny jokes and loving laughter. Even though he sat right beside her, he'd never seemed further away. "I've been having trouble with the battery all week, Teddy," she admitted reluctantly. "When I tried to start the Buick again, it just sputtered and died."

Ted's knuckles were white on the steering wheel; it was obvious that some part of her story had deeply upset him. Was he wondering why she hadn't mentioned her trouble with the car to him earlier in the week...or why she'd gone to Kent's apartment in the first place? Or was he, like Robbin, worried about what had transpired at the apartment after she'd gone? "Shouldn't I have left Kent alone with him, Ted? You don't think Caldwell . . . did anything awful to Kent do you? He sounded so angry!"

"I doubt that Kent's the one who needs to be afraid of Caldwell," he growled. "But by the time I get all the pieces together, I suspect that Joe Chacon is going to be—" He stopped and peered at Robbin as another thought eclipsed his concern for Joe. "What do you mean by 'another' ugly scene. What exactly did Hawthorne do to upset you?''

''Well...he...he had different plans than I did for the...outcome of our evening, Ted. When he realized that I—''

''Did he hurt you?'' Suddenly Ted's eyes were venomous. Robbin had visions of him making a U-turn in the middle of the highway to go back and have it out with Kent. ''Did he try to force himself on you, Robbie?''

Slowly, she shook her head. ''He...was unhappy with me, Teddy. But he didn't...press me—much—after I said no.'' It had taken more than a simple word to convince Kent, of course, but she didn't see any point in hashing it over. What was important was the way *she'd* felt when Kent had tried to kiss her tonight. In hindsight, Robbin realized that she had never particularly disliked Kent's touch; she just couldn't bear the idea of *any* man touching her but Ted.

Ted pulled up to the curb in front of Robbin's house, but left the motor running. ''Are you going to go out with him again?''

''No.'' Her answer was instantaneous. ''I'm not going to go out with anybody but—''

''Good. Sensible move. Give Ruthie my love and tell her I'll come over tomorrow. When Allison and Jarrod get back, I want to sit down with all of you and discuss visitation rights after I move. The system ought to be old hat to them by now.''

He waited for Robbin to get out of the car, but she couldn't seem to move. Visitation rights? He was talking about visitation rights while Robbin was desperate to marry him right away?

''Robbin, I really do have to go,'' he said tersely. ''Your timing couldn't have been worse.''

The motor was still running, and Ted was toying with the keys as they hung from the ignition. His face was dark and sad in the moonlight. Robbin ached for him so much she thought she'd burst.

"Teddy, please don't go back there yet," she begged him, giving up all hope of sliding gently into the subject of their love. "I've been waiting for hours to talk to you. There are so many things I need to tell you. There's—"

"Tell me some other time, Robbin. Or better yet—" his voice dropped as though it hurt him to be so unkind "—why don't you call up one of your other friends? It's time for you to get used to leaning on other people again."

Each word was a fresh rapier thrust of pain, but Robbin refused to give in to the hurt. The only way she was going to get out of this van tonight without Ted was if he roped and hog-tied her and threw her out in the street.

Stifling her anguish, Robbin turned in the bucket seat to face him squarely. She was trembling slightly, but her resolution was strong. "What I have to say to you isn't something I ever plan to say to anybody else, Ted Ballard. It's personal, it's vital, and it simply won't keep for another hour. Now please come inside with me for just a little while."

She watched fresh tension march across his face as he considered her urgent plea. His hands had finally released the steering wheel and were clenching and unclenching in balled fists.

"Damn it, Robbin, this is the reason I have to move away!" he admitted, his frustration vibrant. "I'm not strong enough to say no to you when you need me, but every time I come when you call I feel like a puppet you keep dancing on a string. I just can't keep living like this!"

"Neither can I, Ted! If you'll just come inside with me I—"

"No! I can't come in! I have to go!"

He was so adamant that Robbin stopped, heart pounding to stare at his face. She saw urgency there, and a kind of desperation, but to her relief, he did not look angry with her.

Cautiously she reached out to touch his wrist in the darkness; his skin was hot to her touch. "Why, Teddy?" she asked him gently. "Why can't your business with Lila wait just a little longer?"

He closed his eyes, then opened them as he faced the street and slipped his wrist from her grasp. "I don't understand you, Robbsie," he muttered in a ragged tone. Then he turned back to face her, his eyes haunted and bleak. "You claim you love me, but you're so damn cruel."

"Cruel?" Robbin was stunned. "Ted, I want you to come inside for five minutes so we can straighten out everything that's gone wrong between us! I can't imagine what could be cruel about that!"

"Robbie, stop jerking my chain!" he burst out, anguish shadowing his angry words. "I can't handle five minutes in that house alone with you tonight without begging you to take me to bed! Is that clear enough for you?"

"I *want* to take you to bed tonight, Ted!" Robbin yelled back without thinking. "Is that clear enough for *you*?"

She bit her lip, amazed and a little frightened by her bold words. But it was too late to try to take them back, and she was relieved that she'd confessed her love for Ted at last. But Robbin quaked as she waited for his answer.

By the look on his face, she knew she might have to wait for a long time.

Ted's jaw went slack; all expression but shock faded from his eyes. For an endless moment he just stared at Robbin, grappling with the meaning of her words as though she'd spoken in some alien tongue. His breathing grew quick and shallow, and his head moved side to side almost dizzily in stunned disbelief.

Robbin couldn't move either; the enormity of her confession, couched in the most undiplomatic of terms, still rang in the air between them. She'd laid all of her cards on the table, and there was nothing to do now but wait for Ted to fold his hand or follow suit. And wait she did—for an eon at the very least—while her words swam around in Ted's mind.

Finally he shut off the ignition and pulled out his keys. The jangled sound was magnified by the stillness; he tried to toss them on the dashboard, but he missed the edge and they toppled to the floor. He didn't bother to pick them up.

"All right, Robbie, you've got my attention," he admitted in a low, ragged tone. His hands were quivering; he still looked utterly shocked. "Now you've got about two minutes to explain yourself."

Explain myself? Robbin wanted to cry out. How could she explain that everything that had happened over the past two weeks—the past thirteen years—had propelled her to this special moment? How could she begin to justify her initial hesitance, her uncertainty, her ultimate realization that if Ted Ballard walked out of her life she would never be whole again? How could she tell him that she loved his holey socks, his three-day beard, even missed his pathetic, old Volkswagen bug and the crabgrass in his lawn?

It seemed to Robbin that they'd had far too many words between them; Ted didn't need to be assured that the two of them could talk. It was another kind of assurance he needed, and Robbin needed the same. At the moment, though, she needed far more than verbal promises. Plain and simple, she needed Ted in her arms.

Her fingers trembled as she unhooked her seatbelt and slid over the gearshift to reach his side; it was so dark on the street that only somebody standing right next to the van would be likely to realize that they were sharing the bucket seat. As Robbin approached Ted, she could hardly bear to brave his dark-eyed scowl, which indicated a combination of hope and disbelief and barely banked desire. Gently she lifted both hands to touch his cheeks, then let her fingertips trace the firm line of his jaw. Confident of her own desire, but unsure of how best to convey it, Robbin pulled Ted toward her and kissed him fully on the mouth.

An erotic flush surged through Robbin as she felt his lips on hers. His wiry mustache aroused her unbearably, as did the clean male scent that had always proclaimed the essence of Ted. But those warm lips were not inviting her tonight; Ted's response was guarded, tepid. He was giving her what she asked for, but making no demands of his own.

She knew what he wanted; she knew he had to be convinced of her desire. Bravely she opened her mouth to entice him, extending her invitation with the lightest flicker of her tongue against his lips. After a moment they parted, admitting her sweetness within. Robbin's hands slipped more fully around his head, gripping his thick brown hair as she pulled him yet closer, pressing her breasts against his firm chest.

Still his hands did not touch her, but his resistance began to collapse. His warm tongue talked to hers in the streetlamp's glow; his neck arched hungrily now to merge his tempting mouth with Robbin's. She could feel the thundering beat of his heart against her swelling breasts and longed to feel his warm, square hands there also. But still he held back; still he waited.

"Evening, Robbin! Ted!" Mrs. Griswald called out as she strolled by the van with Peppy. If she saw anything unusual in her two neighbors' embrace, she gave no sign. Robbin decided to ignore the old woman, but Ted broke off the kiss and lifted one hand in nonchalant greeting before he returned his gaze to Robbin.

They sat perfectly still in Ted's bucket seat, their bodies hotly touching, as Mrs. Griswald and her dachshund wandered on down the street. Robbin's hands were still on Ted's face, and his hands still languished at his sides. Need and trepidation shook Robbin to the core, but Ted still made no move to touch her. Only his neck pulse, thudding with desire, gave her confidence.

"That's... an interesting explanation, Robbie," he forced out in a hoarse, breathless tone when their privacy was restored. "It's the most... sensible... thing you've said in a month."

Robbin managed a grin; a tiny seed of hope burst open in her chest. She let her hands slide more beguilingly through Ted's mahogany mane and asked softly, "Does that mean you'd like me to... continue making 'conversation?'"

The tiniest glimpse of a smile found its way to Ted's face. "The ball's still in your court, Robbs."

It was all the encouragement Robbin needed. Her kiss was bold and hungry this time, and Ted's touch was the same. At last she felt his arms slide around her, stroking her back and her ribs and the delicate sides of her full breasts, quickly growing swollen with desire. Her heart throbbed mightily, and her sexual urgency for Ted began to overshadow her earlier need to convince him that her passion for him was real. All she knew was that she ached for him, ached to feel his body above her, below her and within her.

She knew he'd crossed the same line of passion when he gripped her thighs fiercely and pulled her onto his lap. "Robbie!" he cried out in anguished need, cupping her hips with his big, warm hands. "Oh my God, Robbsie..."

The words were lost in the passion of his next kiss. Then, just before Robbin lost all sense of time and place, Ted broke off the kiss abruptly. He didn't pull away from her, but his body grew still. Only his heavy breathing and trembling hands—still clutching her thighs—revealed the ongoing strength of his desire.

"For Pete's sake, Robbie, we can't make love in the middle of Mulberry Lane," he whispered, resting his chin on top of her head. "My kids could rush out here anytime."

Robbin hugged him tightly and smiled against his shirt. "Then let's go inside, Teddy," she begged him, no longer afraid to confess her urgency. "Ruth's at the hospital, and the other two kids will be with their dad all night."

She felt a shudder pass over Ted; he didn't answer right away. For one terrible moment Robbin was afraid he'd changed his mind... afraid she'd said something wrong. Her own needs were exploding in the dark, and rational thought was nearly beyond her.

"Tell me why, Robbs," Ted finally asked her, pulling back to watch her face in the dark. His arms still embraced her lovingly, but his eyes insisted on the truth.

"What's changed? I'm the same man I was two weeks ago."

There were many things she could have told him, but this was not the time. What had started in the van was too new, too precious, too fragile to risk killing it with complex talk. There would be plenty of time for that later.

"You were right when you said that I was already your wife in every way but one, Ted," Robbin admitted in a husky voice that vibrated with desire. Trying to remember his exact words the night he'd asked her to marry him, she confessed, "It just took me a while to realize that...I really did love you...in every way a woman can love a man."

Ted closed his eyes in a wave of relief. His arms tightened around her, and he dropped one sizzling kiss on her throat. For a moment Robbin simply clung to him, too full of love to think past the moment. Ted rocked her softly, as though a simple embrace were not nearly enough to convey his joy.

When he finally opened his eyes and gazed at Robbin's face again, he slipped his fingers through her long hair and tenderly stroked her sensitive scalp. As fresh desire radiated from her head to the rest of her body, Ted struggled for a note of levity as he warned her, "If you're my 'wife,' Robbs, then I've got grounds to warn Ken Hawthorne that I'll kill him if he ever lays a hand on you again."

Robbin had the feeling that he was only halfway teasing, but his new possessiveness only heightened her arousal. She snuggled up closer yet and hugged Ted as tightly as she dared, deciding there was one more thing she ought to tell him before they went inside. It might be hours before rational conversation was possible again.

"Tonight when he tried to kiss me, Teddy, I didn't remember that he looked like Robert Redford; I couldn't even see his face. All I could see was you." She reached up to kiss him softly, as if to underline her words. "I realized that I just couldn't bear the thought of any other man touching me, Ted. It was just that simple."

He swallowed hard, as though he were deeply moved by her revelation. He leaned down to kiss her right below the ear, then burned a trail of tiny kisses from her quivering lobe to her hungry mouth. For a long time they got lost in that kiss; Robbin heard Mrs. Griswald calling Peppy on the other side of the street before Ted pulled back to ask, "Are you sure now, Robbsie? Are you absolutely sure?"

His eyes were so hopeful, so full of desire, that Robbin couldn't bear to speak. Instead she slipped both hands under his collar and loosened his tie. When she tugged it off and tossed it on the dashboard, Ted took a great breath; when she started to unbutton his shirt and slipped one hand inside, he groaned audibly.

"I would sooner die than force myself on you, Robbs, but I need to remind you before we walk into that house that even sitting out here in front of Peppy and Mrs. Griswald, I am—" he took a ragged breath and kissed her hotly in the small dip at the center of her throat "—already very nearly past the point of no return."

Robbin undid her own top button to give him greater access, then pressed herself unreservedly against him as she breathed a husky reply. "As far as I'm concerned, Ted Ballard, we passed that point some time ago."

The ball was back in his court now, and Robbin waited for Ted to make the next move. Here in the van, where they both knew there was a definite limit to their tentative overtures, their foreplay had taken its own direction, and much of the awkwardness Robbin had feared had simply disappeared. But she didn't know what would happen when they slipped into the house. Was she supposed to "slip into something more comfortable"? Or invite him straight to bed? Should she undress herself, or let Ted do it for her? It seemed so strange to be playing this game with Ted after all the years they'd cuddled platonically on her couch. She ached for him powerfully, but couldn't stifle her apprehension about the transition to the new life as lovers, which they'd make together in the next few minutes. After the torment they'd both endured in recent weeks, it was important that everything turned out all right this first time.

Ted slipped one hand under Robbin's blouse in the back, tantalizing her skin with his warm, searching fingers. "In that case, Robbs," he breathed against her throat, "I'll race you to the front door. Last one inside has to explain it all to Mrs. Griswald."

He opened the car door instantly and gave Robbin a tiny push toward her own side of the van.

"Teddy!" she howled with mock indignation, then bolted out the passenger door and raced him to the house.

Peppy was so excited by the commotion that he started to bark, breaking loose from Mrs. Griswald as he waddled across the street to chase Ted and Robbin up the walk. Neither one of them turned around; neither one stopped to explain their antics to Mrs. Griswald.

Ted let Robbin win the race, but the moment she was inside the house he locked the door and toppled her to the floor. There was no time to worry about protocol or grow embarrassed; there was only Ted—laughing, loving, wrestling—as he pinned Robbin a good five feet from the couch. Straddling her on the carpet, he tickled her into a spate of giggling, showing no mercy until she pleaded uncle and gave up the fight. Even then he was not satisfied until his firm lips had kissed her into silence.

"I won the race, Robbs. Admit it," he whispered in her ear.

"You won." Her surrender was complete; her hands were trembling as she reached for his face. "I guess I'll have to let you claim your prize."

Only then, assured of his complete victory, did the playful look leave Ted's face. As he stroked Robbin's quivering throat with his enticing fingers, a different Ted took over their lovemaking...the one she'd watched chase the bear. He wasn't armed with a burning log, and his object was to hold Robbin close, not scare her away. But his urgency left no room for Robbin's prior indecisiveness. This time there was no denying this virile man's desire.

Knees against her sides as he still straddled Robbin on the carpet, Ted started to undo her pink buttons one by one. Like an explorer in virgin territory, he charted each and every inch of the new vista he uncovered, ever so slowly, titillating Robbin beyond endurance as he discovered each round curve and turgid peak of her eager flesh and claimed it as his own.

Each time he detoured from his sensual journey to kiss her soft lips, to whisper his passion, to cradle her head in his hands, Robbin's love for Ted redoubled. It could have been so awkward, this first time, but Ted made it fun and natural; Ted made it right. They were back on the living room floor where they belonged, just inches from the TV and the lofty Siamese on the couch. But this evening—when Ted finally liberated Robbin's pink blouse and tossed it unceremoniously toward the cat—she was certain that a late night movie was the last thing on his mind.

CHAPTER EIGHTEEN

NEARLY AN HOUR PASSED before Ted remembered the world beyond Robbin's living room rug. Their bed of love no longer looked as if it belonged in her pristine house; in fact, the living room looked more like the one in Ted's home—before he'd remodeled it in her image. Although no popcorn kernels littered the rug and nobody had turned on the TV, there were clothes scattered here and there with abandon. One end-table lamp lay broken on the floor—a victim of Robbin's unparalleled enthusiasm at a particularly intoxicating moment in his arms.

Now Ted lay on his side, half-draped over Robbin, his head on a corduroy throw pillow, hers cradled in both his hands. Her long black hair streamed out over the blue pillow, his arms and the rug. Her eyes were closed and sweat glistened on her throat; she was all but purring. Even the corners of her mouth were upturned, making her look like a cat who'd just polished off a saucer of fresh cream. Ted didn't need to ask if he'd taken her to the summit, didn't need to ask himself if she'd put on a show for his assurance. He knew Robbie better than she knew herself, and in the last sixty minutes he'd garnered all the proof he would ever need that she now belonged to him lock, stock, and barrel. He'd never been so sure of anything in his life.

Robbin stirred against him, sliding one warm hand down over the masculine thigh that crossed her body. Slowly she toyed with the fine hairs of his leg, then kissed the dark hollow of his throat in fresh invitation.

"Robbie," he moaned, amazed at the appetite he'd unleashed in her. "We need—" her hand slipped provocatively over his bare hip "—we need to talk."

"Not tonight," she whispered. "Don't you remember? We outlawed talk in favor of a more effective means of communication."

She took hold of his face with both hands and pulled his lips down to hers. Her mouth was firm and demanding; it took all his strength of will to kiss her only once, in promise and regret, before he pulled back again. Reality, unfortunately, was calling.

"Robbie, do you trust me?" he asked in a low, soothing tone.

Robbin's eyes flashed open; wariness replaced the glaze of desire. "What kind of question is that at a time like this?"

He kissed her quickly to still the fear, but he had to carry on with what he'd started. It was incredible that he'd managed to forget his obligations—to all of Coltersville, let alone to Robbin herself—for the sake of his own passion. But they'd enjoyed each other long enough for the moment; he could return in a matter of hours. He didn't relish leaving right now, but compared to the agony he'd endured for the last several months, it would be easy to wait a couple of hours.

"Just answer the question, Robbs. Do you trust me?"

The recent joy in her eyes receded as she cautiously stroked his face. "Of course I trust you, Teddy. But that doesn't mean I have to like whatever you're about to say."

He sighed and cast a longing glance at her beautiful breasts still swollen with passion. He hated to leave them; he hated to leave *her*. But it was imperative that he talk to Joe this evening; imperative that he talk to Kent. From Robbin's description of Hawthorne's interaction with Caldwell, chances were good that one or both of them were about to bolt . . . or take some other panicky action that could only serve to complicate the entire mess. His own sense of urgency was heightened by the knowledge that both Joe and Caldwell would be on duty at Red Rock tonight. He had a gut feeling that when the two of them got together, something terrible was going to happen—unless he found a way to prevent it.

"Robbie, surely you know that about the last thing I want to do right now is get dressed and leave you even for a minute. But I—"

"You're not." Stark disbelief laced her tone. "You're not going to tell me you have to go back to Lila's!"

He held her reproachful gaze. "I thought you said you trusted me. I told you from the minute you called me that I had some urgent business to cope with tonight."

"Lila knows that you're with me. She'll understand. Can't you just call her to say you won't be back?"

"No, I can't. She's not the only one involved. There's another fellow there who—"

"Ted, you don't have to buy or sell a house tonight! Besides, now that we're getting married, I can take over the family real estate problems and Lila won't have to do anything." When he didn't answer right away, Robbin's voice grew a tad shaky as she asked, "We are . . . getting married now, aren't we, Ted?"

She looked so solemn—so desperately serious—that Ted couldn't help but pay her back for all his months of torment. "Well, gee, Robbie, I guess we'll have to now,

now that you've trapped me with the oldest trick in the book. I mean, marriage was the last thing I had on my mind this evening. I hardly know you, lady. Here I was, just minding my own business, when you dragged me into bed and—"

"Teddy!" Robbin feigned a mock slap to his face, then laughed out loud right along with him. "You are terrible. I have no idea why I put up with you."

He grinned; a man could wait a lifetime for an opening like that. "Let me...jog your memory just a bit," he suggested.

While Robbin waited expectantly, Ted slowly bent to kiss one firm breast, then the other. The gesture quickly aroused her passion. She whimpered softly as he lazily licked the dark brown center of the breast in his hand, then tugged his head toward the other one. He gave her what she wanted—at least for a minute—as he nuzzled the other breast, and tantalized the valley between her breasts with his bushy mustache.

It was an effort to pull himself away from her, a struggle to ignore her warm hands sliding down his chest in an eager path toward his thighs. Somehow he managed to catch her wrists and stop her; forcefully, he met her eyes.

"I love you, Robbsie," he said simply, "and that's why I have to go back to Lila's tonight. Your safety comes before our pleasure."

At first Robbin's face showed patent disappointment, but then she hugged him mightily. They kissed softly, a healing kiss, a kiss of love. Then Ted sat up, Indian-style on the carpet. He pulled Robbin into the same position, struggling to keep his mind on his work and his eyes off her beckoning breasts and other tantalizing feminine attributes. He took both her hands and started simply, "It's a long story, Robbs, and I really don't have time to explain it all now. But the long and short of it is that Lila's been dating this fellow named Joe who works at the refinery as a private cop—"

"You mean Erik Estrada?"

"Who?" He met her eyes with some exasperation. Why were these women always bringing up this Estrada character?

"Never mind. Go on. I'm listening."

Quickly he brought her up to date. She listened without interruption until he told her that he suspected Kent of taking a bribe.

"There's no question in my mind that he approved those refurbished valves, Robbin, though I can't prove it until Joe puts me in touch with his friend. There's a chance that he was too scared or too stupid to raise any objections, but—"

"But either way, you're going to ruin him," Robbin finished soberly.

"Yes," he answered grimly. "I am. And until tonight that bothered me a great deal. In fact, I bent over backward to protect him because he used to be a friend of mine... and because I didn't want to be accused of hitting him below the belt just because he stole my girl." He swept a lock of hair out of Robbin's face, then kissed the place it had covered. "But after the way he treated you tonight, I'm going to enjoy—"

"No, Ted," she stopped him quickly, then squeezed his hands. "It's hard to explain what really happened tonight, but Kent... Kent didn't really do anything... too awful. Unwise and immature, perhaps, but... don't punish him because he grew to care for me. Surely you can imagine what it's like to feel frustrated because you want something you just can't have."

Ted growled with feeling, then pressed Robbin back on the floor with a heated kiss. She wrapped her arms around him and pulled him closer, ready to forget his speech about honor and duty. But he pulled back in the nick of time, bracing himself against her breasts.

"I'm never going to get out of here without your help," he confessed, trailing one finger over the nearest pulsing nipple. "Please, Robbie, it really is important. If Joe or his buddy get cold feet before I hear everything I need to know, I'll never clean up this refinery mess. I'm sure Lila's keeping Chacon occupied in my absence, but he's got to go to work tonight, and Caldwell's already starting to lean on him. If Joe gets too scared, my evidence might disappear in a cloud of smoke."

"I think you mean cloud of ammonia," Robbin corrected him, trying not to think about his hands. "If you promise to come back in an hour, I'll let you go." It wasn't an easy promise, he knew; she was already breathing hard.

Reluctantly Ted released her, covering her throat with a last flurry of kisses. "I'm going to get dressed, Robbs. You just stay right like you are and...hold that thought."

Robbin laughed. "I'm going to wait for you in bed like a domesticated wife. After all, you have a key."

He grinned with intense satisfaction, then quickly started to gather his clothes. He took great pleasure from the way Robbin watched him dress, handing him his shirt and pants with considerably more restraint that she'd exhibited while taking them off. When he was finished, he pulled her to her feet and took her in his arms once more—he fully dressed, she totally nude—and kissed her goodbye with fresh passion.

"Teddy, you're the one who's cruel," she scolded as he slid his hands down her naked back to cup her hips.

He chuckled, still marveling at the power he seemed to have over the woman he so adored. "I just don't want you to forget where we left off, Robbs. I'm afraid this is going to turn out like all my other erotic dreams about you where I wake up all alone in my bed."

"Not a chance," she whispered huskily. "If you don't come back soon I'll go wait in your room stark naked and scare Sarah half to death."

Ted teased her ear with his hot tongue as he pressed her soft length against him. "I'll be right back, Robbsie," he promised, enjoying the passionate look on her beautiful, flushed face. "It'll be even better because of the wait."

"It couldn't get any better, Ted," she confessed, her eyes glazed with need. "And I'm going to go a little bit crazier each extra minute you make me wait."

Again he covered her breasts with his big square hands, unable to resist one last caress. Robbin kissed him hungrily, still quivering when he finally set her from him and hurried toward the door.

"Teddy? You will be careful?" He turned back to look at her, surprised by the note of panic in her voice. "I'd just curl up and die if you didn't come right back tonight."

"Give me an hour, Robbsie. That's all. I promise."

He blew her another kiss and opened the door. As the cool evening air brought him back into the outside world, Robbin's last words jarred him into thoughts of caution. *Teddy? You will be careful?* she'd pleaded.

He'd wanted to warn young Joe the same way, and he'd even considered offering protection to Kent if he'd gotten tangled up with Howard Caldwell. But until this very instant, it had never occurred to Ted to worry about himself.

ROBBIN STOOD PERFECTLY STILL in the middle of the living room while she listened to Ted's new van rev to life, then whisk him away. Not one line of her feminine body was free from desire; she'd never been more aroused in her life.

Of course, she'd reached a pinnacle of pleasure more than once in the past hour, but her passion for Ted was so great that each moment of satisfaction only made her need for him more intense. It was inconceivable to Robbin that she'd ever considered herself immune to Ted's masculinity; beyond belief that she'd turned him away more than once and nearly lost him through her folly.

Now, quite suddenly, the shoe was on the other foot. Ted loved her, but he was hardly putty in her hands. Robbin couldn't believe that he had the strength to abandon their lovemaking in order to do his duty. It was not until he was nearly out the door that she grew clear-headed enough to be cognizant of the danger he must have perceived to force himself to leave her alone tonight. And if Coltersville was in danger—let alone Kent Hawthorne and a security guard named Joe Chacon—then Ted was almost certainly in danger, too.

It was an eerie realization, one that shook her to the core. It didn't seem possible that anything could happen to Ted after they'd finally found their way to each other. Robbin tried to push away her fears, but suddenly it seemed too cold in the house to remain undressed, no matter what she'd promised Ted.

What if he can't come back in an hour? she asked herself, rational thought possible now since she wasn't under his spell. *What if he finds some lion in his den, and the lion bares his fangs?*

"Ted can cope with anything, right?" she asked Captain as the Siamese trailed her into the bedroom, where she searched for a warm but sexy robe, and finally picked out a floor-length model in kelly green. She luxuriated in its softness. "Kent's the one who's more likely to get in over his head, Captain. Whatever Caldwell has in mind is—"

The sound of the doorbell startled Robbin, then filled her with relief. She ran down the hall and scampered breathlessly through the living room strewn with clothes. She felt gloriously silly, awash with fresh desire and delight that Ted had returned so soon.

It wasn't until she'd thrown the door wide open that Robbin remembered that Ted would have used his key.

CHAPTER NINETEEN

"HELLO, ROBBIN," Kent greeted her bleakly. "Is there any chance at all that . . . you'd let me come in?"

Nervously he licked his lips, then ran a hand through his uncombed blond hair. He looked terrible. He hadn't changed his clothes since Robbin had seen him last, but there was a tear near his collar and a smudge on one sleeve. Naked fear trampled his suave features. His hands were balled in fists in his pockets.

"What's wrong, Kent?" she asked warily, trying to buy some time. A host of questions were chasing through her head. *Why does he look so frightened? Why is he coming here? What happened with Caldwell after I left? Is there anything Kent could tell me that would be of help to Ted?* But the most important question of all was, *If Teddy comes back and finds him here, will he let me explain why I let Kent in the door before he walks out on me for good?*

"Please, Robbin, I really need your help," Kent pleaded. "I know I owe you an explanation for how...unpredictable I've been. I know I pushed you too hard tonight, but it's only because...I really care for you and I'm . . . damn it, Robbin, I'm scared. I'm in trouble up to my eyebrows! At the very least my career is over if I tell the truth; I might even go to jail! But if I let this hoodlum blackmail me, I'll never stand straight and tall again, and if anything happens to anybody else in this town because of my cowardice, I think I'll just keel over and die."

He looked desperate, almost hysterical, and Robbin did not know how to calm him. As Kent slumped before her on the porch, Robbin realized that he bore no resemblance whatsoever to any famous actor. The only thing he had in common with Robert Redford was blond hair.

"I don't know what to do, Robbin," he whined. "I don't know where to go with the truth even if I'm brave enough to tell it. A month ago I would have turned to Ted, but after ruffling his feathers over you, I think he'd just as soon shoot me at sunrise himself." Too jumpy to notice Robbin's scanty attire—let alone the condition of the living room beyond the open door—he rushed on, "I'm in so much trouble, Robbin. Will you help me? Will you help...clear my path with Ted?"

He looked so sincere—and so pathetic—that Robbin couldn't say no. "Come in and tell me about it, Kent," she offered gently, stilling the panic in her heart. "And when Ted gets back, you can tell him, too."

"GONE?" Ted repeated blankly, unable to accept Lila's report on Joe. "What do you mean he's gone?"

After wrenching himself away from Robbin just to talk to the security guard, the last thing Ted wanted to hear was that he'd returned to Lila's on a wild-goose chase.

"I mean, the more time he had to think about it, the more nervous he got about telling you everything he knew. I did my best to hold him, Ted, but he started mumbling something about his first loyalty being to Red Rock and suddenly took off."

Ted groaned. "You don't think he's gone to warn Caldwell, do you?"

"Maybe. He didn't say. But if I read Joe right, I think it's more likely that he wanted to talk to Gregory. He's the head honcho up there, after all, and Joe likes him."

Ted took a deep breath. "That might be a safe move. But Caldwell was at Kent's tonight, and I have a feeling that he's not going to be any too gentle with the man who crosses him. That gorilla needs to be locked away, and I can't do it without Joe or Kent in my corner."

"Well, I can't produce Joe for you at the moment," Lila admitted sadly. "But Kent Hawthorne has never struck me as too substantial. I suspect that if Caldwell starts leaning on him, he'll be pretty quick to fold."

His eyes narrowed as he thought of Kent claiming credit for his orchid corsage, Kent pawing Robbin as though she were his own. "Caldwell's not the only one who knows how to bait a hook," he answered grimly. "I'll catch you later, Lila. I've got a little fishing to do in Morgantown."

"IT ALL STARTED right after Connie left," Kent moaned when Robbin joined him in the living room.

He'd plopped down into an armchair, utterly disheartened, the instant Robbin had let him in the door. She'd taken a few minutes to gather up her clothes and quickly change into a pair of jeans and a shirt. Kent hadn't moved an iota from his slouched position while she was gone. With just a little prodding, he'd begun to sputter out his tale.

"I just sort of went crazy for a while, Robbin. It was like—well, nothing mattered. Certainly not things like right and wrong. Right was living with my daughter; wrong was being such a lousy father that she didn't even want to spend six weeks with me. If I couldn't have Connie, at least I could have fun being rich, I figured. Part of me thought that if I had more money, I could fly down to see her more often or have her fly up here, but even then I think I knew I was lying to myself. She doesn't care if she ever sees me again, and I don't really blame her."

Robbin knew enough about Kent's relationship with Connie to be fairly certain that he'd never done anything to drive her away; the girl was just responding to adolescent interests and the general stresses of parental divorce.

"Kent, I'm sure that Connie loves you. She's just at an awkward age. With time—"

"Time!" he barked. "That's what I'll be doing when Ted Ballard gets through with me."

Very gently now, Robbin touched his hand. "Tell me, Kent . . . what it is, exactly, that you've done?"

He shook his head, clearly ashamed to continue, but obviously aching for the relief of getting his misdeeds off his chest.

"The day I went up to check on the new equipment at Red Rock in July, Gregory was on vacation. Caldwell showed me around, and I made some comment about how quickly the scuz took over a valve or pipe; the new stuff already looked fifteen years old. He got real edgy and defensive. Even though everything I checked was still in good shape, I had the feeling that he was holding out on me."

Robbin listened without comment, making mental notes for Ted.

"Well, I told him outright that I didn't think the pipes had ever been replaced, and that I was going to check with the company that sold them to Red Rock to verify that they'd actually been installed. He tried to pass it off as a joke, but when he saw that I was serious, he 'mentioned' that he'd once worked at a place where an inspector had been paid five thousand dollars to look the other way."

He covered his face with his hands and moaned. "I told him that anybody who'd get tangled up in that kind of kickback scheme would be heading down a long, dangerous road. He grinned and said he could understand why the inspector had taken the bribe; after all, who couldn't use five thousand dollars?"

"Before I could say anything else, somebody interrupted us, and off he went. I didn't really know what to do—I mean, he hadn't *actually* offered me a bribe in so many words. I decided that maybe I was in over my head and I ought to talk to Ted about it. But I'd been so rotten to him the last time we'd played tennis—it was right after Connie left, remember—that it took me a couple of days to get my courage up. And by then, it was too late."

Robbin adjusted her position on the couch and met his troubled eyes. "Why was it too late, Kent?"

"Because in the morning, there was an envelope with five thousand dollars on my kitchen table. Robbin, I'd slept at home that night—alone; I was there when somebody broke into my apartment. Do you have any idea how . . . creepy that felt?"

"That would be scary, Kent," she admitted, trying to keep him calm. She didn't want to think about the vulnerability of her home; she didn't want to think about how desperately she wished Ted would return.

Kent started tugging on his tie as though it were a hangman's noose. She was afraid he'd balk at any moment and refuse to go on with his tale.

"What happened after that, Kent?" she prodded him.

"Well, I knew what I had to do," he continued sadly. "I went up to Red Rock to tell Caldwell I wouldn't accept a bribe; if he didn't take back the money, I'd call the police."

"And?"

"And Caldwell wasn't there. Now *he* was on vacation. Gregory was back. I should have told him, but I've always hated the man, and besides, I didn't know whether or not he was in on the scam." He turned bleak eyes to Robbin. "Robbin, somebody made a fortune on this deal. At first I couldn't believe Caldwell was clever enough to do it on his own. He looks so stupid! But he . . . he knows what he's about."

Robbin waited in silence, her eyes on her watch. Surely Ted was due back by now. She'd gotten Kent talking, and she ought to have the rest of the answers soon. But she didn't know where to go next—to Gregory, to the police, or to Kent's superiors.

"So what did you do?"

"Nothing. I hemmed and hawed and waited until Caldwell came back from his vacation. When I confronted him, he laughed!"

"He laughed?"

"He said that first of all, I had no proof that he'd given me the money. He'd never actually offered me a bribe, never placed one red cent in my hot little hand." He slammed one fist into the other. "Which was true!"

"But you had the money, Kent. And as long as you had it—"

"I know. I was still guilty of something if I kept it and didn't report my suspicions about the equipment." He turned beseeching eyes on Robbin. "And I only suspected there was a problem, Robbin. I had no proof. I did the proper testing on all those valves, and they were all adequate. Of course, I knew they could have been refurbished, which would have accounted for enough construction activity that maybe nobody realized that nothing had been replaced. But when I threatened to reveal what I knew, Caldwell pointed out that I'd only be cutting my own throat. After two weeks sitting on that money, he said I had already accepted a bribe. If he went down, I'd go right with him."

"Oh, Kent," Robbin murmured sympathetically. She knew he was in the wrong, but she could see how it had happened. Especially at a time when he'd been so mixed up and vulnerable.

"Well, I still didn't know what to do. I never spent the money, but I couldn't bear to get rid of it, either. And Caldwell wouldn't take it back! And then when the plant exploded, I really got mad. I confronted Caldwell while Ted was busy and told him we had to know the truth. And then he—" Kent closed his eyes "—he reminded me that he'd had plenty of time to search my house the night he'd left the money there while I was sleeping. And he knew... what I valued most... and where to find it."

"Kent—"

"I wasn't sure just what he meant until he...told me—from memory—Connie's address in Colorado."

Kent's eyes grew red; he fought back the wave of feeling. "Oh, Robbin, what could I do? It wasn't just my own neck I was risking anymore—or even yours or the lives of Ted's kids! My baby was being threatened by this hoodlum! I was terrified!"

Robbin rubbed his shoulders, fighting tears herself. What hell this poor man had been through in the past two weeks! And she certainly hadn't been much help.

"So I hoped and prayed that Ted would figure out that something was wrong with the valves without implicating Caldwell or me. He's so damned good at what he does that I can't believe it's taken him this long. I know he suspects me, but he's still trying to come up with some other way to explain those old valves. He doesn't want to accuse me if there's any way around it, even though he's...still mighty sore about the way I tried to steal you away from him."

He studied her grimly. "I really did like you, Robbin, right from the start. But I also knew that you were the best pipeline to Ted, and you could help me keep tabs on what was going on in his head. After a while, I got so scared that I—I just needed a friend." He glanced away, embarrassed. "Tonight, when I saw the way Caldwell looked at you, I realized that if he thought you were special to me, he might threaten you, too, just to keep me quiet."

He stood up impatiently and began to pace the room. "But I can't keep quiet any longer; that man is more dangerous than the plant! He came to see me tonight to tell me I had to get Ted off the scent. Somebody else at Red Rock has been asking questions—somebody who shouldn't even care—and he's sure that Ted put him up to it." He jammed his hands in his pockets and literally broke out in sweat. "He said that if Ted points a finger in his direction, he's going to hurt my little girl!"

And Ted's going to pull the rug out from under Caldwell tonight, she could have told him. But that wouldn't have helped the frightened man before her; it would only have pushed him over the edge of hysteria.

"He can't hurt your daughter if he's in prison, Kent. And you know that's exactly where he should be."

"I know! Damn it, I know!" He sighed again and stopped pacing. "Where the hell is Ted? He can tell me what to do."

"He's due here any minute, Kent. He promised me that he'd be right back."

"You said that an hour ago, Robbin. Isn't there anywhere you can try to reach him?"

Robbin thought a minute; under the circumstances, Ted would probably forgive her for interrupting him at Lila's again.

Quickly she found the number and dialed it, but Lila reported that Ted had come and gone. She suggested that Robbin might be able to reach him at Kent's or at Red Rock.

Robbin called the refinery next, hoping that sheer dumb luck would help her find Ted. If he'd already gone back to Morgantown, he wouldn't return for another hour, and poor Kent would surely rupture if he waited that long to confess his part in this sorry mess to somebody in a position of authority.

Ted wasn't there, the man on the other end of the line told her, but he'd take a message if by chance Mr. Ballard should show up there... an unlikely event on a Friday night. Before Robbin could give him her number, he was interrupted by someone in the office who apparently had overheard the conversation.

"Hello. This is Lowell Gregory, plant manager," a new voice greeted her a moment later. "We rarely see Mr. Ballard here in the evening unless he's conducting a spot check, but if there's some personal emergency I'll check with the boys and see if he's been here or is expected."

"Mr. Gregory?" Robbin could hardly control her relief as she realized her stroke of good luck. "This is Robbin Walker; I'm Ted's... fiancée. I'm trying—"

"Gregory's there?" Kent interrupted her, eyes alight as he heard her say the name. "Gregory's at the plant?"

Robbin nodded. "Hold on just a moment, Mr. Gregory." She waited for Kent. "Ted says he trusts him, Kent.

Doesn't like him much, but he thinks he's sincere about getting to the bottom of this mess."

Kent nodded warily. At this point, trusting anybody seemed a bit risky. "Ask him what he's doing there."

"Kent, it's none of my business why—"

"He's never there at night."

Robbin sighed and turned back to the phone. "Mr. Gregory, I'm glad I caught you. I didn't expect to find . . . the top man in so late at night."

"Neither did I," he answered seriously. "I've been home for hours. But I just got a very strange call that may have something to do with Ballard. Did he tell you he was coming out here tonight?"

"Well . . . indirectly. It's sort of a long story."

"I'd sure like to hear it. All I know is that one of our security guards called me and asked me to meet him at the plant. I'm here but Joe Chacon isn't. And I haven't seen hide nor hair of Ted."

Robbin was sure that Joe wouldn't have called Gregory if he hadn't been sure that the plant manager was innocent of any wrongdoing. She was also sure that if Joe hadn't arrived, it was because Caldwell had found a way to stop him. And that meant that Caldwell could find a way to stop Kent, too . . . or her beloved Teddy.

"Mr. Gregory," she declared boldly, "I've got somebody else who wants to see you."

Kent shook his head in panic. "I can't face him alone! He'll love it! He'll make me bleed, Robbin. I only agreed to tell Ted!"

But Ted's not here. Robbin pushed away all the frightening potential reasons for that indisputable fact...along with all the possible dangers that could still befall him until Caldwell was locked up. She had no more time to worry about Kent's pride, or his squeamishness. Ted's safety was at stake.

"If you can wait at the plant for just a few minutes, Mr. Gregory, I think we can clear up this whole mess."

"In that case, young lady," he answered stoutly, "I've got all night."

Robbin grabbed her sweater and purse, then all but dragged Kent out of the house. She took a minute to leave a message for Ted with Sarah, certain that he would be proud of her initiative. After all, he'd made it emphatically clear that tonight was a time for action.

The Mercedes was already inside the refinery gates before it occurred to Robbin that Joe Chacon might not have decided to share his knowledge with Gregory out of a noble surge of honor. She didn't know the man; he might just have been greedy enough to use his knowledge to ask for a slice of the pie. And if Gregory had any reason to pay for Joe's silence, then he was the last man on earth to whom Kent should reveal his story tonight.

CHAPTER TWENTY

TED PULLED INTO ROBBIN'S DRIVEWAY feeling as though he'd wasted half the night. No trace of Joe at Lila's, no trace of Kent at home. Joe was due to go on duty any minute, and Ted wanted to make a quick run to the refinery, but first he had to stop and tell Robbin. It was dangerous to think he could get in and out of the house without making love to her again, but he *had* promised her he'd be back in an hour, and it was already over that now. Considering how uneasy she was about having him leave her to visit Lila, it was only prudent to offer some reassurance.

Go ahead and lie to yourself, Ballard, he thought grinning to himself. *You just want to see if she's still waiting for you in the buff.*

Disappointment came hard when he entered the dark, empty house. Not one trace of their lovemaking still remained. No clothes on the couch, no lamp on the floor. No sign of Robbin anywhere.

He found a green robe flung over her bed as though she'd dressed in great haste, but since he hadn't been in her room today, he had no idea when the robe had found its way to her bed.

Did I dream it again? he asked himself. He closed his eyes and felt the urgent call of his body, the memory of her warm, full breasts in his hands.

Damn it, it was real! he told himself. Then, in a wash of relief, he remembered that Robbin had threatened to wait for him next door if he took too long. He bolted out the back door, cursing the nails he'd put in the short cut gate, and hopped the picket fence.

"Robbie?" he called out as he entered the house through the screen door.

"Mr. Ballard?" It was Sarah's voice, shaky, a mere whisper as it reached him from the hall. "Mr. Ballard, is that you?"

He tromped quickly down the hall, unable to stifle a vague sense of foreboding. He found Sarah in Tina's room cuddling a sleeping Larry in her arms. The children looked peaceful, but Sarah looked white-faced and terrified.

"Sarah, what's wrong? Where's Robbin?"

Sarah shook her head numbly, then burst into tears. "At the refinery! She told me to tell you she was going there with Mr. Hawthorne—"

"Hawthorne!" He felt black with rage.

"Yes, that's what she said. But right after she left a snazzy red sports car pulled into Robbin's drive."

"Red?" Instantly the description triggered his earlier discussion with Robbin. Caldwell! Caldwell right here at Robbin's door!

"Yes. When he couldn't find Robbin, he came over here. Tina answered the doorbell—he woke her up with all the pounding on the door and I was on the phone—and he grabbed her hair and told her to tell her father to 'keep his big mouth shut' if he wanted to leave his children home alone!"

Sarah was crying so hard it was all Ted could do not to comfort her, but the fear within him was so great he knew he couldn't take the time. Caldwell's boldness could only mean one thing. With a second-degree murder charge hanging over him, he didn't think he had much to lose. Whatever scruples he might once have had had clearly gone by the wayside.

"Do you know where he went? The man in the red car?"

"No, but Tina told him where Robbin said she was going. Tina feels so guilty, Mr. Ballard, like she betrayed a friend. But she was so scared that—"

"Tell Tina not to worry." Since his daughter was asleep, Ted didn't take the time to console her, either. "Lock the doors, Sarah, and call my mother. Tell her I want her to come over here and stay with you and the kids until I get back . . . and have her warn Doug Walker to keep a sharp eye on his kids. But first call the police and tell them to meet me at Red Rock right now!"

Calling the police was the kindest thing Ted could do for Howard Caldwell, he thought grimly. If he got to the man before the cops did, there was a good chance he'd kill him with his own bare hands. And depending on what shape Robbin was in when he found her, he might yet do the same to Kent Hawthorne.

ROBBIN HAD SEEN THE REFINERY AT NIGHT, of course, but never up close. In fact, she'd only been inside it once in all the years she'd lived in Coltersville, and that had been in broad daylight with herds of people milling around. And, of course, Ted had been there; nothing was very scary when Ted was around.

Where is he? she asked herself again. *Why is it taking him so long?*

Kent gave the security guard a long, hard stare as they drove in. He was an older man with a balding hairline. He looked weary and ready to go home.

"Is Mr. Gregory still here?" Kent asked him.

"As far as I know. Caldwell's shift starts at eleven so I don't know why the boss came back this late."

Robbin was nervous now, no longer sure what had motivated Gregory to return. "You're sure that . . . Gregory doesn't have anything to do with this mess, Kent?" she asked uneasily. "Caldwell never said—"

"I'm not sure of anything, Robbin. But I can't for the life of me imagine Gregory threatening little girls. I don't particularly like the man, but he's had a dozen chances to offer me a bribe or threaten me with exposure, and he's bent over backward to look scrupulously clean. If Ted's sure he's innocent, that's good enough for me."

Robbin shivered; it was summer, but the night air was cool. She thrust away any other reason for her urge to draw her sweater yet closer. It was a dark night; the spiraling towers and jutting metal made for an eerie background. And only the lights of their incoming car broke the infinite darkness that separated the refinery from the nearest houses. Even the school was shrouded in darkness.

"Well, let's get this over with, Kent. As I recall, the office is over in the back."

"Just behind the ammonia processing unit," Kent replied, tugging on his collar as he escorted Robbin through the dirt and gravel.

"That's where the valve blew up before, isn't it?"

"Yes. We're lucky so few people were in that area. When one of those valves bursts open, anybody close enough to breath in a deep gulp can just about kiss life goodbye."

They were awesome words to contemplate as the two picked their way through the darkness. It seemed to Robbin that even an oil refinery ought to be better lit than this, and she wondered if they'd had some sort of power blackout.

It was one of many questions that tripped through her mind as they took a shortcut through the ammonia processing unit. The noise up close was tremendous; the rattle and bang so forceful that when the valve first blew, Robbin didn't realize that she was in grave danger.

It was a full five seconds later, as the scent of one hundred proof ammonia scorched her nostrils, that she realized what had happened. In a kaleidoscope of noise and panic, she heard a bell clanging and men shouting warnings; saw Kent cover his face and knew she had to do the same. There was a sudden lurching of relief when she saw a man rushing toward her from the main valve area. Unlike she and Kent, utterly unprotected as they slumped half-conscious to the earth, he was covered from head to toe with a Tyvex suit and oxygen mask, which surely meant that he had the resources and the savvy to rescue them. She wondered how on earth he'd had time to don the suit just seconds after the alarm had rung.

She was still wondering when the heavy, ape-shaped man bolted over Kent and Robbin as though they were mere obstacles in his path. Although she was too far gone to contemplate the full dimensions of what he must have done, she realized, in a desperate rush of panic, that this time the explosion at Red Rock was not an accident. And this time, more than one man would probably die.

TED PULLED UP TO THE REFINERY just seconds before the valve blew. He'd only discovered that Caldwell hadn't checked in yet when Red Rock went crazy and the guard started talking to somebody on his walkie-talkie.

"Yes! Ambulance alert! I'll be ready."

Too stunned at first to think, Ted wanted to run from the overpowering stench of ammonia. It burned his eyes and made him gag, and the screech of the bells added to his sense of terror. Yet he had but one blinding need—to find Robbin and get her home safe and sound.

"Sorry, sir!" The guard blocked him quickly at the gate. "Nobody can go in there! You'd only become a casualty yourself. We've got everybody logged and—"

"Did a man and a woman just come through here? Kent Hawthorne from—"

"Yes. But—"

"Then tell somebody! Your people won't be looking for civilians!" He realized, in sudden clarity, that the timing of the accident was just too perfect. Oh, it would sell to the public—after all, Red Rock had just had a similar accident, right? Clearly there was a problem up there . . . a problem that would land on Lowell Gregory's doorstep when the old valves were discovered. But Gregory, he was certain, had been an innocent dupe.

"I can't just sit here!" he shouted at the guard. "I've got to find out if—"

"Move your vehicle, sir!" The elderly man commanded him. "If you want to help, clear this path for the ambulance! Your friends will need the oxygen right away."

Jamming the van into reverse, Ted backed away from the gate and pulled over a safe distance away. The van jerked to a stop as he bolted back to the fence to see what was happening; the ammonia gas burned his eyes so badly that he could hardly see. Nonetheless, he was contemplating crawling over the barbed-wire fence when he noticed that somebody else had the same idea. Only this somebody was going the other way.

He couldn't recognize a face in the Tyvex suit, but the giant form had a familiar gait as it stumbled down the hill. No responsible employee of Red Rock would ever run away from a disaster when his co-workers could be dying...especially when inside that uniform he alone was perfectly safe!

Ted didn't give Caldwell time to make his getaway; he didn't even take the time to think. The man was twice his size and might be tougher in a fight, but Ted knew he could outrun him, especially in that bulky suit. Once he caught up with the bastard, he'd have to trust his adrenaline to do the rest. Caldwell, after all, was only fighting for money and his freedom from a prison term; Ted was fighting for Robbin, for his children, and for the public he'd promised to protect. It didn't bother him in the least that he might also end up fighting for his life.

ROBBIN CAME TO VERY SLOWLY. Tears streamed down her face from her burning eyes, and she gagged every time she tried to breathe. An oxygen mask covered her nose and throat. She could hear a wild crush of noises, but she couldn't quite see. Yet she knew the touch of the hand on her forehead, and it gave her the strength to push away the fog of fear.

She drifted in and out of consciousness for several hours. When her vision finally focused, she realized that the oxygen mask had been removed. The very first face she saw was Ted's.

At least it looked like Ted; the last time she'd seen him he'd looked clean and dapper, and now he was covered with dirt. He had a black eye, a badly swollen lower lip, and a roaring anger in his eyes that she'd never seen before. The anger, she knew instinctively, was not directed at Robbin, but at someone else on her behalf.

"Teddy?" she murmured groggily, reaching out for him with both hands.

Instantly he took her in his arms and buried his face in her hair. "Oh, Robbsie," she heard him whisper from some place deep within his heart. "I should have killed him when I had the chance."

Robbin struggled to make her breathing even while Ted took her hands and pressed a firm, reassuring kiss on each palm. Vaguely she realized that she was in a hospital room, but she had no clear recollection of arriving there.

"You're going to be okay, Robbie," Ted promised her at once. "They got to you in time." And then, in answer to her next unspoken question, "It looks like Kent's going to be all right, too. I called his daughter and told her what happened. She told me to tell him she loves him very much. Lila's going to meet her plane."

Robbin nodded and breathed deeply, clinging to Ted with all her might. There were so many questions she wanted to ask him, but she felt too weary to speak. Fortunately, she didn't need to say very much. Ted had always been able to read her mind.

"The doctor says you'll need to stay here for a day or so, Robbs, just to make sure everything's all right. So I'm going to take Ruthie home in a little while—it's already morning, you know—and my mother's going to stay with us for the duration so I can come visit you." He gave her one of his embarrassed grins as he promised, "I'm going to buy you a teddy bear of your very own to keep you company whenever I'm not around, but Ruthie says you can borrow hers till I have a chance to go shopping."

Deeply moved, Robbin reached out a loving hand to touch Ted's cheek. He covered her fingers with his own as he continued to speak.

"You don't have to worry about a thing, Robbie. I just want you to rest." His tone was gentle as he gave her the basic information she needed to know; he didn't bog her down with details. "Caldwell is in custody, and Gregory has shut down the plant until the old equipment can be replaced. Everything's going to be okay at Red Rock," Ted assured her, "and everything's going to be okay at home."

Overwhelmed by fatigue, receding terror and Ted's great tenderness, Robbin began to cry. She loved him so much; she wanted nothing more than to slip away with him immediately so they could begin their new life together.

Ted slipped one hand gently through her hair, then bent over to kiss her cheek as she clung to him fiercely. "I know, Robbsie," he whispered. "You want to go home and tell the kids we're getting married; you want to start the paperwork on the Crescent Heights house. But I'll be here every minute that Ruth can spare me, and you'll be home in a day or two. Then we're never going to be apart again." He kissed her lips once, ever so gently, then smiled at her with the promise of a fresh dawn's sun. "I know it doesn't seem fair, Robbs. But you know what I always say. Life isn't fair, but . . ." Determined to make her smile, he waited expectantly for Robbin to finish his favorite saying.

Despite her grogginess, her love for Ted lifted her from the hazy world of last night's terror into the vibrant light of their joyful future together. She touched his mustache, then slipped one hand through his hair before she whispered, ''As long as I'm with you, Teddy Bear, life may not be fair, but—'' she grinned as she paraphrased his slogan ''—it's going to be absolutely terrific.''

This time when Ted fiercely wrapped his arms around her, he didn't need to say anything at all.